T

Bill and Katherine turned to the mug shot of George Webster. The man who had corrupted Gerry Birch. The man who had masterminded the smuggling of six million pounds worth of gold into Britain. And the man who had covered his tracks so well that, when Bill's team had cracked the racket, there was not a shred of evidence to be found linking him to the smuggling.

The silence weighed heavily as Bill and Katherine contemplated the smiling face. Then Bill turned to his newest deputy.

'He's walking about free somewhere.'
'Somewhere?'
'Yes. He vanished.'

Tom McGregor is a journalist and the author of twelve books. He lives and works in London.

*Also by Tom McGregor
and available in Mandarin*

The Knock (series one)

TOM McGREGOR

The Knock

Series Two

Mandarin

A Mandarin Paperback

THE KNOCK: SERIES TWO

First published in Great Britain 1996
by Mandarin Paperbacks
an imprint of Reed International Books Ltd
Michelin House, 81 Fulham Road, London SW3 6RB
and Auckland, Melbourne, Singapore and Toronto

Based on the series created by Anita Bronson
and written by Geoffrey Case
A Bronson Knight production for LWT

Copyright © Tom McGregor 1996
The author has asserted his moral rights

All the characters and events in The Knock
*are fictitious, and no resemblance to actual persons,
living or dead, is intentional*

A CIP catalogue record for this title
is available from the British Library
ISBN 0 7493 3640 4

Typeset by CentraCet Limited, Cambridge
Printed and bound in Great Britain
by Cox & Wyman Ltd, Reading, Berks.

This book is sold subject to the condition
that it shall not, by way of trade or otherwise,
be lent, resold, hired out, or otherwise circulated
without the publisher's prior consent in any form
of binding or cover other than that in which
it is published and without a similar condition
including this condition being imposed
on the subsequent purchaser.

One

Tommy Maddern, although generally down on his uppers, was having a good day. He was on his home patch in South London. He was doing the job he liked best. And he was sure that, in a baseball cap and shell suit, he was looking as anonymous as was possible for anyone of his build. Tommy was very keen on preserving his anonymity. And after today's little chore, he would need it more than ever.

Smiling to himself, he jogged down Peckham High Road towards the little parade of shops at the bottom. Although Peckham was hardly the high life, it was the life he had grown up with. People knew him there. More to the point, people in Peckham knew not to mess with him. Those who did usually lived to regret the experience. Some of the worst offenders didn't even live.

Tommy's casually ruthless methods of doing business had got him into trouble many times – and not just with the police. The more sophisticated members of London's criminal fraternity had learned to steer clear of him. Tommy knew that, and it rankled. Two years ago he had been part of the big time; a mover and shaker who dealt with enormous sums of money, and made large amounts for himself. And then it had all gone horribly wrong.

Tommy's employer at the time hadn't quite seen it like that. He had known Tommy for years and it hadn't taken him long to realize that Tommy's uses were exclusively in the brawn department. He had always been, and would always remain, a hired hand. He was too lacking in brains and too much of a loose cannon to go further. He was one of many – albeit a more than usually effective one – and that made him expendable. It was purely a matter of luck that he had escaped from the fiasco of two years ago. His employer had, from the beginning, covered his own tracks. Everyone else involved had been arrested by Her Majesty's Customs and Excise. Some of them had been sentenced to eight years in jail. But not Tommy Maddern. He had battered his way through the ring of police and customs officers who had sprung the operation. His methods had included throwing iron bars at anyone who approached him. Brute force was his forte; a brutality as innate as his employer's cunning. Both men had a complete disregard for other people. Tommy's employer had hidden that trait under a veneer of wealth and sophistication; Tommy hadn't bothered even trying to hide it.

He didn't bother trying to hide it today either. Reaching the small supermarket in the middle of the parade, he slowed his pace and put one hand into the voluminous pocket of his trousers. That movement brought an ever broader smile to his face. Then he walked into the shop and straight towards the till at the back. A small Indian man emerged from behind the counter. His name was Arjun Malhotra and he usually smiled at his customers. But this time it was Tommy Maddern who was wearing the smile as he pulled a sawn-off shotgun out of his pocket and shot Mr Malhotra in the chest from a distance of three feet.

'I heard about the replacement, by the way.'
'Replacement?'

'Yeah. Gerry's replacement.'

'Oh.' George Andreotti found himself most unusually at a loss for words. The name of Gerry Birch, while not exactly taboo at the Soho office of London City and South Customs and Excise, still had a peculiar effect on his ex-colleagues. Even after two years, none of them quite knew how to handle the issue. Bill Adams, the senior officer, had encouraged his team to talk about it: the last thing he wanted was for the dent in morale it had caused to become permanent. But Andreotti, the most junior officer, was still uneasy about the subject. Barry Christie didn't find it so difficult. While the episode had affected him, he had never been as close to Gerry as the others. He had quietly suspected Gerry of being racist. Something about Gerry's attitude had implied that Barry should be on the streets committing crimes, not solving them.

Barry looked down at Andreotti. The look had nothing to do with attitude, just height. Everyone was obliged to look down at Andreotti. 'The replacement,' he said with a grin, 'is a woman.' Andreotti immediately looked more interested. He liked women. And if women didn't seem so keen on him, well, it was just a matter of time, wasn't it? 'A woman boss for you,' continued Barry. 'Make your hair curl.'

Andreotti glared at him. Barry had pounced on Andreotti's other great weakness. He spent more at the hairdresser in a month than most people did in a year. The unkinder of his colleagues thought it a complete waste of time and money. His thick black hair *was* curly – despite his repeated and expensive attempts to straighten it. Deciding – rightly – that Barry was spoiling for a teasing session, he chose to ignore the jibes. 'What's her name?' he asked.

Barry shrugged. 'I don't know her. Katherine Roberts? Mean anything to you?'

Andreotti frowned. 'Rings a vague bell ... Christ! Yeah, I remember. Worked at Heathrow and then transferred to Harwich. I went out with a friend of hers once.'

'So what's she like?'

Andreotti looked wistful. 'The friend is gorgeous. Katherine,' he added with a grimace, 'is very bright, very ambitious – and as hard as bloody nails.'

A new, unexpected voice broke the short silence that ensued. 'And,' it said in withering tones, 'I'm pretty tall as well.' Both men looked round in complete shock. Barry's surprise was tempered with amusement: Andreotti's with a desire to vanish through the floor.

Katherine Roberts was looking straight at Andreotti. In another place at another time, he would have looked back and smiled. Five minutes later he would probably have made some sort of pass. But this time he failed to meet her eye and stood, shifting his weight from one foot to the other.

Barry broke the uneasy silence. 'Hi,' he said as he extended his hand, 'I'm Barry Christie. You must be Katherine.' He smiled. 'Good to meet you. This,' he added as he turned to Andreotti, 'is George Andreotti. But we never call him George. Always Andreotti.'

A faint smile played at the corners of Katherine Roberts's mouth. 'Rhymes with spotty,' she said as she shook hands. Andreotti flushed.

'We didn't think you were starting till next week,' said Barry, privately wishing that she wasn't starting at all. She did indeed look as hard as nails. Pretty, though, with tumbling curly blonde hair and big blue eyes. But looked older than her years. His sources had informed him that Katherine was twenty-seven.

Katherine seemed unaware of the frosty atmosphere

in the room. 'Well,' she said as she looked around her, 'Harwich let me go earlier than I anticipated, so I thought I'd come straight here.' Anyone else, thought Andreotti, would have gone straight on holiday. And she was a fool to have sprung her arrival on them. She should have informed Bill.

On cue, Katherine finished her scrutiny of the room and addressed Barry again. 'Is Bill Adams around?'

'No. He's in court. Hearing the verdict on a child pornographer we've been investigating for months. He should be back soon.' What Barry didn't add was that Bill was likely to come back in a towering rage. The defence counsel for the pornographer was one of the best QCs in the land – and Bill was sure he would get his client acquitted. Bill was furious about it. Worse, the judge hadn't allowed Bill's evidence of imported videos to be shown in court. If Katherine Roberts poked her superior nose into Bill's office when he returned, she was likely to have it bitten off.

'Oh well,' said Katherine, blissfully unaware of impending disaster. 'I'll wait.'

'Fine.' Barry certainly wasn't going to wait with her. 'We've got to go off to some South London incident, haven't we, Andreotti?'

'Er... yeah. Yes! We do.'

'See you then,' said Katherine in a 'class dismissed' tone of voice.

Bill Adams collided with the two men at the main door of the building. He looked thunderous.

'How...?'

'We lost. We bloody lost.' Bill's incredulity rivalled his fury.

'But how?' Barry couldn't believe it either. 'The guy's...'

'Guilty as sin. A paedophile.' Bill clenched his fists and glared at the hapless Andreotti. 'We're going to get that bloke. We are. We're going to bloody nail him if it's the last thing we do.' Stomping around in anger, Bill looked through the glass partition and caught sight of Katherine. 'Who's that?'

'Katherine Roberts.'

Bill frowned. 'She's not due till next week.'

'Eager,' said Andreotti with a smile. He knew from Bill's expression that he wasn't going to welcome her with open arms.

Then he turned and, followed by Barry, headed towards the staircase. 'Oh,' said Barry, turning back to Bill. 'Alan Jackson phoned to cancel your meeting. He said you can cover everything at your review interview.'

That was the last straw. Bill looked as if he were about to explode. 'For crying out loud!' he yelled. 'What do these damned people think we do here all day? Jesus Christ. I should have taken his job when I was damn well offered it.'

Barry and Andreotti decided, as one, that their absence would be the better part of valour. They headed downstairs, both of them thinking they were heartily glad that Bill hadn't accepted Alan Jackson's job. The regional director of the customs service, his job was largely an administrative one. Bill's job was much more 'on the street'. Although in charge of City and South, he never stood on ceremony, seeing himself as part of a team as well as head of it. And, his present state of mind excepted, he was thoughtful, sympathetic, sensitive and fair.

Feeling none of those things, Bill walked into his office where Katherine Roberts was waiting.

'Hello.' Katherine's greeting was altogether warmer than her introduction to Barry and Andreotti.

Bill's wasn't. 'I didn't expect you so soon,' he said as he strode over to his desk.

If Katherine was surprised by his offhand manner she didn't show it. 'I'm up sorting out a place to stay,' she said with a smile. 'Thought I'd look in. Say hello.'

Bill tried, and failed, to return the smile. Something told him that this confident, smartly-dressed creature was going to be trouble. 'Well, it's not a very good day, as you can probably see.'

Katherine nodded. 'A child pornography case. The file's open on your desk.' Katherine missed Bill's expression. 'You lost?' she finished.

Bill took a deep breath. 'Yes. We lost.' Sitting down at his desk, he nodded for her to do likewise. 'In your interview,' he continued, 'you said you couldn't join us until the 23rd.'

'That's changed.'

Bill subdued his irritation. After all, he was extremely busy and very short-staffed. His other deputy, Jo Chadwick, had been sent on MoD training and then on a computer course. The timing had been lousy, especially as she wasn't due back for another two weeks. 'Well,' he said, this time with a smile, 'we can certainly use the help. Where are you staying at the moment? Settled in?'

But Katherine didn't want to waste time on pleasantries. 'Hotel. I'm looking for a flat.'

'Fine.' Bill decided to tackle like with like. 'Well,' he said with a nod towards the other room, 'there's a desk. Sixteen case files. Might as well hit the ground running.'

Katherine looked delighted. 'Great. I'll start reading.'

Bill suddenly felt extremely weary. Enthusiasm was

one thing. Obsession was another. He had a horrible feeling he was looking straight at the latter.

But Katherine's attention had been drawn elsewhere. 'Are those current cases?'

Bill followed her glance to the surveillance photographs on the noticeboard. 'No. Well... no. Reminders.'

Katherine raised an eyebrow. 'Of ones who got away?'

'Two did.' Bill's mouth was suddenly a thin, hard line. 'Including the big one.' Then he looked again at the biggest photograph with an expression of infinite sadness. 'That's a surveillance photograph of Gerry Birch. You'll no doubt have heard...'

Katherine had heard. 'Oh yes. The one who went crooked.'

'Who was corrupted.'

But Katherine missed the extreme frostiness of Bill's reply. She stared with renewed interest at the photographs. 'You did a good job catching him. Got eight years, didn't he?' Katherine's mouth curled in distaste. 'He deserves every day of it. I can't stand anyone who goes bent.'

'He was once a very good officer.'

'There are a lot of very good officers. They have strong enough characters not to get greedy and betray the whole service.' Katherine smiled across the desk. 'You turn crooked, you go to jail. Simple.'

'Yeah. Simple.' Bill reckoned he could grow to dislike Katherine intensely. 'So why didn't the man who turned him crooked go to jail?'

In unison, they turned again to the photographs. One of them was of the man who had learned of Gerry Birch's unhappy personal life and financial difficulties, who had offered to 'help him out', and who had gradually and skilfully drawn Gerry into his world. At first Gerry had had no idea that the man was a criminal.

By the time he had realized, he was so deeply enmeshed that he had seen no way out. The man who had corrupted him had been very, very clever. And he had had brawn to back up his brains. Brawn in the shape of a vicious, unscrupulous and extremely unpleasant hired hand. A man called Tommy Maddern.

The photograph of Maddern was one of the reminders of the ones who got away. But it was another photograph that captured both Bill's and Katherine's attention. A mug shot of a tanned, smiling, balding man of about fifty. He looked as if he didn't have a care in the world. He probably didn't. George Webster was the man who had corrupted Gerry Birch. The man who had masterminded the smuggling of six million pounds worth of gold into Britain. And the man who had covered his tracks so well that, when Bill's team had cracked the racket, there was not a shred of evidence to be found linking him to the smuggling.

The silence weighed heavily as Bill and Katherine contemplated the smiling face of George Webster. Then Bill turned to his newest deputy.

'He's walking about free somewhere.'

'Somewhere?'

'Yes. He vanished.'

Even Tommy Maddern realized he had gone a bit far by shooting Arjun Malhotra. His instructions had been to intimidate the man, to frighten him into continuing to toe the line. Tommy's loose interpretation of those instructions had infuriated his 'employer'.

'You're going to have to lie low for a while,' Eddie Davies had told him.

Tommy had snorted in derision. 'I've been lying low for two years, haven't I? Nobody's come anywhere near me. It'll be all right.'

'No. The Paki will be all right. God knows how he managed to survive, but *it* won't be all right for a while. You've gotta get out of the country, Tommy.'

Tommy had looked at the elderly, world-weary Eddie and decided that, yes, he had better get out of the country. Working for Eddie was a bore. Small-time stuff. It was a good enough scam – and you got a bit of Paki-bashing into the bargain – but it was hardly the most exciting stuff. Not like working for George.

It was then that Tommy had the brainwave. Eddie was right; leaving the country was probably a good idea. Living in Deptford and only ever working in Peckham was really beginning to get to him. He would go away to the sun and settle a few old scores. He would go to see George Webster. It had penetrated even Tommy's often-dormant brain that George had dumped him like a hot potato. In a way he couldn't blame him: he *was* a hot potato. Yet George hadn't made the slightest attempt to find out how he was or even where he was. For years George had protested that Tommy was his most valued friend. While Tommy had always had his suspicions about that – he was always asked to vanish when George's other friends appeared – he had believed that George would always need him. The last two years had proved him wrong.

But if George neither knew nor cared where Tommy was, Tommy knew where George had gone. He had made sure about that one. Two days after his chat with Eddie Davies, Tommy alighted from a plane in Portugal. He grinned as, blinking in the blinding sunlight, he tried to visualise the expression on George's face when he arrived, unannounced, at his villa high in the hills above Faro.

Tommy had imagined several expressions, ranging

from delight (unlikely, he knew), to surprise and even to shock. What he hadn't envisaged was the look of complete horror on George's face as he opened the heavy wrought-iron gate to the courtyard of his luxurious residence.

'Hello George!' Tommy was grinning from ear to ear. 'How's your luck?'

George stared at his erstwhile henchman. 'How the hell,' he asked after a moment of stunned silence, 'did you find me?' His face fell.

Two minutes later George had recovered his composure. Two things helped him do this. One was that Tommy was on his own. The other was that he had arrived on, of all things, a mountain bike. Nobody in their right minds would do that. Unless, of course, they were practically broke. Tommy's clothes helped corroborate the latter view. When working for George, he had always worn smart and expensive, if slightly sharp, suits. Two years down the line, it was apparent that Tommy's budget could no longer sustain smartness. He looked a mess. Tommy, George realized, hadn't come to threaten him or exact revenge for being abandoned. He had obviously come for a job.

Relief sweeping through him, George ushered Tommy into the villa and towards the swimming pool on the other side. Give him a drink, he said to himself, be nice to him – and then get rid of him.

'Well,' he said as he produced two gigantic gin and tonics, 'I can't get over this!' He beamed at Tommy and handed him a glass. 'Here you go, get your laughing gear into that, as the Bishop said to the actress.' Thinking that he might just have gone over the top with his hail-fellow-well-met tactics, he reclined back onto the sunlounger beside Tommy's and asked him what brought him to Portugal.

Tommy looked around him: at the azure sky, the water glinting in the sunlight and at the villa sprawling in front of him. 'Well . . . it beats Peckham.'

George nodded. 'What doesn't.' Good, he thought. I was right. Tommy's going through rough times.

Suddenly Tommy turned round and looked him straight in the eye. 'I thought you was gonna shut the door in me face.'

'Tommy,' scolded George with a sad shake of his head. 'Tommy!'

But Tommy wasn't convinced. 'Well,' he shrugged, 'there's still a ticket out on me. I'm a wanted man.'

Again George shook his head. 'Not in my house you're not. No, no, I was surprised to see you, that's all. What's it been – two years? And,' he added reproachfully, 'you did leave Blighty on the hurry up. No forwarding address.'

Tommy smiled at the other man. It was a smile that failed to reach his eyes. George was overdoing it a bit. 'So you would've dropped me a line, would you George?'

But George pretended he hadn't heard. 'Who told you,' he said with a sweeping gesture at the house, 'about this place?'

Tommy shrugged. 'Ray Fowler said something to Eddie Davies.'

'Eddie Davies? Christ, I thought he was dead.'

'Nah. He's running bootleg booze in from France.' Sensing that George was about to make a disparaging remark, he pressed on. 'Well, he's sixty-two. It's a living.'

George was intrigued. 'Is that worth the aggravation?'

'About twelve long ones a week.'

'Twelve grand?' George's tone was scathing. 'He could make more than that legal.'

'Yeah, but he don't know how. He knocks it out to the boozers. Asian shops.' Tommy took a deep slug of his drink. 'You know the sort of thing. Makes them buy a grand's worth whether they like it or not.' He thought fleetingly of Arjun Malhotra. The little Indian hadn't liked the idea at all. No doubt he had come round to it by now. Then, as he turned his attention back to George, he noted a faint smile playing on the other man's lips.

'Are you involved in that, then?' asked George, knowing full well what the answer was. Tommy, as usual, had opened his big mouth too wide.

'Nah.' Tommy shrugged and took another, slightly desperate slug of his drink. 'I just have a drink with him now and again.'

So, thought George, he's working with Eddie Davies and earning very little. And he's a wanted man. And now he wants something from me. But what?

Anxious to change the subject, Tommy looked around again and smiled ruefully. 'You're doing OK, George. But then you always did.'

George grinned. 'Retired. Why knock myself out? I have a little business that keeps me ticking over, but nothing ... well, you know.' He left the word 'illegal' hanging in the air. Tommy wasn't altogether sure if he believed that. If there was one thing he knew about George, it was that the man was a mover and a shaker. And people like that didn't tick over on a 'little business'.

'How long,' asked George in a deceptively casual manner, 'do you plan to be in this area?'

Tommy shrugged. 'Few days. Unless you invite me to stay for longer.'

George's silence was an answer in itself.

Tommy looked again at the villa, the pool and the several acres of cultivated garden – this time with undisguised envy. 'When I legged it, I got out with nothing.'

Ah, thought George. Here we go. But if Tommy expected pity, he certainly wasn't going to get it. He grinned. 'Well Tommy, I heard you got to South Africa via Florida. Didn't swim, did you?'

Tommy turned and looked him in the eye. 'So you knew where I was then, George.'

George shrugged. '"Tommy Maddern, South Africa" wouldn't have found you, would it?' Not, he could have added, that I would even have tried. I lost interest in you after that.

Tired, jaded and almost sick with envy, Tommy was beginning to feel sorry for himself. Why did George always manage to come up trumps? He gestured to the vista in front of him. 'So how's all this come about, then?'

'Building trade. I bought a firm selling timeshare apartments and villas. They were going skint. Now we're building luxury places for the Hong Kong Chinese market.'

'Lucky Chinese. I'm living in Jack Foyle's place in Deptford. He's banged up again.'

George smirked. 'Well, if these people *will* get caught...'

Tommy lapsed into silence once more. George's words merely depressed him further. No longer able to sustain his bravado, he buried his pride and asked him if he had anything on the go.

'Eh?'

'Y'know; anything I can help you out with.'

George sipped his drink, savouring not the gin but

the moment. Tommy was back where George wanted him. Begging. 'Well,' he said with a grin, 'you're not a trained plasterer, are you?' Then he noticed the expression on Tommy's face. 'I'm only kidding. No Tommy, I'm out of everything now. The past is the past. It's done. If you need a few quid, I'll see you OK, but anything else...' With a shrug and something of a smirk, he looked expectantly at Tommy.

The other man was clearly not pleased. Not only was he wasting his time, he had managed to humiliate himself into the bargain. That had not been part of his plan. He looked at George, dismayed. 'Well ... I just thought I'd look you up, y'know.'

'Where are you staying?'

Tommy told him. It was, George remembered, an armpit of a place. 'Tell you what,' he said with the air of one bestowing a great favour. 'I'll take you out to dinner. Can't do it tonight, but let's say ... Wednesday. You here then? Course you are, must be.' Then he frowned. 'Oh no, hold on. Not Wednesday. Thursday.'

But Tommy had had enough. He deposited his empty glass on the marble table and stood up. 'Yeah, well ... we'll see. Sounds like you're busy.'

Still smiling, George got to his feet and, rather too quickly, led Tommy back towards the villa and the outside gate. 'We'll certainly go out before you have to go back.' He opened the gate and grinned at Tommy's mountain bike, propped against the wall. 'Don't go falling off that thing.'

'No.' Tommy eyed the vehicle without enthusiasm. 'I won't.'

George patted him on the back. 'Great to see you, Tommy. I'll be in touch about dinner.'

That, thought Tommy, was as genuine a statement as George's claim to have gone straight. Quietly seething, he gave his ex partner in crime a farewell salute and mounted the bicycle. 'Yeah. Cheers, George. Be in touch.'

As he pedalled down the dusty road in the midday heat, he vowed that one day – one day very soon – he would see George again on different terms. On *his* terms. He wanted to have George eating out of his hand.

Two

Diane Ralston was used to people playing games. Used to it, but also fed up with it. She supposed she would be even more fed up with it were it not for the fact that she usually won those games.

The young woman opposite her obviously thought that Diane was going to lose this one. Diane knew otherwise. Yet she did grudgingly admire the woman's composure. Nadine Charles still seemed only politely interested in the fact that she had been found walking through the green channel at Heathrow customs with half a million pounds worth of cocaine in her luggage.

The cocaine had been found 'suspended' in the three bottles of rum that Nadine had been carrying in her suitcase. It was a common way of smuggling the drug, but the cocaine was detectable first by the smell and secondly by a chemical test that, if positive, turned clear liquid blue. Diane had just done the test. The sample of rum had turned a brilliant blue. 'Pretty colour,' she had observed.

'What is it?'

'It's cocaine, Nadine, and you're carrying it.'

But Nadine greeted that information with a small shrug of her elegant shoulders and settled back in her seat, crossed her legs and lit a cigarette.

Diane had already got the measure of Nadine. She was extremely attractive and extremely cool. Tall, fine-boned and very well dressed, she was also, thought Diane, used to being admired; used to bending men to her will. She was no doubt irritated that the senior customs officer at Heathrow was a woman.

Had Diane but known it, Nadine was most irritated by the fact that Diane was the more beautiful of the two. Worse, she was obviously of West Indian extraction. Nadine loathed competition. She would have disliked Diane in any situation. In this particular situation, sitting opposite her in a Heathrow interrogation room, her dislike was profound.

And now Diane was asking her to give a urine sample – another test for drugs.

'You can keep staring all you want, but I'm not having no peeing test.'

Diane shrugged. 'Fine. But you've got to go sometime.'

'Yes, but maybe on the floor.'

Diane just smiled. It was hardly the first time she had heard that particular remark. No doubt it wouldn't be the last either. 'Well, a sample's a sample.' Then the door to her right opened and Kevin Butcher, her bluff, laconic deputy, walked into the room.

'I've got him,' he said in his broad Yorkshire accent as he handed his mobile phone to Diane.

'Good. Thanks.' Still smiling, and with a charming 'excuse me' to the scowling Nadine, she left the room.

'Him' was Barry Christie. Diane had asked Kevin to contact him about the Vodaphone number and address they had found in Nadine's purse. She hoped that either one or both would lead them to whoever Nadine had been courier for. For all the girl's arrogance and air of superiority, Diane had no doubt she was a woman of little importance to her employers. Couriers were never important. And they were usually expendable.

But Diane was now silently regretting that she had asked Kevin to contact Barry. Barry was not just a colleague: he was her lover of the last four years. Years that had seen their relationship change from blissful passion to contented companionship – and latterly to stagnation. And Diane knew that most of it was her fault. She worked too hard. Although they lived together, they rarely saw each other. And Barry was very sore about it. More reflective than Diane, he was well aware that love of her job wasn't the only reason why she worked such long hours.

Yet he seemed pleased to hear her voice on the phone. 'Hi! Why'd you get Kevin to call me?'

'Couldn't do it myself. I was interviewing someone we stopped this afternoon.'

'Oh. Well, I'm glad you called.' From his tone of voice it was clear that he thought this was a personal call.

But Diane failed to register that. 'I tried calling Bill at your office, but he's not around.'

'Oh.' Barry now sounded weary. 'Right. So this is a work call or something?'

'Yes. We're holding a woman for suspended coke in three bottles of white rum.'

'Where from? The West Indies?'

'Jamaica. But the other thing we've found is a Vodaphone number and an address.'

Barry sighed down the line. Why, he asked himself, could he ever have imagined that Diane would call him for a chat? After all, they lived together, didn't they? They could chat at home. Except they didn't. 'OK,' he said. 'What's the address?'

Diane told him. But as he repeated it back to her, she detected a new sharpness in his manner. 'You OK?' she asked.

'Just dandy,' lied Barry. 'See you later, will I?'

'Er . . . I may be pretty late.'

Barry was silent for a moment before replying. Then, deciding it wasn't worth remonstrating with her, he told her to take care. But the line was already dead. Diane had gone back to work.

It was with a heavy heart that Barry replaced the receiver at his end. He could pinpoint exactly neither where nor why their relationship had started to go wrong: all he knew was that he and Diane had grown apart. What he feared was that Diane had grown out of him.

To outsiders, their relationship had, from the outset, seemed unequal. Barry was the South London boy from a lower-class, broken home. And while there was no denying that he had 'made good', he was still a long way behind Diane. She was the graduate daughter of a doctor and a lawyer; she was three years older than Barry and she was also senior to him. Up until now, none of those things seemed to have mattered. Barry and Diane had confounded their critics. Now, however, he was beginning to experience the unfamiliar and uncomfortable sensation of feeling inferior to Diane: both personally and professionally. Although he did not technically work for her, the fact that the Heathrow Division worked so closely with London City and South meant that he was occasionally at her beck and call. Like now.

Sighing, he made his way to Bill Adams's office to clear Diane's request with him. While Diane was Bill's equal, he had first call over his own staff.

Seeing that Bill was busy with Katherine Roberts and Arnie Reinhart, another member of the City and South Division, Barry merely popped his head round the door and, after a quick apology for the interruption, explained the situation.

Bill frowned. 'Where's this address of Diane's, then?'
'South London.'

Bill sighed. 'Why is it *always* South London?' Then, grinning at Barry's expression, he nodded. 'Sure. Half a million pounds worth of coke; sounds like worth following-up. Take Andreotti with you. He'll blend in nicely with the scenery.'

'Thanks, guv.' Barry smiled his acknowledgement and closed the door – but not without noticing the expression on Katherine Roberts's face. As soon as Barry had mentioned how much cocaine Nadine Charles had been found with, her ears had pricked up. No doubt she would be wanting to get her teeth into that case as well. As Barry clocked her expression, Arnie winked at him. Barry grinned. Arnie, tall, blond and – as his colleagues kept reminding him – bookish, was clearly finding Katherine as much of a trial as everyone else. Still grinning, Barry went off in search of Andreotti.

Arnie, in fact, was finding Katherine extremely trying indeed. Still smarting from the acquittal of the pornographer the other day, Bill had decided to tackle the subject from another angle: the source of many imported pornographic videos. And that source was Sweden. Already he had had reports faxed to him from that country about Britons suspected of receiving hardcore films involving children. And one report looked extremely promising indeed. He had decided to choose two of his team to follow it up. Arnie was still trying to work out what he had done to deserve being 'volunteered' with Katherine. She had already made it quite plain that she was senior to him and that he would have to clear every action and every finding with her. It wasn't the way Bill operated: it wasn't the way any of them operated. Arnie secretly suspected that Bill was quietly monitoring Katherine's high-handed tactics in order to work himself up to giving her a right royal bollocking. As yet, there was no sign of that. To Arnie's discomfiture, Bill was being extremely pleasant to Katherine.

'The information from Sweden,' he said after Barry had left the room, 'is still rather vague, but one name has been confirmed.' He looked up at Arnie and Katherine. 'A man called Eric Short.' Arnie was more than a little startled by that information. Katherine appeared not to recognize the name. 'Ex-footballer,' explained Bill.

'Oh.' Katherine wrinkled her nose in disapproval. In her book footballers and child-pornographers were equally distasteful.

'And,' continued Bill, 'a name that came up during the investigation Arnie and I were just working on. Higson.' He looked grimly satisfied as he spat out the name.

'Ah! The porn case you just lost.'

Bill shot Katherine a warning look. 'I'd rather we referred to it as the Higson case.' Without waiting for a response from her, he then pulled some photographs out of the file in front of him. 'Short's name coming up once in the trial doesn't mean much, but now hearing it again from Swedish customs, we could have something. He's involved with various charities apparently. Children's Sportsaid, football schools, that sort of thing. He's highly thought of, but this new information may put him at the centre of a major importation racket.'

Arnie refrained from commenting. Bill, he thought, was being wildly over-optimistic.

Katherine, however, nodded her approval. The words 'major importation racket' appealed to her –

especially if she could take the credit for cracking it. 'Another pillar of society,' she said, 'with a crack down his middle.'

This time it was Bill who nodded. 'That's exactly what we need to find out.' He looked from Katherine to Arnie. 'I want you two to put some time in on him and see what you can come up with.'

Arnie grinned. He already knew what Katherine felt about that. On cue, Katherine looked condescendingly at him and then turned to Bill. 'If I am on this, Bill, I would prefer to take it on myself, at least in the early stages.'

Bill looked at her. Wasn't she aware that Arnie had just spent four months working with him on the Higson case? He decided to give her the benefit of the doubt. 'Er ... I can understand you wanting to do that, but as Arnie's just spent four months on a case that might well overlap with this, pooling your efforts could save us a lot of time. You may find some of the same names crop up. OK?'

Katherine nodded. Even she understood that the last word was not a question – it was a command.

While Barry, accompanied by an unwilling Andreotti, went to investigate the address in South London that Nadine Charles had been carrying, Diane, back at Heathrow, made another discovery. Unable to resist nature's forces, Nadine had finally succumbed and, much against her will, had provided a urine sample. Diane and Kevin Butcher had wasted no time in requesting an EMIT test on the sample: a test for the presence of drugs. The test was positive. Nadine had taken a great deal of cocaine over the past twenty-four hours. That, and the half million pounds worth of the drug in her luggage, about which she claimed total ignorance, gave them a great deal of evidence against Nadine. Certainly enough for her to be formally charged with the suspected importation of cocaine into the country. Diane then contacted customs in Kingston, Jamaica, to ask them to pursue an enquiry at their end. It was only a routine and polite question. She doubted very much that Kingston would come up with anything.

Then she and Kevin requested that Nadine Charles be taken from her detention room at Heathrow to an interview room to be informed of her fate. Once there, Nadine looked from Diane to Kevin and then back again. Where most people would have sobbed or screamed with rage, Nadine smiled. Then she asked for a lawyer.

'We can arrange that for you,' said Diane.

Nadine smiled again. Then she reached into her bag and extracted a slip of paper. It contained a phone number, nothing else. 'I want,' she said with the air of one who is used to getting her own way, 'to see this lawyer.'

Diane took the paper and grinned. 'Came prepared in case of bad luck, eh?'

Nadine just stared at her.

Diane coughed and then read out a statement she now knew by heart. After a quick look at Kevin, she addressed Nadine. 'Nadine Charles, you'll be taken by myself and this officer to a police station, where you will be formally charged with the suspected importation of cocaine into this country.'

Nadine didn't even blink. Diane, her expression suggested, was boring her.

A few days later, Diane made a discovery that made her revise her opinion of Kingston customs and of her counterpart in Jamaica, one Matthew Eldridge.

Matthew's voice on the phone had been soft, musical and, in a typical Jamaican manner, unhurried. But his actions had belied the tone of his words. Nadine Charles, it turned out, had left a very interesting trail behind in Jamaica. For a start, she and her boyfriend had long been of interest to the Jamaican authorities. Neither of them, it transpired, was a stranger to drugs, and the boyfriend had twice been behind bars for dealing in them. Nadine, however, had gone one further.

'That,' said Diane after Matthew explained what they had found, 'explains why she was so surprised that we only found three bottles in her luggage.' She smiled to herself. With Matthew's evidence, there was no way any court of law could find Nadine innocent.

Diane went off to relate Matthew's news to Kevin. 'You remember,' she began without preamble, 'how surprised Nadine Charles was about the bottles of rum?'

Kevin shot his boss a lugubrious look. 'I remember how surprised she *pretended* to be.'

'No, no, I don't mean about the cocaine. I mean about the number of bottles.'

'What? That there were three?' Kevin stroked his chin. 'Mmm. It did strike me she thought there were more.'

'She did. She thought there would be four. There *were* four,' explained Diane as she walked towards the computer terminal in the corner of the room, 'when she left Kingston. Matthew Eldridge thinks the taxi driver who took her to the airport swiped one of them.'

'What on earth makes him think that?'

'Because a bottle identical to the ones in Nadine's suitcase – foil wrapping and all – was found in the taxi.

Eldridge reckons the driver somehow managed to swipe one of the bottles and took a drink.'

Kevin looked even more sceptical. 'You mean somebody drank Wrey and Nephew rum spiked with that coke? Jesus! That'd be like being hit by a train from the inside.'

'It was.' Diane grimaced. 'The man's dead.'

Kevin let out a low whistle and then looked Diane in the eye. 'So we've well and truly got her.'

But they didn't have her. Not quite. The evidence against her looked irrefutable on paper. Yet, on one count, she had a huge advantage. The solicitor she had requested was one of the most high-powered in the land. And he had wasted no time in briefing an even more high-powered barrister to handle her defence in court.

'Bloody hell!' Diane threw the piece of paper onto her desk and glared at Kevin. 'Andrew Ryan, of all people.'

'Oh blimey.' Kevin looked up and made a face. 'Andrew Ryan, QC. How on earth can she afford...?'

But Diane was jabbing angrily at the photograph of the rum bottle found in the Jamaican taxi. 'A hundred and sixty thousand pounds worth of coke in each of those bottles. Do you have to ask? That woman has wealthy connections. And who can we afford?' She began to pace the room in irritation. 'It won't be Perry Mason, that's for sure. We've got about four hundred pounds a day in the budget for a barrister.' She looked hopefully at her deputy. 'Heather Hirst? Bill Adams swears by her.'

'She just lost for him. That porn case. Maybe,' he mused, 'we should throw all the money we've got at a top QC and hope the trial's over inside two days.'

Diane gave him an old-fashioned look. 'We'd look a bit silly if it wasn't. The papers would love it. Can't you just see the headlines? "HM Customs and Excise run out of money for QC". Terrific, eh? And I don't think we exactly qualify for legal aid.'

'But it should be over quick, Diane. I mean, even at a grand a day Ryan is going to have his work cut out trying to get her off. She was full of cocaine and she was carrying those bottles. Four hundred and eighty thousand pounds of coke,' he said, emphasizing each figure. 'She'll go down.'

'As long as we second-guess what Ryan's defence is going to be.'

Why, Diane asked herself, did it have to be Andrew Ryan of all people? It wasn't just his professional reputation that annoyed her – it was the man himself. He annoyed her because, in their previous few meetings, he had made no secret of the fact that he found her extremely attractive. But what really upset Diane was that she was also attracted to him. Much as she would have liked to agree with Kevin that he was a slimy bastard, she couldn't. Andrew Ryan was a good-looking, straight-talking Irishman with a great deal of integrity. And Diane found his company unsettling. There was something in his eyes that told her he knew she was taken by him. He was one of the few men she had ever met who was not the slightest bit intimidated by her. And now, just as her relationship with Barry was at its lowest ebb yet, he was coming back into her life.

Three

'What I've done so far,' said Katherine, 'is I've concentrated on an in-depth analysis of Eric Short's private and business life. I always like to know what I'm up against.' She looked up at Bill and smiled. Bill remained expressionless. Did she, he wondered, realize just how much she was using the word 'I'? As Katherine bent once more over her neatly-typed notes, he looked over to Arnie. Arnie's expression was one of polite interest in what Katherine was saying. He probably *was* interested, thought Bill. This was possibly the first time that he – although supposedly working with Katherine – was being made aware of the progress of 'their' investigation.

'The first, and most obvious question,' continued Katherine, 'was, why would a man like Short get involved...'

'*Allegedly* involved,' corrected Bill.

Katherine ignored him. '... in importing the kind of material we suspect him of importing. So I started by looking into his company affairs. The health clubs – J. P. Leisure – were purchased for a cost of four point two million, and refurbished at a cost of seven hundred and thirty-eight thousand pounds only weeks before Black Monday.' Katherine grinned. 'That really knocked them for six. Their shares fell from well over a pound to less than fifty pence. They're still in business, but they've been trading at a considerable loss ever since.' Katherine turned the page revealing, Bill noted with dismay, several rows of facts and figures – and at least another four pages underneath. The art of being succinct was evidently, like the concept of sharing, completely alien to Katherine.

'Short,' she continued, 'is into three banks for just under eight hundred and thirty thousand. But that's only one company. For an ex-footballer,' she concluded as she indicated the mass of company names and figures on her notes, 'he has some pretty sophisticated business interests.'

'It hasn't been all flat caps and rattles for a long time, Katherine.'

At Bill's words, quietly yet damningly spoken, Arnie broke out into a huge grin.

Katherine, however, was anxious to press on. 'Maybe Short wishes it was. His parent company, E.S. Holdings, is more feel good than real good. I checked with Companies House. Judging by the last set of accounts available, he was in serious financial trouble from the year 1992.'

Bill leaned forward in his chair. 'So, in a word, you've found a motive. Our man could be involved in a very suspect area, trying to make fast money.'

'Well, the threat of bankruptcy is certainly a motive, but what's more interesting is the fact that he hasn't gone bankrupt, and the fact that certain individuals have advanced him very sizeable, unsecured loans.'

'Friends.' Bill didn't like the sound of those friends.

'Yes. Some really rather well-known ones. But even very good friends would want to know they'd get their money back. They've taken a big risk on him.' Eyes shining, Katherine sat back and looked at the two men. 'Unless, of course, they know he has another, very profitable way of earning money. Then they've taken no risk at all.'

Bill looked at Katherine. She was, he thought, trying to run before she could walk. 'So you're suggesting these friends are backing him in this racket?'

'Yes. It's possible.'

Bill nodded and looked at the mountain of material Katherine had gathered on Eric Short. 'All right. What else have you found out about him?'

Katherine had certainly not been idle. She had done her research, and done it well. Eric Short, ex-footballer, was, at the age of fifty-four, a high-profile and seemingly wealthy public figure. He had been respectably married for twenty-eight years and his two married daughters had been educated at Benenden. Everyone in his family was involved in the management of his health clubs, the original ones having belonged to his wife's family. Somewhere along the line, Eric had assumed control of the clubs. 'That,' said Katherine as she sifted through her notes, 'is how he became chairman. You know,' she continued, 'about the charity work; the holidays for the disabled, his children's football foundation and the rest.'

'Mmm,' said Bill drily. 'Very respectable.'

'As is the large house in Totteridge and the flat in the West End. But what's not so respectable is, if our suspicions prove correct, Eric Short is also the main importer of snuff movies into the UK.'

'OK.' Bill straightened and looked over to Arnie. 'So how much do we think this investigation might cost, Arnie?'

Katherine opened her mouth to reply but, seeing Bill's expression, thought the better of it.

Arnie looked sheepish. 'Er . . . I gave my preliminary budget to Katherine.'

Without a word, Bill gestured for Katherine to hand the budget over. He perused it silently for a moment and then shook his head. 'Well ... you're not going to get four man days, I'll tell you that right now.'

Katherine was ready for that one. 'But it'd be quite a splash if we get him and some of his friends for importation. It'd be the biggest scandal since ...'

'Let's remember,' cautioned Bill. 'Famous or not, he's just another suspect.' He looked pointedly at Katherine. 'This is an investigation, not a career move. Get good evidence first, and the "splash" will take care of itself.' His tone implied that he would brook no argument. He stood up, tacitly dismissing them. 'And keep your receipts,' he called as they sidled out the door, 'And I don't want to see any for lunch.' Then, seeing the look on both their faces, he relented. 'But you can,' he finished with a smile, 'have four man days.'

Sighing, Bill sat down again and eyed his paperwork without enthusiasm. Two years ago, he had never considered his work an uphill struggle against unfair odds. Yet recently, and increasingly, he found himself thinking just that. The Gerry Birch episode had started it. The fact that Alan Jackson, the regional director, had seen fit not to replace Gerry had meant that manpower as well as morale had been lowered. When Nicki Lucas, Katherine's predecessor, had left three months ago, he had threatened to resign if she was not replaced. Alan Jackson had taken the point – and had taken on Katherine. Bill sighed again and picked up his pen. Katherine. She had hit the office like a typhoon, rubbed everyone up the wrong way, and now looked like embarking on a one-woman crusade, not so much in the pursuit of Eric Short, but of furthering her own career.

Bill wondered why he had capitulated so quickly about giving her four man days. Then he remembered. Bloody Jackson's assistant had been on the phone again, banging on about cost-cutting – and telling Bill that Alan wanted, due to 'pressure of work', to defer his review meeting. Bill had nearly exploded. Pressure of work indeed. They were all pressured, his team especially. They were so pressured they had to quibble about four man days to do a job that, in reality, merited far more. And Bill had had enough quibbling. Despite his reservations about Katherine, he suspected she knew what she was doing in her investigation into Eric Short. But she needed time – and time was money. Money that Bill had now allocated to the investigation. He hoped Katherine appreciated what he'd done. Annoyed with himself for focusing too much on Katherine, he forced his thoughts back to the paperwork. He hated administration, preferring to be on the streets with his team, investigating and finally 'knocking' their targets.

Two minutes later his phone rang. Last time he had been glad of the interruption. This time he was just irritated. The paperwork had to done *sometime*.

But as he listened in horror to the voice on the other end of the line, he knew that he would get nothing more done today. After he replaced the receiver he sat motionless, head held in his hands, for a full minute. Then he picked up the receiver again and dialled a familiar number.

'Diane Ralston please.'

'Just a moment.'

A few seconds ticked by and then Diane's strong, well-modulated voice came down the line.

'Diane. It's Bill.'

'Oh hi. What's up?' Diane's was a light-hearted enquiry, not an expression of concern. Clearly Bill didn't sound as sombre as he felt.

'Bad news, I'm afraid. I've just had a call about Gerry Birch.'

'Oh?' This time Diane was guarded, wary.

'He committed suicide in Almhurst Prison last night.'

Bill was still in the office an hour after he had promised his wife to be home. He couldn't get Gerry out of his mind. He couldn't help blaming himself for the whole sorry mess. He had known, two years ago, that Gerry was in financial distress. He had known that Gerry's divorce was messy; that his wife was making impossible demands and that she was denying Gerry access to their seven-year-old son. Yet Bill had failed to realize just how desperate Gerry had been. It mattered not that everyone else agreed that Gerry had made light of his plight and that he had begun to live a secret double life. Bill blamed himself.

Himself, and another man. For the umpteenth time that evening, he swung his chair round to face the photographs that had so interested Katherine. He couldn't bear to dwell on the one of Gerry. Soon he would take it off the wall. But he had already vowed not to remove the smiling face of George Webster until he had personally wiped that smile of the man's face. He had neither seen nor heard of Webster since Gerry's incarceration, but now he vowed to see him again. Soon. In his eyes, Webster wasn't just a crook who had got away: he was now a murderer.

And then Bill looked at the other photograph. The brutal, thuggish face of Tommy Maddern stared back at him. Bill had been in his job long enough to know that Webster would have dropped Maddern – a wanted man – like a hot brick. Then, if he had any sense, he would have left the country; leaving Maddern to fend for himself. And men like Maddern didn't make money by taking in laundry. They survived in the only way they knew how.

Bill pursed his lips and unconsciously clenched his fists. Maddern was out there somewhere. Doing something illegal. Bill was going to find him. And through him he would find Webster. Webster was going to regret that.

Several miles away in Deptford, Tommy Maddern was also thinking of wiping the smile off George Webster's face. George had really annoyed him in Portugal. He hadn't, of course, made any attempt to contact him after his abortive trip to the villa. Tommy had been anyway too proud to reveal that he could afford to stay in the country for only two days. He had spent those days seething with anger, torturing himself with images of George at the country club, George by the pool, George playing golf with his rich cronies. And images of George laughing about him; about poor old Tommy who was back in his old stamping ground earning pin money through a bootlegging racket.

On his return to London, Tommy had released some of his anger by beating up another Indian shopkeeper in Peckham. The shooting of Arjun Malhotra hadn't, he conceded, been a good idea. It had very nearly lost him his job with Eddie Davies. The little Indian's recovery, while a blow to Tommy's pride, had at least one advantage: he was still around to be intimidated; still there to support, whether he liked it or not, the bootlegging operation.

Tommy had spent part of the afternoon reminding him of that. Tommy had walked into Malhotra's shop with an exaggerated swagger and a smug smile. The Indian probably thought that, after the shooting,

Tommy would leave him alone. More the fool him, thought Tommy as he walked up to the counter.

Malhotra had indeed thought just that. Still scarcely able to believe that he had been shot in the chest – and survived; still bandaged underneath his clothes and in considerable pain; he had nevertheless assumed that the brutish man who had made his life such a misery for the last year would now leave him alone. He assumed that the man who had shot him would be lying low, hiding from the police.

So when Tommy came into the shop, the terror came back with him: Malhotra started to quiver like a jelly. Why, he asked himself, was this happening to him? Why had this gang picked on him, forcing him to buy a thousand pounds worth of lager every month or so? Lager that he couldn't afford and that he couldn't sell unless he offered it at a massive discount. It was ruining his business, and his life. Refusal to co-operate with the gang was, he now knew, both useless and dangerous. Seeing Tommy, he unconsciously put a hand to his chest; to the wound that was a result of his one and only refusal to co-operate.

Tommy noticed the gesture. It made him smile. 'Wotcher, mate,' he said, 'how's the injury?'

Malhotra just stared. The man, he thought, was inhuman. Then Tommy leaned over the counter: a very human, and very frightening presence. 'I ... I can't ..' stammered the Indian.

'Yes you can.' Grinning from ear to ear, Tommy jabbed a finger at Malhotra's face. 'You're going to co-operate now, aren't you? You wouldn't want,' he added, pointing to Malhotra's chest, 'another little hole in there, would you?'

'*Please!* You're ruining my business! My family ...'

'Ah!' Tommy stood up to his full height. 'Now *there's*

an idea. You wouldn't want the wife nipping along to casualty, would you? Or your daughter. Bit of all right, your daughter, isn't she? Nice face. You wouldn't want it . . . rearranged, now would you?'

Malhotra recoiled in horror. He could cope with what had happened to him. He could deal with the fact that his business was slowly being bled dry. But endangering his family was a different matter. Never, he thought as he looked at Tommy with pure hatred. I will never let you get your hands on any of my family. I'll kill you first. 'No,' he said in a small, defeated voice. 'Please. Not my family. I'll do anything. Anything.'

Tommy laughed out loud as he noted Malhotra's expression. 'Good. But don't worry, we don't want you doing anything except stocking up on a bit more of that.' Grinning, Tommy gestured towards the crates of unsold lager at the back of the shop. 'Not exactly doing a roaring trade in it, are you? Here,' he added as he moved towards the pile, 'I'll help you out.' Reaching over, he plucked two cans out of the crate at the top. Roaring with laughter, he slipped them into his pockets. 'Cheers, mate.' Then he turned on his heel and walked out of the shop. As he reached the front door, he suddenly turned back. 'Oh – and I'll be in touch about the next delivery. Couple of weeks or so? Keep the chequebook handy.' Still laughing, he made his way out to the street, leaving a terrified Arjun Malhotra alone to contemplate his ruination.

Now, back in Deptford, Tommy found his thoughts straying to Malhotra's daughter. He had been lying when he had said he found her attractive. Malhotra probably thought she was the bee's knees – but she wasn't Tommy's type. Her friend, however, was a different story. She had a twinkle in her eye that appealed to him. He had noticed it on one of his previous visits to the shop when she had been helping the Malhotra girl behind the counter. Tommy had been careful, on that occasion, not to reveal the true nature of his business. He had, he reflected with a laugh, been careful to keep it in the family. The friend, he had been glad to see, didn't seem to suspect anything. She had just looked on in amazement as the big white man had entered the shop. White men didn't usually go into the shop. Then the daughter, who knew full well what Tommy was up to, had ushered her out. She'd shown a nice bit of leg, recalled Tommy. Pity she was black.

Thinking of women had the effect of making Tommy even more irritated with Webster. The man always pulled the most attractive ones. His ex-wife, for instance. She'd been a bit of a stunner. If she'd been Tommy's, he'd have looked after her. Not set her up and pretended to be shocked when she'd ended up in the nick. Bastard.

Tommy punched the TV remote control with more than his usual savagery. Some crappy game show. Typical. Same on ITV. Couldn't get the other channels on this poxy portable thing. Feeling increasingly sorry for himself, Tommy looked around him. Poxy flat as well. 'Jesus!' he said out loud. Here he was, aged thirty-four, dossing around some friend's gaff, bootlegging to earn a crust and spending half his time looking over his shoulder. Not much of a life. Not the life he had imagined for himself when he'd run away from the remand home all those years ago.

Tommy reached down to the bare floor and found another beer can. Drowning his sorrows may not be the best answer, but at least it dulled the pain. Then the telephone rang. As always, it startled him: and as always he didn't answer it. Instead he looked suspiciously at the answering machine as it clicked on. The voice on the other end was the last one he would ever have expected. It was deep, rich and unmistakably South African. Afrikaner South African.

'I bet you're bloody well sitting there, aren't you Tommy?' the machine boomed. 'It's your old pal here...'

With a whoop of delight, Tommy snatched the receiver. 'Conny! Conny, you old sod! How are you? Where are you?'

The other man chuckled. 'Where you should be, mate. On the Cape. I was in the Harbour Bar last night,' he added, unconsciously rubbing salt in the wound. 'They all send their best.'

Tommy was silent for a moment, imagining the sound of the sea as it lapped at the cliffs below Conny's house. It had been nearly two years since he'd been there, but he would never forget it. The sun. The sea. The cheap booze and fantastic fish. The birds. 'Wish I was there, mate,' he said with audible envy. 'Wish I was.'

On the other side of the world, the bluff, burly South African ex-policeman laughed the hearty, booming laugh that Tommy remembered so well. 'Listen,' he said. 'You could be, sooner than you think.'

Tommy drew a sharp breath. Then he exhaled deeply. This had happened to him before: hopes built only to be shattered moments later. 'Whadd'ya mean?' he said with a mixture of suspicion and hope.

Unseen by Tommy, Conny Devooght cradled the telephone receiver under his chin and lit a cigar. 'I might be able to put something your way,' he said between puffs.

'In South Africa?'

'No, no. In Europe. But Tommy, it'll mean you'll be

able to take early retirement.' He chuckled again. 'Live in luxury down here.'

'Yeah?' Tommy had heard that one before.

'Definitely. Biggest thing ever, but it needs cash up front.'

'Conny...'

'Yeah, yeah, I know. You don't have two brass farthings to rub together. But you know people, Tommy.'

Tommy's suspicions were now fully aroused. Men like Conny didn't phone up old mates – destitute old mates at that – out of the blue to ask for their help in 'the biggest thing ever'. When he said as much Conny, in a blasé, offhand way, explained that he'd had a 'little setback'.

'My deal went up in smoke, so to speak,' he explained. 'Need to go again with it. You, er ... you had a finance friend, am I right?'

How the hell, thought Tommy, did Conny know about George? 'Yeah. I, er ... yeah. I know a guy.'

'Webber? Webb? Was that his name?'

'No, that's not his name, but I know who you mean.'

Conny was silent for a moment. 'Well,' he said as he puffed again at his cigar, 'if he's a real player, not just a wrist merchant, this could be something for him. But,' he added with a hard edge to his voice, 'it's like Lloyd's of London. You have to buy in.'

'Well, my bloke's got long pockets. But he don't like parting with much. What're we talking about?'

'About three quarters of a million.'

Tommy whistled down the line. 'The take?'

'No. That's to buy in.'

Tommy laughed out loud. 'Give over, Conny. Nobody's going to go in that much – especially if they don't know what it's all about.'

'Yeah, I know. But,' added Conny in a lower voice, 'there are sixteen million good reasons why it's a deal worth talking about.'

Two days later Tommy went to see an old friend. The old friend was appalled. And surprised. And not a little scared. Tommy wouldn't come back into his life unless he had something very big to talk about. Tommy was a wanted man and he, David Archer, was an inmate of Ford Open Prison, on weekend leave at his sister's house. If there was anything good about Tommy's visit, it was that Archer's sister was not there to witness it: and that his weekends were unsupervised.

After his initial paralysed shock at Tommy's appearance on his doorstep, Archer quickly and reluctantly ushered him inside. The parole board wouldn't take kindly to the sighting of a wanted man lurking on his doorstep.

'How the hell,' he asked by way of greeting, 'did you know where to find me?'

'Asked.' Tommy was extremely pleased with himself. 'I should have been a detective.' Then he looked around the shabby though tidy little house. 'Heard you was on weekend leave. Society getting ready to receive you back, is it? How's it in Ford? Met many judges?' Tommy bellowed with laughter at his own humour. Seeing old Dave cheered him up: the man looked old, wizened and defeated. He made Tommy feel strong, powerful and in control.

Archer glared at his unwelcome visitor. 'If anyone knows you came here, everything could be ruined for me. You're a wanted man.'

'Yeah, yeah.' Tommy shrugged. 'They may want me, but they can't have me.' Then he looked the little man in the eye. 'I've got a proposition for you.'

'I'm not interested.'

'Sixteen million quid.' Tommy smiled and loomed over Archer. 'That sound interesting?'

'Go away. I don't want to have to stay in prison. I want my life back.'

Tommy looked extremely put out. He hadn't expected such a vehement brush-off. 'Look,' he said, dropping his previous cocky superiority, 'I need to raise three quarters of a million. You know people – people with money. Who do I talk to?'

Archer fought back the smile that was playing on his lips. 'George Webster.'

Tommy shook his head. 'Nah. Forget George. This is my deal.' He prodded his chest to illustrate the point. 'Mine. Bring George in and I finish up on wages. I want to talk to people who can put together three quarters of a million. I don't know these sorts. You do.'

This time the supercilious look was on Archer's face. 'Aren't you getting rather out of your depth?'

Every muscle in Tommy's face – and in his fists – tightened in anger. It was only with supreme effort that he resisted the urge to throw the little man to the other end of the room. 'No offence taken,' he eventually said with a forced smile. 'But Dave, your whack could put you in clover for the rest of your days.'

Archer shook his head. 'I can't help. Please Tommy, leave me.' Then he looked up in alarm as he heard the sound of a key at the front door. 'Tommy!' he begged. 'That's my sister. Please, she'll be . . .'

But she was already. The door opened to reveal a short, squat woman huddled against the cold in a depressing grey coat and hat. Surprised to find a stranger in the house, she looked to her brother for enlightenment.

Archer was literally hopping from one foot to the

other. 'Hello Margaret.' Then he nodded towards the towering Tommy. 'A friend of mine from, er . . .'

'From hell,' spat Tommy, already making his way out. 'And,' he added with a last, disgusted look at Archer, 'I might come back.'

As he left the house, Tommy's supercilious snarl gave way to a worried frown. So much for David Archer. He should have given the creep a hiding – and thumped the old bag of a sister into the bargain. Going to him had, he realised, been a mistake. He and Dave had always disliked each other. The only consolation for his fruitless journey was that Dave looked as if he had really suffered from being in prison. And it was a real laugh that he thought he could go straight after so many years being bent. He'd been a rotten crook anyway. Suddenly Tommy laughed out loud. At least he had his freedom. Open Prison or not, Dave was still a lag.

Back at his sister's house, the lag was embarking on a telephone conversation that Tommy would have found extremely interesting. And very worrying. He had just dialled a number in Portugal.

'Hello? Yes, hello; I'd like to speak to Mr George Webster please. Archer.' He pursed his lips as he listened to the voice at the other end. 'No, just Archer. He'll know.'

George did know. 'Dave! Well, well, if it isn't old home week! How're you doing?'

Annoyed by George's ebullience, by his happy-go-lucky tones, David Archer frowned and gripped the receiver more tightly. 'You said,' he began without preamble, 'I should call if there was ever anything.'

'Ye . . . es.'

'Tommy Maddern has just been to see me.'

'Gets about a bit, doesn't he? Anything in particular – or was it just social?'

'Something about putting together a deal worth several million. One go, scoop the pot is what he said.'

'Oh yeah.' George was unimpressed. Tommy was all talk and no trouser, that was his problem.

'Yeah. But he needs three quarters of a million seed money.'

George burst out laughing. 'Tommy? Nobody'd give him five bob. When was this, anyway?'

'Just now. He said it was something very big. I suggested he speak to you but he, er . . . he didn't seem too keen.'

George laughed again. Poor old Tommy. He was obviously sore about being turned down in Portugal. Well, let him be. He'd come crawling back. 'I give him three days, tops,' he said down the line, 'and he'll be on the trumpet to me. You mark my words.'

David Archer didn't reply.

'Appreciate the call,' said George, figuring it would look good to show a little concern. 'You out yet?'

'No.'

George's chuckle was involuntary. 'Oh well, keep smiling.'

But in the small suburban council house on his weekend leave from Ford, David Archer did not have a great deal to smile about. He wondered why he found himself incapable of escaping George's clutches.

Four

Diane and Kevin were convinced that Nadine Charles would be found guilty. They had a huge amount of evidence against her. They had the three bottles of rum she had been carrying: they had the lab report about the amount of cocaine suspended in them: they had a witness who had seen Nadine check her luggage in at Kingston and who had sat next to her on the plane: they had the EMIT test relating to her own consumption of the drug. They were so confident that they had Matthew Eldridge flown over from Jamaica to give his own evidence about the fourth bottle and the dead taxi driver. They reckoned their case was unassailable.

But they had reckoned without Andrew Ryan. Throughout the trial and in the lobby of the Crown Court, Diane had been deliberately frosty towards him. Kevin had seen nothing odd about that: Ryan was the enemy. And if he noticed Ryan being overtly flirtatious with Diane, he assumed it was just part of his tactics; to lull her into a false sense of security. Diane, of course, knew otherwise. She knew that Ryan was upset and not a little surprised by her offhand manner. And she knew she couldn't afford to let her guard down in front of him. He was extremely personable – and extremely persuasive. He was also exceptionally charming; a charm enhanced by his sparkling blue eyes, lilting Irish brogue, and almost boyish enthusiasm for life.

The first blow he delivered was to tell the judge, just before the trial started, that he would accept all the prosecution evidence. It was left to a furious Diane to bite her lip and explain to her witnesses that they could all go home. Matthew Eldridge was appalled. 'Whaddya mean? I've only just got here. I got evidence to give.'

'I know. But I'm afraid you can't give it. Because Ryan has accepted all our written evidence, it will simply be read by the jury and you won't be called as a witness.'

'What? Me neither?' Mrs Slattery, the large lady who had flown over with Nadine looked affronted. 'But I've come all the way from Leicester!' She looked indignantly at Matthew. He was unimpressed. Kingston, Jamaica was a hell of a lot further than Leicester.

Ryan's next coup was to make Nadine out to be vulnerable and naive: a helpless innocent on whom the drugs had been planted. Nadine's appearance in court certainly helped his cause. She looked stunning, absurdly young – and she proved herself a mistress of the trembling lower lip. The predominantly male jury was impressed. Diane was livid. She sat tight-lipped as Ryan addressed the court with theatrical flourish.

'This young girl,' he said as he gestured towards his client, 'was duped into bringing items she thought were perfectly legal into the United Kingdom by a man who, as you see, is not in this court today. He gets away with it – she suffers the consequences.'

If only, thought Diane, they had been able to get their hands on that man. They knew his name was Rufus Teague; that he was known to his friends as Uzi because of the weapon he always carried, that he had a shaven head, that he drove a black BMW and that he was an extremely nasty piece of work. But the only 'evidence' they had to connect him to Nadine was that she had been in possession of his mobile phone number, and that was too flimsy even to be allowed in court. Diane's asking Barry and Andreotti to put Teague under surveillance had led, as yet, nowhere. Although he was a highly visible character, he also had several people to help him with his dirty work. People, thought Diane with contempt, like Nadine Charles. There Diane differed from Ryan: she knew that Nadine had knowingly smuggled the drugs.

But what Diane didn't know – and would have been extremely interested to learn – was that Rufus Teague was keeping tabs on what was happening in court that day. He wasn't foolish enough to come himself. Instead he had sent his girlfriend. She was sitting in the public gallery, watching intently as Ryan continued his impassioned plea for Nadine's innocence.

'This young woman,' Ryan almost shouted, 'has never had any involvement with crime, has never been involved with drugs, and those – whether the prosecution chooses to accept them or not – are the facts.'

Diane had to admit his performance was impressive. It was with a mixture of appalled disbelief and grudging admiration that she listened to him refute the evidence that she had so painstakingly garnered. He scoffed at the idea that Nadine, as a hard-nosed smuggler knowing her booty was worth a fortune, would give a bottle to the taxi driver who had taken her to Kingston airport. And, with a sidelong glance at Matthew Eldridge, he dismissed the notion of Nadine being responsible for the driver's death. If the Jamaican authorities had anything like a decent case against her, they would have had her extradited from the UK.

'Nadine Charles,' he went on to conclude, 'gave that taxi driver a bottle of white rum because, as she has said in her statement, the man had told her he'd recently had a birthday.' He looked at Nadine and smiled. 'It was a gift. A gift.'

Nadine smiled back. It hadn't been a gift. The wretched man had stolen it from the case, she supposed, when he was hauling her luggage out of the boot. The case had sprung open before she'd left for the airport. Stupidly, she hadn't checked to see if she had closed it properly the second time. Served the piece of trash right, she thought.

'But,' continued Ryan, 'the prosecution aren't interested in the simple truth. No, they've made up their minds about Nadine Charles.' He shook his head in disgust. 'Black girl. West Indies. Drugs. Guilty. So they ditched logic and pursued her in order to get what I believe they refer to as "a right result".' Shuddering with distaste, he looked at Kevin and Diane. Then he looked one last time at the jury. 'I mean, the police don't believe she's a killer, or they'd have arrested her – and nobody believes smugglers give their goods away. Except, of course, the customs team who started this little fiasco.'

There was a minute of stunned, admiring silence; a silence which Diane broke by leaning over to Kevin and whispering in his ear: 'I could have been at a funeral.'

'Sorry.' Andrew Ryan did indeed look extremely contrite as, ten minutes after the jury announced their verdict, he sidled up to Diane.

She just stared at him for a moment. Two thoughts simultaneously entered her head. One was that he had gorgeous eyes. The other was that she hated him with a vengeance.

'How can you sleep at night?' she spat.

Ryan grinned. 'There's an answer to that.' Then he registered that Diane was not even remotely amused. 'Oh come on, Diane. Don't be so angry.'

That just made her even angrier. The words 'not

guilty' were still ringing in her ears. 'What the hell do you expect? And,' she added as she drew herself to her full height, 'I was not motivated to "get a right result" as you put it. Why do you always adopt that kind of voice to quote us?'

God, thought Ryan, she's attractive. He looked into her eyes and lowered his voice. 'What did you expect me to do? Lose? I was only doing my job.'

Diane held his look. 'She was guilty.'

'The jury didn't think so.' He shrugged. 'You've got your cocaine, she's probably had the fright of her life. You won't see her again. Everyone's had . . .'

'A right result.'

Ryan had the grace to look abashed: and to remain silent.

But Diane, despite her anger and her vituperative attack on Ryan, seemed reluctant to depart. For a moment they stood together, their awkwardness relieved by both of them, quite unconsciously, watching the departure of a nervous-looking young girl from the court's public gallery. She had an intent look on her face and, as they watched, extracted a mobile phone from her jacket pocket.

'D'you think,' said Ryan as he turned back to Diane, 'that there's ever a chance you and I might get together on neutral ground?'

'Not a cat in hell's.' Diane regretted the harshness of her words the minute she spoke them.

They appeared to surprise Ryan as well. 'Shame,' he said, meaning it. 'It's never personal.' He gestured around the court lobby. 'This, I mean.'

Diane smiled without humour. 'It is when you lose.' Then she turned abruptly on her heel and went in search of Kevin, leaving Andrew Ryan looking and feeling more dejected than he had in years.

Outside the court, the girl from the public gallery was on the phone to her boyfriend. 'She tried to do you. She only brought three bottles through. Seems the taxi driver nicked one from her luggage – but the other two never even got packed.' She cocked her head as she listened to Rufus Teague's explosive reply. Then she smiled. 'No, no, she was acquitted. I'm sure she'll welcome a visit from you.' Then she laughed.

Two days later Matthew Eldridge phoned Diane from Jamaica. His first-ever trip to Britain had proved a bitter disappointment. His hopes to fit some sightseeing into the visit had been firmly dashed by Andrew Ryan's tactics in court: not needed in the witness stand meant not needed in Britain, and Matthew had been despatched back to Jamaica while still suffering jet lag from his arrival. But more galling for Matthew had been Nadine Charles's acquittal. It insulted his professional pride that the girlfriend of a well-known crook should walk away from the crime she had committed. And it enraged him that a Kingston taxi driver had died as a result of Nadine's activities. The minute he landed in Kingston he resolved to call Andrew Ryan's bluff: to investigate the driver's death and level a charge of murder against Nadine.

'Matthew!' Diane was more than a little surprised to hear from him so soon. 'How's it going?'

'Tired.' Matthew sounded exhausted. 'Dunno 'bout this jet leg business.'

Diane laughed. 'Happens to the best of us.'

'Yeah, well, on that subject, I got so mad about coming all that way for nothing and not getting tickets for anything and not seeing any sights that I decided we'd have a word with Nadine's boyfriend again.' As he spoke, he looked through the glass partition of his office where said boyfriend was being interrogated by three West Indian customs officers. He was not having a happy time. 'We mentioned,' he continued to Diane, 'a possible charge of murder for him, and he's being really helpful all of a sudden.' He grinned. 'He's blaming Nadine for everything, naturally, and offering to give us names of contacts in London. If I were you, Diane, I'd watch Nadine. You may want to arrest her again pretty soon.'

Diane could think of nothing she'd rather do than arrest Nadine Charles again. But first she had to find her. She knew, from Matthew, that Nadine wasn't back in Jamaica. She knew that Nadine would be unaware of the latest developments in that country. And she suspected that, if the girl had any sense at all, she would be trying her best to get as far away from Rufus Teague as possible. That led to the logical conclusion that Nadine had booked herself onto a flight back to Kingston. There was, reflected Diane as she picked up her phone again, a very easy way to find out. Working at Heathrow was not without its compensations.

Rufus Teague, however, had already found out everything he needed to know about Nadine Charles's plans. He wasn't very pleased with Nadine, and Diane's assumption that she would try to avoid him had been correct. He had, therefore, instructed his girlfriend to follow Nadine out of the Crown Court two days previously, and hadn't been surprised to learn that she had taken the Underground to Heathrow and checked into a hotel. It had taken him longer to discover which room she was staying in – and what flight she was taking to Jamaica. Yet, by the time Diane received her call from Matthew, Rufus was armed with all the information he needed. And by the time Diane received the information that Nadine was staying in an airport hotel and was leaving that evening for Jamaica, Teague was ready to 'pay her a visit' – accompanied by five of the men who knew him as Uzi. Nadine, he thought as he drove towards Heathrow in his BMW as dusk began to fall, was a very stupid girl. To lose thousands of pounds of cocaine was bad enough: to think she could escape unpunished was even worse. She would have to be taught a lesson.

Nadine didn't stand a chance. She was shocked into paralysis by the six men who burst into her room, and only started to struggle after they had thrown a duvet over her head and lifted her off her feet. A hefty thump from one of the men quietened her down – but not before she heard Rufus's voice. And it wasn't the soft, caressing voice he used for hotel receptionists. 'You're in trouble, girl,' he snarled. 'Where's my stuff? Where the hell,' he added as he kicked her dangling legs, 'is my stuff? I want what I paid for. I paid for six bottles.'

The irony of the last statement wasn't lost on Nadine. She had been stopped at customs because of three bottles. She had thought she had four. Now she knew that there had been six. The only person who could have stolen the other two was her boyfriend in Jamaica.

Diane Ralston and Kevin Butcher arrived at the hotel two hours after Nadine had been abducted. One look at Nadine's room told them what had happened.

Diane swore like a trooper, surprising even Kevin, as she took in the scene of the struggle. Then she turned to him and grimaced. 'Teague?'

'Yeah. Teague.'

Diane bit her lip. It had all seemed too easy a few days ago. Now the whole scenario was infinitely more complex – and probably off her patch. She sighed and shook her head. 'Then I suggest we get straight to City and South. The only address we have for Teague is on Bill's patch.'

Bill smiled in genuine pleasure as Diane, with Kevin at her heels, rushed into his office. He and Diane enjoyed a good friendship as well as a harmonious working relationship, and, in the latter respect, complemented each other perfectly. As head of the City and South office, he was often asked to follow-up a case that began at Diane's Heathrow headquarters. Likewise, he and his team regularly alerted Diane about cases that they had begun and that resulted in activity at the airport. Furthermore, Bill and Diane frequently swapped both information and staff. Had either of them been remotely territorial or resentful about such encroachments, their relationship would have been a completely different story. As Bill acknowledged Diane's friendly greeting, he couldn't help comparing her to Katherine. If she ever found herself in Diane's position, the latter would, he suspected, muddy the waters and create an altogether different working relationship between the two branches of Her Majesty's Customs and Excise.

'So?' Bill gestured for both of them to sit down. 'What gives?'

'Nadine Charles.'

'Huh?'

Diane raised an amused eyebrow. 'The West Indian we found with half a million pounds of coke. Not an easy one to forget.'

'Oh. *Her*.' Bill grinned. Fancy forgetting that. 'But I thought,' he added with a frown, 'she'd been acquitted?'

'She has,' said Kevin. 'And now we think she's been abducted.'

'Isn't that her problem rather than ours?'

Diane shook her head and sat down. 'Sorry. Dropped you in at the deep end. The thing is, Bill, the information we're getting from the West Indies suggests we may be in a position to arrest her again. Customs over there picked up her boyfriend and he's offering them any information they want.'

Bill looked sceptical. 'And how reliable will that be?'

'Well, he's saying that the cocaine we lifted Nadine for had been paid for by Rufus Teague, and was part of a regular operation.'

'Mmm.' Bill turned towards the open door of his office and called to Barry in the main office. 'Barry! Can you bring the stuff you've got on that Rufus Teague bloke?' Then he addressed Diane again. 'So you reckon it's Teague who grabbed the girl?'

Diane nodded. 'Yep. And I have to find her to confirm what the boyfriend's been saying. If Teague's got her, she may be in danger.'

'Not our problem.'

'Quite. But if she disappears as a possible witness against Teague – assuming she'll give evidence – then it *is* our problem. One dope smuggler grassing up another,' she finished, 'may not stick. Two telling the same story, Nadine and the boyfriend I mean, probably will.'

'So what are you asking us to do? Watch her? Arrest her?'

'She's disappeared, Bill. I want you to find her.'

'Please!' On her knees and choking back the tears, Nadine tried to fend off another blow from Rufus Teague. 'I'll do anything you want,' she pleaded, 'but don't hit me again. I didn't rip you off. He gave me four bottles. I did everything he told me.'

But Rufus Teague didn't believe her. Not only had

the lying bitch stolen two bottles of the suspended cocaine, but she'd lost one to a taxi driver and the other three to HM Customs. He looked down at her; at her ripped dress and bloodied face. Then he looked around the room. It was bare, save for the mattresses lining the walls and floor. A strange method of decoration – but useful for soundproofing. None of the neighbours in the run-down council block could hear Nadine's screams. And Nadine was going to be screaming a lot more before he'd finished with her.

'So,' he said, looking back at Nadine. 'The taxi man took one bottle. I'll give you that.' Then he hit her again. 'That's for being so fucking stupid. But somewhere,' he continued as Nadine fell to the floor under the weight of his punch, 'there's two bottles more worth about three hundred and twenty grand. You'll stay here till you tell me where they went, bitch.'

Barry's file on Rufus Teague contained four addresses. 'He uses them all on a regular basis,' he said to Bill and Diane. 'Andreotti and I got all that when we did the surveillance. The guy's not too secretive. Deals on the streets, throws his weight around. Nobody messes with him.' He looked Bill in the eye. Somehow he couldn't quite meet Diane's. Looking at each other – let alone talking to each other – seemed to have become a thing of the past. 'If we're asked to arrest Teague,' he said in a low voice, 'we'll need armed police back-up.'

But they couldn't get the back-up until they'd located Teague. And, if Diane and Kevin's suspicions were correct, locating him was a matter of extreme urgency.

Manpower being at an all-time low, Bill and Barry were obliged to carry out the search on their own. Kevin and Diane were needed back at Heathrow: Katherine and Arnie were somewhere – God knows where, thought Bill – investigating Eric Short, and someone – Andreotti – had to man the fort. 'When the hell,' Bill asked Barry as they made their way to their separate cars, 'is Jo coming back?'

Barry shrugged. 'Dunno. But her leather jacket's still on the back of her chair, so I guess the answer's sometime.'

'Hmm.' Unimpressed, Bill concentrated on the task in hand. 'Which addresses do you reckon are the most likely?'

'Newnham Road and Stanhope House. Both in South London.'

'Surprise, surprise. OK. You take the first and I'll see what's happening at Stanhope House. If he's got the girl, you can bet he's got some of his heavies lurking outside wherever she is.'

'And that glossy BMW of his.'

'Registration?'

Barry looked at the notepad he was carrying. 'Foxtrot 341, Alpha, Romeo, Tango.'

Twenty minutes later it was Barry who found the car. It was parked outside the Newnham Road address. Barry parked round the corner and strolled casually past the BMW. There was a duvet in the back seat. And on the duvet were spots of blood.

Barry sprinted back to his car and phoned Bill. Bill muttered a curt 'I'm on my way' and then phoned the police. They, too, said they were on their way.

Because Barry was already *in situ*; because he knew that time was of the essence, he didn't wait for either Bill or the police before going into the building. He didn't plan to do anything other than establish which flat Teague and his henchmen were in – but neither did he plan on being seen by them.

It was when he reached the sixth floor that he heard

the screams. He had heard many screams during his work with customs – but never ones that communicated such terror and pain. Something about them impelled him further, up another flight of stairs, closer to their source.

On the landing of the eighth floor he ran straight into a large, wide-eyed West Indian lady who was standing at the open door of her flat. Panting from his exertions, he nodded and then flashed his ID card at her. 'The screams,' he asked without preamble. 'Which floor?'

The lady, clearly relieved that someone other than herself was going to do something about them, pointed upwards. 'Top,' she said. Then she looked Barry in the eye and shook her head. 'The gangster's flat. Knew he was trouble the minute I set eyes on him – but would the council listen to anything I said? We folks're living in terror, I tell you. And when I saw that girl they took up this afternoon, well, I just knew...'

But Barry had heard enough. In a normal situation, the woman's response would have had him running back downstairs to await the arrival of Bill and the police, ready to inform them of the whereabouts of their target. But this was no ordinary situation; the screams, louder now, were urging him ever upwards.

Barry should have heeded his professional training instead of his conscience. He should have realized that one of Teague's henchmen had witnessed even his very quick examination of the BMW and had put two and two together. He should have been prepared for the fact that Teague had posted a guard on the landing of the twelfth floor. And, most importantly of all, he ought to have realized that Teague was utterly ruthless and would take no prisoners. But as Barry reached the eleventh floor, none of those considerations entered his mind. He had, through the landing window, just witnessed a scene that would stay with him for months. The screams had stopped – and now he knew why.

'Why,' asked Diane much later, 'did you go rushing into the building all on your own? You could have been killed.'

'I very nearly was. Teague *does* carry an Uzi: he blew half the plaster off the wall behind me.'

'So why didn't you wait for the police?'

Barry shook his head. 'Couldn't.' He turned to Diane. 'I was propelled up the stairs by uncontrollable anger. Couldn't really believe what I'd seen.' Diane nodded in sympathy. She could hardly believe it either – but she knew it was true. So did Barry: he'd written it in his report.

Nadine Charles, bleeding but still very much alive, had been thrown out the window of the twelfth floor of Stanhope House.

Five

'You did *what*?' Bill was already in a foul mood. Katherine was making it much worse. 'You entered Eric Short's building by dubious – no, illegal – means, and you expect me to congratulate you?'

'No. I'm just telling you that I'd like to gain access again.'

Bill just stared. What was it, he wondered, with Katherine? Why did she have this desperate need to prove herself, at seemingly any cost? And how on earth could one person have so much brass neck? Then a small smile flitted across his face. He supposed he should be thankful that his new deputy was obviously impossible to intimidate. Still without replying, he looked once more at the surveillance photographs she had brought in. Some of them were of Eric Short. Others were of a man who according to Arnie was called Alex Britain and who was involved in football charities. But the most interesting were of the interior of Eric Short's office. Katherine and Arnie had, according to the former, entered his office by picking the locks. She had imparted this information to Bill in a guileless, matter-of-fact manner, as if it was something she did every day. But then she probably did.

Bill had to admit the photographs looked promising. Why would a man whose main activities were in leisure clubs and charities have banks of video recorders in his private office? And why would that office be so heavily secured? He flipped through the photographs and stopped at the one of the Chubb locks, the bolts and the chains that protected Eric Short's inner sanctum. Interesting. Very interesting. Then he looked over to Katherine. She was waiting patiently, expectantly and, he thought, confidently for his response.

'Are you ready to knock the place?' he asked.

Katherine looked uncertain. She obviously hadn't expected quite such a positive response.

'Well? Are you ready? Have you got evidence?' Bill thought he detected a flicker of annoyance in Katherine's expression.

'No,' she said after a short silence. Then she pointed at the photographs. 'I think everything we want is in that office.'

'So knock it.'

'We . . . ll.'

Bill looked at Katherine. Katherine looked at Bill.

'You're not sure, are you?' he prompted.

'I'm . . . pretty sure.'

'What does Arnie think?'

'Arnie?' Katherine looked extremely surprised. Bill might as well have asked her Santa Claus's opinion on the matter.

'Yes, Arnie.' Bill looked at her through steely eyes. 'He has opinions as well.'

She flinched. Yet rather than back down, she went on the offensive. 'I am the senior officer, Bill.'

'Yes, but he's working with you, not *for* you.'

She didn't reply.

'Look,' said Bill with a sigh. 'Just keep observing our Mr Short for the moment. Not too gung-ho, Katherine. We're Soho,' he added with what he hoped was a conciliatory smile, 'not the Lone Star State.'

'Yes. Thank you,' she said through pursed lips. Then

she stood and turned to leave the room, leaving Bill's olive branch on the floor.

Bill stared after her for a long moment. Was it his fault, he wondered? Had he gone wrong somewhere along the line, or was he losing his touch? He certainly wasn't having much luck recently. The escape of Rufus Teague and his gang after the appalling death of Nadine Charles was just the latest in what he now considered a long line of disasters. Disasters that, as far as he was concerned, stretched back two years.

He glanced again at the photograph of George Webster on the pin-board. There was now an empty space beside it. Gerry's photograph had gone. Bill had removed it that morning, after he had returned from Gerry's funeral. Katherine hadn't known that she had chosen the very worst time possible to grind her axes about Eric Short.

Bill had been the only one from City and South to attend the funeral. It had been a short, dismal affair with very few mourners. Gerry, thought Bill with regret, would have been horrified. The young man who had been seconded to Bill at City and South seven years ago had been a popular extrovert with a wicked line in humour and an eye for the ladies. A pity, thought Bill, that the lady he had chosen to marry had let him down so badly. Bill blamed the snobbish, grasping Carol for many of the things that had gone wrong in Gerry's life. But not as much as he continued to blame himself.

When Katherine had marched into his office, Bill had been in the process of depressing himself even further. A month previously, a young female customs officer had been blown to bits while examining a container recently arrived in Harwich. The tabloids had gone to town, competing with each other in their alternately mawkish and sensational stories about her job and her domestic situation. It had transpired that the young woman had been twenty-six, a divorcée, and the sole source of support for her seven-year-old daughter. On an otherwise quiet day the newspapers still ran the odd story about the 'tragic orphan', whose plight they exposed but did nothing to help alleviate.

While as appalled as anyone else by the manner of the young woman's death, Bill was even more surprised by the lack of progress in discovering what had been in the container that had blown apart in her face. The national press had made no progress in discovering the cause of the explosion. Internal investigations within the customs service had likewise come up with nothing. Bill thought it most peculiar – and not a little suspicious.

Still, Harwich was nothing to do with City and South or Heathrow, and there were other matters to attend to. There was paperwork; there was his forthcoming review with Alan Jackson; there was next quarter's budget to prepare ... and there was George Webster. Gerry's funeral had made Bill even more determined to run the man to earth: so much so that, on the way back from the crematorium he had taken a diversion – a long one – to Webster's last known address. It hadn't surprised him that the affluent young woman who answered the door knew nothing about Webster. She had been charmingly apologetic but equally vague: she even had trouble remembering through which estate agent she and her husband had purchased the house. It had been, she recalled, 'the one down the road. You know ... Whatsit and son.'

Luckily for Bill, there turned out to be only one estate agent on the nearby main road. Taking his cue from the vague woman, Bill entered and chatted in an aimless way about wanting a house 'like the one up the road. You know, the one that used to belong to old Webster.' The aged agent, whom Bill took to be Whatsit and not the son, nodded and said what a pity it was the only house like it in the neighbourhood. Then he had brightened somewhat and said that it had changed hands twice since Mr Webster had sold up and retired to Portugal.

Bill had had difficulty in suppressing a triumphant smile. Bingo, he thought as he made his excuses and left. Portugal.

Later, back in the office, he wondered what on earth he had been doing. The files on Webster – both the police one and the Customs and Excise one – were closed. Officially, the man was not and never had been a criminal. But Bill did not and never would believe that. And he certainly didn't believe that Webster had retired to Portugal. In his experience, master criminals never retired.

Bill was still wondering what to do with his knowledge of Webster being in Portugal – certainly nothing official, he knew he would get severely reprimanded for that – when Barry interrupted him. It was a mere ten minutes after Katherine's stormy departure. Bill looked up without enthusiasm. The last thing he needed was another of his employees with an axe to grind.

'Bill?'

'Mmm?'

'I have a bit of a problem.'

Oh God, thought Bill. Not another one. He looked at Barry's worried face. He hoped Barry wasn't coming to him with his personal problems about Diane. Everyone in the office knew things weren't going too well between the two of them but everyone, thus far, had respected the couple's privacy.

Barry took Bill's silence as an invitation to continue. He sat down with a token apologetic smile. 'That shooting I told you about.' He registered Bill's blank expression. 'You know, my sister's friend's dad?'

'I'm afraid you've lost me completely.'

'An Indian shopkeeper in Peckham.' Barry frowned. 'I'm sure I told you.'

'Oh, yeah... yes you did. Remind me again.'

Barry reminded him.

This time Bill sounded sure of himself. 'What was his name... Mal... Marabar...?'

'Malhotra. His daughter is my sister Charmian's best friend.'

'I see.'

'Everybody thought,' continued Barry, 'that it was a racist attack. The guy that shot him was apparently a thumping great bruiser. Fascist. You know the sort.'

'Unhappily I do.'

'Well, the thing is, it wasn't a racist attack at all. It's tied up with a bootlegging racket in South London.'

'Oh?' Now Bill's interest was genuine. For one horrible moment he had thought Barry was about to tell him his life story, and that of all his relations. 'Have we anything flagged up about it?'

Barry shook his head. 'Nothing.' Then, frowning again, he looked at Bill. 'The problem I've got is protecting the source of information.'

'Ah. Your sister?'

'No. Her friend. The daughter of the man who was shot. Obviously we're going to want to interview him, but how can we without him knowing it was his daughter who put us onto it?'

Bill was silent for a moment. 'How exactly did she put you onto it? And what is "it" anyway?'

Barry scratched his head. 'It's a bunch of guys who buy cheap wine and beer in France – all legal, like, in the hypermarkets – and then force Asian and black shopowners to buy a thousand quids worth at a time.'

'And if they refuse?'

Barry nodded. 'They get beaten up – or, in the case of Arjun Malhotra – shot.'

Bill folded his arms on the desk in front of him. 'We'll have to inform the police, Barry.'

But Barry didn't want to hear that. He wondered if Bill knew that the ethnic minorities of South London were far more afraid of the police than of the local gangs. If Arjun Malhotra didn't want to tell the police about what was happening to him, it was because he had been told in no uncertain terms about what the bootleggers would do if they found out he had squealed. It had been Charmian, who spent a great deal of time with his daughter Indra, who sussed out something was wrong in the little Indian corner store. It wasn't just that there always seemed to be much more lager than anything else, it was the look on Indra's father's face when 'that man' walked into the shop. And it was also the proprietorial look on 'that man's' face when he looked at Charmian's legs. Eventually, Charmian tackled Indra about the whole set-up; and Indra told her the story that Barry was now relating to Bill.

Barry wondered if Bill knew just how little the police cared about people like the Malhotras. 'But Bill,' he said, 'the police are already investigating it as a racist attack. Well, they're *filing* it as one.'

'But we know different.' Bill shook his head. 'And we'll have to tell them, Barry.'

'Look, Bill, Arjun Malhotra's lucky to be alive. If the bootleggers find out that he's...'

Bill held up a hand. 'OK, OK. Malhotra owns the shop, yes?'

'Yes.' Barry raised a puzzled eyebrow. 'But...'

Bill smiled. 'Just leave it with me, OK?'

The smile would have been much broader if Bill had known his wish was about to be fulfilled and he had unwittingly stumbled on the trail of George Webster.

Six

Katherine Roberts's brashness was, as only the few people who knew her well could testify, a cover for her shyness and insecurity. An only child and the daughter of an army major, she had had a peripatetic childhood, throughout Britain and abroad. As soon as she had settled into one school and made friends, the family would be on the move again, uprooting her and transplanting her to another environment, another country. She had, to a large extent, enjoyed that existence: the foreign travel had been exciting; there were always new sights to see, new sensations to experience. Yet gradually and unconsciously, Katherine had developed a defence mechanism to deal with being parted from her friends: she stopped making any. Self-reliant by nature, she enjoyed her own company and the company of her parents' friends: that of her peers she learned to do without.

When she returned for good to Britain to take up a place at university, it bothered her that she seemed to lack many of the interests and social skills of most of the other students. And she found them immature. They found her stuck-up; and after various attempts – especially by her male counterparts – to get behind the beautiful façade of Katherine Roberts, people stopped trying.

Katherine compensated for her isolation by working herself into the ground. She emerged from Edinburgh University with a first-class degree in psychology and, after a year of training to be a chartered accountant, she jumped ship and joined Her Majesty's Customs and Excise. The change suited her: she could spend most of her day in the company of other people whilst at the same time keeping her distance from them. And because she again worked hard, her promotion was rapid. It stopped bothering her that she rubbed many of her colleagues up the wrong way: she was by now completely accustomed to being considered bolshie and snooty.

But even she realized that she had made a pretty poor impression at City and South. The closeness of the rest of the team irked her and, thinking she would never be able to make friends with them, she made up for that in the only way she knew how: by working. She knew she could impress Bill with her professionalism. She knew that if she persevered she could nail Eric Short.

Still smarting from what she perceived as her defeat by Bill over knocking Short's premises, Katherine determined to make absolutely sure of her target. She decided that she would get to know Eric Short. And she decided to do it without telling Bill or Arnie; neither would approve of such unorthodox tactics.

Her method of introduction was quite simple. Two days after her meeting with Bill, she followed Eric Short to his tennis club. She saw him ease his Bentley into the car park and then depart, racket in hand, towards the clubhouse. Then she left the club. When she returned an hour later she very carefully backed her car up against Short's Bentley. She didn't cause any damage, but she did succeed – by hand – in transferring some of the newly acquired mud from her car to the

Bentley. At first sight, it looked as if she had made a dent in the bigger vehicle.

Ten minutes after that, Eric Short emerged from the clubhouse to find a distraught-looking Katherine frantically scribbling a note and trying to fix it onto the windscreen of his car. Immediately furious, he bellowed at her and asked her what the hell she was doing.

Lower lip quivering, she turned to the older man. She was surprised to see he was much better-looking than his photographs suggested. 'I'm sorry,' she wailed. 'I'm really sorry...' Lapsing into silence, she gestured towards his car. Short followed her gaze, took in the touching bumpers, and the mud. 'Oh my God...' he shouted as he ran to inspect the damage.

'I didn't realise,' Katherine all but sobbed, 'that I was in reverse. It's a hire car, you see. I'm sorry.' She indicated the note. 'I was leaving my name and address. I'll pay for anything. I am so sorry.'

But Short had now finished his examination and had realized there was no damage. He looked at the distraught woman and smiled. She was, he now noticed, extremely attractive. 'You, young lady, are very lucky. It's dirt, not damage.' He grinned as he saw her sigh with relief. 'Shaken, not stirred.'

'Thank the Lord for that. I thought I'd have to use all my savings to pay for it to be resprayed or something.' She managed a shy smile. 'I really am sorry.'

'Don't worry.' Short was now the picture of affability. 'I appreciate your volunteering to leave your name and address. Most people,' he added with a barely-disguised smile of appraisal, 'would have driven off.'

'Oh but I couldn't have done that. I would have been on my conscience.' Katherine bit her lip to stop herself saying any more. She feared she was going slightly overboard.

But Short found the little-girl gesture extremely attractive. 'That's very nice to hear,' he said as he looked her straight in the eye, 'in this day and age.'

Katherine smiled back. It was now or never. 'I'm so relieved it's okay,' she said with a broad smile. 'If I wasn't driving,' she added disingenuously, 'I'd have a brandy to calm me down.'

Four brandies later – and very much against her will – Katherine found herself drawn to Eric Short. She knew what she was doing was both potentially dangerous and definitely dishonest. She knew she was investigating the man and she knew he was married. She also suspected that he was ruthless. What she hadn't expected was that Eric Short, suspected importer of snuff movies from Sweden, would be charming. Another surprise was his gentle manner and the fact that he looked considerably younger than his years. Slight of build, he had a full head of dark blond hair and a slightly impish, endearing smile.

As she looked at Eric over the rim of her glass in the quietly grand hotel bar, she realized that she was – for one of the few times in her life – flirting outrageously. A frisson of pleasure tinged with fear shot down her spine. It felt good. It felt like living.

'You've got the most devastating smile, you know.'

Two pink spots appeared on her cheeks. She hadn't realized she'd been smiling at him. She was unaware she was still smiling.

'So,' said Eric, breaking the spell. 'You're looking for a job?'

Relieved that the moment had passed, Katherine forced herself back to the task in hand. 'Not doing too well, so far.' She made a face. 'I find I'm either overqualified for the kind of jobs I'm interested in, or totally uninterested in the things I'm being offered.'

Eric looked thoughtfully at her. 'What sort of things interest you?'

Katherine grinned. 'Well, nothing to do with cars.'

Eric laughed. 'No, I think you and cars should keep a respectful distance.'

'I've been working in France,' lied Katherine, 'so I've lost the contacts I used to have here. I worked freelance for a fund raising company.' She looked Eric in the eye. 'Children's charities.'

'Really? What, here or . . .'

'In France.'

'That's extremely interesting.' Eric leaned forward in his chair. 'One of my companies is involved with several charities. Holidays for disabled children.'

'Good for you.' She hoped he couldn't hear her heart beating. It was all so pat: would he later begin to have doubts about this extraordinary coincidence?

'Well, good for the company image is probably nearer the mark.' He made the admission, thought Katherine, with a charming honesty. 'Makes sense tax-wise as well.'

'But at least you're doing something.'

Eric shrugged. 'Well, the kids get something for our efforts, of course. It's swings and roundabouts. A friend of mine,' he added as he leaned further forward, 'runs one of the charities. I'll have a word with him, if you like.'

'That really would be enormously kind.'

'I like to be kind.'

Later, in bed in the hotel where she had been staying since her arrival in London, Katherine woke up in a cold sweat. What on earth had she been doing? She had been flirting with a suspected criminal. Worse, she had been congratulating him on his work with children: children like the ones who were used and abused in the pornographic videos she was investigating. Children who wouldn't reach adulthood because they appeared in snuff movies.

Yet, after a fitful sleep, and in the cold, rational light of day, she came to the conclusion that she was simply running an investigation and, if her methods were a little unorthodox, she was still completely in control of the situation. She needed to find out more about Eric Short, and he had made it quite clear that he wasn't averse to her company. Satisfied and justified, she resolved to continue with her investigation. On her own, of course.

For his part, Eric Short had not been lying. He *did* like to be kind, especially to very attractive women who appeared lonely and in need of a helping hand. And he liked Katherine's company. While she didn't appear to be overly bright – a plus in his book – she was entertaining and, he thought, attracted to him. He had great expectations of Katherine which was why, when she phoned him two days later, he suggested dinner that evening. She accepted with alacrity.

Any lingering thoughts about her unprofessional conduct disappeared over a sumptuous dinner washed down with excellent claret. For the first time since her arrival in London, Katherine found herself enjoying herself, and the company of another man. At first, and as on her previous drink with Short, she had been acting up to a point. Yet after an hour in his company the gulf between acting and enjoying herself narrowed – and then disappeared altogether. Eric Short, whether he realized it or not, was weaving a spell around her. A spell that worked. By the time her main course arrived,

Katherine had forgotten about his alleged involvement with child pornography and snuff movies. It just didn't seem appropriate. Or possible. Her only qualms over dinner were over Eric's wife. Again and again, she found herself contemplating the prominent gold wedding band on his left hand. Finally, unable to contain her curiosity any longer, she broached the issue. 'What,' she asked bluntly, 'about your wife?'

'Ah.' Eric looked down at his hands. 'My wife understands me, Katherine. I let her do what she wants to do; she lets me do what I want to do. Anyway,' he said, dismissing the subject with a wave of his hand, 'that's not what we're here to talk about. I am really not trying to ... well,' he looked up and grinned at her. 'If I can help you find a job, I will. That's all.' She felt a sudden and sharp pang of disappointment. 'You won't be chased around the furniture,' he continued. 'I mean that. You're just great to talk to.'

The talking continued over coffee in Eric's flat. And it was there, in an up-market high-rise with stunning views over London, that Katherine forced herself back to reality and to the reason why she was with Eric in the first place. When, ten minutes after they entered the flat, Eric excused himself to take a 'private' phone call in his study, Katherine saw her opportunity. The minute he left the drawing room, she pounced on his address book and copied as many names and addresses as she could into her notebook. Eric Short, she mused as she did so, had a lot of friends, and a lot of high profile ones at that.

Hearing him leave the study, she snapped the book shut and retreated to the window to admire the view. 'I didn't buy a flat,' said Eric quietly as he watched her, 'I bought a view.'

'It's terrific,' said Katherine without turning.

Eric joined her. 'Great at night. Watch the planes on the flight path to Heathrow. I sit here for hours sometimes. Looking the other way,' he continued, touching her shoulder and turning her round, 'you can see where I was born. Holloway Road.' Then he laughed. 'But you have to stand in the bathroom to get a proper view. Not quite the same.'

She didn't reply. Eric still had his hand on her shoulder. She was beginning to feel most peculiar.

Then he walked back into the middle of the room. 'Look, I'm sorry but I have to go. I have a meeting with the woman who might be able to give you a job.'

A meeting, thought Katherine. At eleven o'clock at night. Very strange. 'Maybe,' she said, 'I'll see you again . . . ?'

Eric grinned. 'If you weren't going to suggest it, I was.'

She thought for a moment. 'I'm free on Friday.'

'No. Sorry, not Friday. Meeting.' He reached into his jacket pocket for a pen. 'Look, I don't even know where to call you.'

'It's a hotel.' She grimaced. 'Still trying to find a flat.'

He didn't reply. Instead he looked around the room and then back at Katherine. His meaning was abundantly clear.

Katherine smiled. 'Thank you, but no. I don't think you'd want your "bachelor" haven invaded. Not every night anyway.'

'Hmm. Maybe not every night, but . . . Phone number?'

Katherine gave it to him. Then she picked up her bag. Eric nodded and walked her to the door and, as she crushed past him, pecked her on the cheek. That's OK, she told herself. Just a social kiss. But as she pulled away, Eric suddenly grabbed her and kissed her full on the mouth. She was so completely taken aback that it was a good few seconds before she rebuffed him. And she did so with regret.

Then she left the flat and walked to the lift in a state of complete confusion.

'Who the hell,' shouted Bill, 'said you could make contact with the suspect?'

Katherine shrugged. 'How else am I supposed to push the investigation on?'

Bill stared at her in disbelief. First she breaks into the man's office. Then she makes friends with him. Jesus! 'And has this ... this making contact pushed the investigation on?' He sighed and began to pace the room. 'We watch, Katherine. We observe – and we build up our evidence.'

But she was unimpressed. And scathing. 'And six months later the suspect walks free from court because we didn't get close enough to get watertight evidence.'

Bill rounded on her. 'If you're referring,' he barked, 'to the child porn case Arnie and I spent several months on, let me tell you that we had all the evidence we needed. It was the judge who decided it was inadmissible. It wasn't bad investigation; it was bad law!'

Katherine knew she had gone too far. She had never seen Bill so angry. She looked him in the eye. 'I apologise,' she said, meaning it.

Bill took a deep breath. At last, he thought. She apologises. Her next statement, however, took his breath away. 'The suspect,' she said without any trace of contrition, 'does want to see me again.'

'I beg your pardon?'

'The sus ...'

'I heard what you said.' Bill's voice was deceptively calm. 'Why?'

Katherine didn't answer.

'I thought,' he continued, 'you said you'd only spoken to him. What,' he added with a feeling of dread, 'were you speaking about?'

Her gaze wavered, confirming Bill's suspicion that something was not quite right here.

'Katherine!' Bill banged his fist on the desk in front of him. 'He wants to see you again? If he finds out you aren't who you say you are, any future investigation could be totally jeopardized.'

But she had got over her temporary embarrassment. Now she was looking mutinous. 'Everything I've told him has been the truth, Bill. Except for what I do. I'm still living at the hotel until I find a flat.'

But Bill just stared at her. 'What the hell's going on, Katherine? *Why* does he want to see you? What on earth's the arrangement?' Angry and frustrated, he made a gesture of helpless irritation. 'What's . . .?'

'He likes me.'

Bill just stared. So it was true. The bloody stupid woman had been flirting with Short. Batting her eyelids at a pervert who dealt in snuff movies. Now that really *would* look good if it ever got into the press. With a terrible pang of sorrow he remembered what had happened the last time a member of his staff had become involved with a suspect.

But Katherine interrupted his thoughts by voicing some astonishing ones of her own. 'I know what I'm doing, Bill. I suggested we meet on Friday evening. He said he couldn't make it. I've ... er, Arnie and I, have already observed him meeting people at his office building in the West End some Fridays. That could be the time they copy or distribute the material.'

Bill, however, was still appalled by, and fixated on, her last statement. 'Because he likes you?' He held both hands up in the air. 'Because he *likes* you? Jesus,

Katherine! If this ever gets to court, and if he's got a clever lawyer – which he undoubtedly will have – I hope you won't have to answer the question "Did you lead this man on?" or "Did you act as an *agent provocateur*?".'

'Bit old fashioned, isn't it?' challenged Katherine.

'We're an old fashioned service.' Bill fixed Katherine with a steely glare. 'And quite often we get an old fashioned roasting in court! Usually because some ... some gooey individual thinks they know how to handle an investigation better than ...' Realizing he was about to lose it completely, Bill checked himself and lowered his voice. 'You speak to me before you do anything, Katherine. Do you understand?'

Two pink spots had appeared on her cheeks. Gooey individual, indeed! Suddenly she stood up and started shouting at Bill. 'Look, I respect your views, but I have to tell you that we, as a service, glorious past or not, will lose today's battle completely if we don't shape – and I don't mean break – the rules to fit a shifting situation.'

Bill could hardly believe his ears. He was still staring, mouth wide open in disbelief, when she turned on her heel and walked out of the room.

He was *still* staring when, two minutes later, his phone rang. He looked at the instrument in annoyance. Another problem, no doubt: another one of his staff staging a mutiny. Then he grabbed the receiver and barked an angry 'Yes?' down the line.

'Bill, it's me.'

'And who is me?' retorted Bill, knowing full well who it was.

'Er ... Andreotti.'

'Ah! How's it going?' Andreotti, he knew, would never mutiny; although he had been less than delighted about the project Bill had just assigned him to. Investigating small-time bootleggers in Peckham wasn't his idea of heaven. Yet Bill, true to his word to Barry, had decided to follow up the story behind the shooting of Arjun Malhotra. He had, two days previously, deputed Andreotti to hang out in the pubs where – according to Barry's sister – the bootleggers organized their business.

'Going great, Bill.' Andreotti sounded immensely pleased with himself.

'That's terrific. Just great.'

'Thanks. The thing is it's all happened quite quickly...'

'All the better.'

'Yes, well ... you see ... I'm sorry, Bill, but I need to buy a van.'

At the other end of the line, Bill was silent for a full ten seconds. Then he took a deep breath. 'A van. I see. And why do you need a van, Andreotti?'

Andreotti, glad that Bill was several miles away, also took a deep breath. 'Eddie Davies's mob have recruited me to pick up some of their hooch from France. I ... well, I told them I had a van.' Bill's failure to reply prompted Andreotti on. 'It was the only way, Bill.'

It was, indeed, the only way. Despite his protestations about being unfamiliar with South London, Andreotti had surpassed even his own expectations (and they had been high) of blending into the scenery of Peckham. He had modified his slight London accent into true Cockney tones and, more importantly, had struck up a 'friendship' with Eddie Davies's eldest son Chris. After that it had been plain sailing. Establishing a contact address where the Davies mob could find him, he then dropped heavy hints about being unemployed and 'not being able to get a job worth having, not for love nor money'. He had also managed to drop into the conversation the fact that he owned a Transit van. The next day Chris Davies told his father they'd found another driver.

And now Andreotti – or rather Bill – had to put his money where his mouth was and come up with a van. Bill's silence on the phone wasn't due to his unwillingness to provide Andreotti with one: it was due to his inability to do so.

He sighed down the line. 'I can't get you a van, Andreotti. The budget...'

'I need one *now*, Bill. Today. I'm on for a drive to France tomorrow.'

'Bloody hell, Andreotti! You were supposed to keep me informed every step of the way!'

'I could hardly phone you from the pub, could I? It happened so quickly, Bill ... I'm sorry,' he added in genuine contrition, 'but it was just too good a chance to miss.'

'Yes. You're right. But I still can't buy you a van. You'll have to use a pool one.'

Andreotti was aghast. 'Christ. That's traceable to HM Customs! If Davies's lot ...'

'But they won't, Andreotti. You've already said they think you're clean as a whistle.'

Andreotti silently cursed himself. It was true. Not only had Davies and his men accepted him as one of their own, they had also insisted that there was nothing illegal in what they were doing. And they had made no mention to him about bootlegging or protectionist rackets. All they had told him was that his, Chris's and one other van were needed to do a run the following day. The fact that Andreotti was being paid fifty pounds for his efforts made it look highly unlikely that anyone would investigate him: he really wasn't worth bothering about.

But still he was unhappy. A pool van was not what he had in mind. 'Is that really my only choice, Bill?' he asked down the line.

'Yes. I'm sorry. I'd love to buy you a great big spanking new one, but ... it'll have to be a pool van or nothing.'

'Yeah. Well, how about a pint instead?'

Bill grinned. 'Done.' Why, he asked himself as he replaced the receiver, weren't more people like Andreotti? Why wasn't Katherine, for instance, willing to play the game like he was? And then he remembered why. Katherine didn't play as part of a team. She played solo – and to win.

Bill looked at his watch. It was about time he started thinking of how he was going to play the game in the future. Today, at last, was the day of his review with Alan Jackson. Alan preferred to call it an 'informal chat', but Bill knew better. The words could be informal, but the subtext was deadly serious. And Alan already knew that Bill was deadly serious about increasing manpower at City and South.

Alan Jackson was looking out of the window when Bill entered his office at York House, the nerve centre of Her Majesty's Customs and Excise. Without turning round, he started speaking in a wistful, far-away voice. 'You were wise not to take this job, Bill. You get an odd view from up here.' Then he turned to Bill with a half smile.

But it was the other half of Alan's expression that registered. It was a look of embarrassment. So, thought Bill, something's up; and that talk of me not taking his job was a sop to that something. Everyone had known Bill hadn't wanted the job.

Alan gestured for him to sit down. It was the gesture of a tired man; a man grown old before his time. Bill thanked his lucky stars that he had aged better than Alan. Both men were approaching fifty: everyone said Bill looked ten years younger and Alan ten years older.

'Shame,' said Alan as he fiddled with the pencil in front of him, 'that these can't be informal chats any more.'

Bill smiled politely but remained silent.

'We're all,' explained Alan with an apologetic shrug, 'under the cosh nowadays. Even those of us who appear to be wielding it. Still, not such a bad thing, I suppose. I think greater team competence is something we'd all agree with.'

For a moment Bill thought Alan had gone mad. Perhaps he had. 'Sorry Alan,' he said, 'but I haven't brought my buzz word book with me.'

'No? Well, you won't really need it. I'm afraid,' continued Alan on a far more serious note, 'there isn't any possibility of increasing, permanently increasing, the number of officers at your unit.'

Bill had expected that – but not quite so suddenly. Pausing for a moment, he then leaned forward towards Alan. 'Alan, my team is desperately under-manned, not sure which directive of the week to follow, and worried they might not have a job when they next turn up for work. And,' he added, 'I had Jo Chadwick away at the MoD for three weeks – now she's gone straight onto a damned computer course. I mean . . .'

'Well, yeah,' Alan stalled him in mid-flow, 'but in the long term that's going to save time and effort, isn't it?'

'Alan,' said Bill with a sigh, 'we've been using the new computer system for five months. She doesn't *need* a course. I have to tell you that I have some very disgruntled...'

'Yes, yes, I know.' Alan waved a dismissive hand. 'Nobody likes change.'

Jesus! thought Bill. Doesn't he realize what I'm saying? 'There are one or two of them seriously considering packing the job in – and I know just how they feel.'

Alan shrugged. 'Well, make sure you tell them there's no shortage of graduate applicants.'

Bill couldn't believe his ears: couldn't believe that Alan was taking such a cavalier, unconcerned attitude to what he was saying.

'The reorganization currently under consideration,' continued Alan without meeting the other man's eye, 'will mean ... well, could mean a few changes for you, you know. It's not going to be the way it was.'

'You sound like you know something I don't.'

'No. No. Nothing's been decided.' At last Alan looked up. 'Er ... have you seriously thought of jacking it in?'

Bill just stared. There was something distinctly ominous about the way Alan looked at him as he said the words.

'You're fifty next year, aren't you?' continued Alan.

'No. I'm thirteen months younger than you are.' Which makes me, he could have added, forty-eight.

'We ... ll. Geoff Smith took early retirement. Never felt better. I mean, I'm not saying you should. Just wondered if you'd ... considered it.' Alan was rushing his words. 'City and South will probably be amalgamated with another ... well, you know. Who'll be running it is ... er ... it's not clear at the moment.' Clearly embarrassed, both by his words and the lack of tact with which they were spoken, he nevertheless finished with the words that rang in Bill's ears for the next few days: 'Early retirement's something to think about, you know.'

Bill was so stunned by Alan Jackson's words that he couldn't bring himself to repeat them for a full two days. Two days during which he tortured himself with visions of unemployment, of sniggers from his colleagues and, worst of all, with pitying looks from his wife. He could cope with most things, but not the thought of losing Libby's respect.

As soon as he told her about the meeting with Alan, he realized what he should have known all along: that she was concerned for him, sympathetic to him, and appalled by Alan's words. She was also extremely surprised by the timing of Bill's abrupt announcement. 'But I thought,' she said, 'you saw Alan the other day. Did...?'

Bill gave his wife a sheepish smile. 'I know. I should have said earlier. Took a while to sink in, to tell the truth.' Then he looked away. 'They sure know how to make you feel wanted.'

'What on earth did you say?'

He shrugged. 'I was a bit too surprised to say anything.'

Libby sighed. Early retirement. She still regarded Bill as a young man. What on earth would he *do*? What, come to think of it, would they do as a family? Libby only worked part time and the girls, at ten and twelve, were still ... Libby frowned and shook her head. Then she walked over to Bill and put her arms round his shoulder. 'Oh you poor thing. That's really put the tin hat on a lousy month for you, hasn't it?'

'Yeah. Topped up my losing streak nicely. That child porn case – watching that bloody man walk free. I suppose,' he added bitterly, 'I'm not to think of him as a criminal these days. He's just a customer I've lost.' He pulled away from her embrace. 'Then, of course, there's poor old Gerry Birch.'

Libby looked at him with real sorrow. Like him, she had been extremely fond of Gerry. Like him, she hadn't been able to bring herself to hate Gerry after what he did. But unlike Bill, Libby didn't bear an almighty and all-consuming grudge against George Webster. And, although he never mentioned it, she knew perfectly well that Bill was being eaten up by his obsession to get back at Webster. Of all the 'customers he had lost', Webster was the one who mattered most. As she looked at Bill's intense, set expression, Libby felt a twinge of unease, a frisson of fear. For the first time it occurred to her that Bill was prepared to go to any lengths to avenge Gerry Birch's death: lengths that could have a disastrous effect on his career.

Seven

At the same time as Andreotti inveigled himself into the company of Eddie Davies and his bootleggers, Tommy Maddern re-established contact with George Webster. He had forgotten his earlier qualms about becoming a 'hired hand' and was now feeling very pleased with himself. After all, he held all the cards, didn't he? For the first time in his relationship with George, he had the upper hand. George would be working for him and Conny Devooght.

George thought otherwise. While not remotely surprised by Tommy's phone call – it had come within the three-day period he had chuckled about to David Archer – he was irritated that, after making a few enquiries among old contacts in London, he was unable to establish what on earth Tommy was up to. Tommy had crowed that there was 'twelve million at stake'; a remark that had both aroused George's interest and convinced him that, whatever pool Tommy was swimming in, he was way out of his depth. Employing his favourite game with people like Tommy – the waiting game – George asked him to call back the following day on a different number. He had been extremely displeased that Tommy had called him at home at the villa and had the number changed the minute he replaced the receiver. Remaining one step ahead of Tommy was essential.

Four days later George deigned to answer Tommy's call. Tommy was extremely put out – and obviously anxious. 'Where've you been, George?' he wailed. 'I phoned you when you said to. They told me you weren't there. Then I tried phoning your house, but it's out of order or something.'

'Really?' In the bar in Portugal where he took 'sensitive' calls, George smiled into the receiver. 'Wonder why that is?'

'I've been trying to get you for four days, George.'

On the other end of the line, George smiled again at the hint of desperation in Tommy's voice. 'Well,' he said at last, 'I'm here now.'

'Where's here? Is this your office number?'

'No. It's where I take phone calls. Now, what's all this about?'

Tommy told him about his call from Conny Devooght.

'Who?'

'Geezer I knew when I was over there.'

George laughed. 'Oh, that would have been in your colonial days, then, eh?'

'He hasn't,' said Tommy through gritted teeth, 'gone into detail.'

George sighed. 'Either he's told you what it's about or he hasn't.'

'Well, the profit sounds...'

'Never mind the bloody profit! I wanna know exactly what...'

'He hasn't exactly said.'

George's amusement gave way to annoyance. Tommy was even more hopeless than he remembered. 'Knowing what it's all about is ever so slightly to the point, don't you think? I suggest you get a bit more out of him and get back to me.'

'Can we meet?'

George's shrug was almost audible. 'Can if you like,

but I'm not travelling. Anyway,' he added, relishing the moment, 'I can't meet you in the UK: I understand you're a wanted man there. Something to do with smuggling gold bars?'

George howled with laughter at his own humour. Tommy, while sorely tempted to hang up, just managed to control his temper. He needed George. Conny needed George. He would, he said down the line, get back to George.

Three days later Tommy flew to Portugal and met George in a quiet waterfront bar. George was accompanied by his armed bodyguard. Tommy, to George's horror, was not alone. He was also, as he approached, the soul of bluff affability. 'George,' he said as he approached them, 'I thought to save time and put you in the picture, I'd bring the 'orse so you can hear the deal straight from his mouth.' He gestured towards the florid, hulking South African at his side. 'George Webster, Conny Devooght.'

'Pleased to meet you, George.' Conny was all smiles; George looked harmless. Loads of dosh and not enough brain was what Tommy had told him. He seemed to fit the bill.

George's lack of expression was, however, a mask to hide his fury. He looked at Conny through steely eyes and then turned on Tommy. 'What the fuck are you playing at?' he demanded.

Tommy was appalled. 'What, what? But George, he's the –'

'I don't give a flying fuck who he is. I don't want to know him.' Conny flinched as though he'd been hit. Suddenly George didn't look at all harmless.

'This,' George said as he went up to Tommy and

thrust his cold, furious face towards him, 'had better be the first and last surprise you ever pull on me.'

Tommy suddenly looked like a lost, pathetic child. 'I thought you'd want to talk to him.' He looked from George to the increasingly puzzled Conny. 'He's wondering what's going on. You're making me look bad.'

No, thought George, it's you that's making me look bad. For I know Conny Devooght is a wanted man in five continents. 'Tommy,' he said with a weary sigh. 'I always want to know who I'm meeting. You said you were coming alone.' He gave Tommy another cold, furious glare, wondering, as he did so, whether or not to give Tommy the benefit of the doubt. He decided he would. Tommy was a wanted man himself and not even he would be stupid enough to expose himself to the scrutiny of Interpol. He turned to Conny with the beginnings of an apologetic smile. 'You surprised me, that's all. Now, shall we order something to drink and you can tell me what this is all about?'

'The business we are talking about,' began Conny as he sipped a bilious looking cocktail five minutes later, 'is the transportation of "rare earth metals".'

George raised an eyebrow.

Conny put his drink down. 'You've never heard of such things?'

'No.'

'Well, they're exactly what they sound like. Natural minerals from the earth. Found in South Africa, Russia and South Dakota in the States. Caesium 133,' he said after a short pause, 'is the one I'm interested in.'

'What's it do?'

'It can be used in the manufacture of rocket fuel.'

'Hold it right there.' George eyed Conny with distaste. 'Is this to do with the weapons industry? Because if it is . . .'

'George, George!' Conny smiled and shook his head. 'Caesium is not an illegal substance.'

Tommy nodded in agreement. 'You can buy it from Fisons.'

George leaned back and looked from one man to the other. 'So why don't you?'

Tommy looked at Conny. Conny nodded. 'Caesium,' he repeated, 'is not illegal. But large shipments going to ... well, certain countries ...' He finished with an eloquent shrug and a conspiratorial smile.

'You say Iraq,' replied George, 'and you can leave.'

Tommy looked at George in surprise. Fancy him having scruples. 'The destination of the load,' said Conny, 'would be Guinea in Africa.'

'Oh yes? And who do we know there?'

Conny shrugged again. 'It would be sold on from there. The deal could be worth ... ooh, total fifteen million sterling.'

Quick as a flash, George rounded on Tommy. 'You told me twelve.' Tommy shrugged. 'You know me George – can't remember big numbers.'

'You remembered my phone number,' snapped George. Then he turned back to Conny. 'Why are you doing me the favour?'

'Tommy knows you. I need a backer.'

'Yeah, but who are you selling the stuff to?'

'George, with respect, I need your money, not your opinion on who I do business with.' For the first time, Conny looked as if he were wresting control of the situation from George. 'For an investment of three quarters of a million, you could walk away with seven. That,' he said with a broad smile, 'would be your profit. Sounds too good to be true, huh?'

'Yeah. It does a bit.'

Conny shrugged. 'Well, I want to move several kilos. I have a buyer ready and waiting.'

'You done this before?'

Conny didn't quite meet George's eye. 'We ... er, we had a problem with the last load.'

'A financial problem?'

'It's become a financial problem. Kind of went up in smoke.'

George was looking even more doubtful. 'And how would I collect my vast profits?'

'COD. The cargo would be shipped by sea container. At the docks it would be checked. Before you or your appointed agent allowed it to leave the dock, the money would be paid to you. Cash or bank draft.'

Although becoming increasingly interested, George maintained a cool façade. 'All this happening in Guinea?'

'Yes.'

'Well ... call me Mr Cautious, but I need to know a little more about it.'

Conny nodded. 'We can all fly to meet the other interested parties, and to see exactly what we are talking about.'

'Where'd we have to fly to?'

Conny grinned and took another sip of his pink cocktail. 'Place they now call the Wild East. Latvia.'

In London, Bill was having a slightly better day than of late, if only because no disasters had yet struck. It even looked, as he replaced the telephone receiver in his office and turned to Arnie, that something akin to success may be in the offing.

'That was customs at Ipswich,' he said with a grim smile. 'They have a Swedish bloke in custody. He was trying to bring in a particularly nasty consignment of videos.'

Arnie raised an eyebrow. 'Snuff movies?'

'The same.'

'Any connection with Eric Short?' Arnie had a personal as well as a professional interest in the Short investigation. That was the reason he was in Bill's office in the first place: to request being taken off the enquiry. Arnie was too polite to say that Katherine was getting on his nerves as well as sidelining him, but Bill had read between the lines. He knew Arnie's 'You don't really need two people on this enquiry' meant 'Katherine doesn't want me.' Yet despite the fact that having two people on the case was a touch extravagant, Bill had no intention of letting Katherine handle it on her own. Especially after the phone call from Ipswich.

Bill looked at Arnie and shrugged. 'Dunno ... but apparently the Swede's made a statement. He was to deliver two packages. One to a holding address and one' – he looked at the notes he had just taken – 'to a courier firm called Goldwing. Ipswich have kept the original tapes and repackaged a trashed set.'

'So he'll still make the delivery?'

'Yes.' Bill looked Arnie in the eye. 'Ipswich are handing the fella over to us. He's co-operated so far, Arnie, but I don't want him getting cute at the last minute. You stick with him: he may lead us to Short.'

'I, er ...'

'You're needed, Arnie. You've more experience in the field than Katherine. Use it.' The implication was clear. Keep an eye on Katherine. 'And make sure,' continued Bill, 'that the Swede doesn't give anyone the nod that we're on to him. But first,' he finished as he handed Arnie a piece of paper, 'get to this Goldwing place and have a quiet look around outside.'

'Right.' Arnie took the paper, gave Bill a brief smile, and left the room. Enthusiastic was not the word Bill would have used to describe him.

Bill looked pensive as, also without enthusiasm, he eyed his in-tray. He was thinking about Ipswich. That was where the young female customs officer had been blown to bits. Two days ago Bill had learned that the enquiry into that was now being dealt with at a higher level. That meant no one was likely to hear anything more about it. Unless, of course, it was in some way connected with the importation of snuff movies. That, in Bill's experience, would be highly unlikely. The explosion no doubt concerned something altogether more sinister.

Arnie moved quickly and deftly – and without telling Katherine. He established the whereabouts of Goldwing Couriers and then made contact with the taciturn Swedish seaman, who had been escorted to London at the same time as Arnie's interview with Bill. Then he asked Barry to help him with the surveillance of whoever picked up the substitute videos from Goldwing. Barry was the only member of the City and South team who possessed a motorbike and was therefore the most mobile when it came to negotiating the streets of Central London. He was also, despite what Bill had said to Alan Jackson, underemployed.

They arranged the drop for the following day. Arnie accompanied the Swede to Goldwing while Barry, clad in black leathers and sitting astride his Triumph, was positioned round the corner.

The Swede, as instructed, spoke only one word to the receptionist at Goldwing: 'Delivery'. The receptionist seemed totally uninterested. Annoyed that the two men had disturbed her scrutiny of her bright red fingernails, she merely nodded, took the distinctive yellow package and threw it into a wire basket marked 'Despatch'. Disappointingly as far as Arnie was concerned, she didn't write a delivery address on it. The numbers '243' that had been on the original package found in Ipswich had been faithfully reproduced for the dummy package – but presumably it was the province of someone in the despatch department to link them to an address held by Goldwing. If it was the receptionist's job, reflected Arnie with dismay, the operation was going to move very slowly.

It didn't. It moved extremely quickly – almost too quickly for Barry to follow the courier who, ten minutes after Arnie left the building with the Swede, emerged with the yellow package. But follow him Barry did – straight to Eric Short's office building.

Bill was delighted when Arnie and Barry reported back after lunch. Katherine, however, was not so thrilled. Miffed that Bill had given the task to two junior officers, she wasted no time in complaining at being sidelined in what she saw as 'her' case.

'I wasn't even aware,' she said as she glowered at Bill, 'that anything was happening until an hour after it was all over.'

Bill knew that. He also knew that, when he had briefed Arnie that morning, Katherine had been inexplicably absent from the building. 'If you'd thought it necessary,' he retorted, matching her hauteur, 'to tell me where you'd be, I could have contacted you.' Then he turned to address the two men. 'So, we know that the first package went from Goldwing to Short's building.'

As he spoke, Katherine looked with interest at the photograph he was holding. It was of Eric Short's building, and it had been taken without her knowledge. It suddenly occurred to her that Arnie, or Barry – or indeed anyone at City and South – could, unbeknownst to her, be tailing Short. And if they were, they would know who Short had been seeing. Katherine felt quietly sick.

'Unfortunately,' continued Bill, 'we don't know for sure that the package went to Short. There are six companies in that building, so it could, arguably, have been going to any of 'em.'

No one in the room, not even Bill, believed that. Yet tracing the package to the building wasn't the same as tracing it to Short. Without concrete evidence, they would be laughed out of court.

Shaking off her brief moment of unease, Katherine addressed herself to her professional, not her personal interest in the investigation. 'Who addressed the package?' she asked.

Bill nodded. 'Exactly. Someone at Goldwing Couriers. Whether they're actively involved or not remains to be seen. Arnie,' he barked, turning to his left, 'get the PAYE slips of all Goldwing employees. They're a proper outfit; they'll keep proper records. You,' he said to Katherine and Barry, 'go back to our smiling Swedish friend and accompany him to the holding address with the second package. If that one also goes anywhere near Short's building then we're really going places.' Bill addressed his final words to Barry, so didn't notice the thunderous look that passed over Katherine's features. It was the word 'we' that annoyed her.

The holding address on the second package was of a company called, appropriately, Hold All. Barry and Katherine arrived there two hours after the briefing with Bill, and in the company of the increasingly dour Swedish seaman. He had repeatedly claimed, both to customs in East Anglia and to Bill's team, that he was an innocent party in whatever game they were playing. While nobody believed that was the whole truth, the consensus of opinion amongst the customs officers was that he was merely a pawn – but a paid one. No one believed his story that he had intended to make the deliveries to London out of the kindness of his heart.

There was, however, still the possibility that he would prove his greater involvement by tipping the wink to someone at Hold All. But as Arnie escorted him to that company while Katherine waited outside, it seemed that Hold All, like Goldwing, was nothing more than a staging post in the journey of the package.

The receptionist was altogether more alert than her counterpart at Goldwing. She was competent, smiling and friendly: partly due, concluded Barry, to the birthday cards and the bunch of red roses on her desk. He hoped to God the package wasn't a birthday present to her. Then he really would have seen it all.

She smiled as she took the package from the Swede. 'From?' she asked.

'Sweden.'

She checked the reference number of the package against the list in front of her. Frowning, she looked up again. 'Wasn't this supposed to be delivered before today?'

'Yes.'

Barry grinned at the Swede's monosyllabic reply. He had been under strict instructions to say nothing more than was absolutely necessary: nothing that could be construed as some sort of password or warning. He was obeying his instructions to the letter.

The receptionist didn't know what to make of him.

'Oh,' she replied after a moment. 'Right. Well, thanks.' Then, to Barry's intense interest, she wrote the initials 'L.C.' on the package and left it on the desk in front of her.

The moment he and the Swede left the building, Barry was on his mobile phone to Katherine. 'Package in position at front desk. Wait one.' Then he looked up in relief as the undercover policemen who were 'looking after' the Swede arrived to take him back into their care. He didn't envy them. 'Thanks,' he smiled as they invited the seaman to accompany them. 'What're you going to do with him now?'

One of the policemen smiled. 'Keep him in custody until you guys get to the bottom of this.'

'Oh well.' Barry's smile was much broader. 'Don't hold your breath for his wit and repartee. I reckon his conversation starts and finishes with fish and suicide.'

The Swede glowered. But then glowering was his habitual expression.

Barry went straight back to the phone. 'The receptionist wrote L.C. on the package.'

At the other end of the line, Katherine looked over to Arnie, now in the passenger seat of her car. His investigation into Goldwing's PAYE records had not taken long and, after reporting back to Bill, he had been given new and surprising instructions. Without quite meeting Arnie's eye, Bill had asked him to stay with Katherine. 'You know,' he had said, 'new girl on the block and all that. Perhaps you could . . .' Bill didn't even need to finish the sentence. Arnie, smiling, knew exactly what he was getting at.

Katherine would have been livid had she known. It would have spoiled her mood: a mood that surprised Arnie. Katherine was not only friendly – she was actually making jokes. 'The initials L.C.,' she said as she turned to Arnie. 'What's that mean? Leather Correction?' Arnie's eyes nearly popped out of his head. Katherine with a sense of humour? That *was* a turn up for the books. Soon she'd be admitting she was human. Then it struck him that she was also proffering an olive branch. He took it. Grinning, he informed her that L.C. was probably someone's initials.

'Oh. Right. Of course.'

Arnie remained lost in thought for a moment. 'How,' he suddenly asked, 'do we know the package isn't for somebody who works there?'

Katherine shrugged. 'Perhaps we should go in?'

Arnie looked at her. Again he was startled by her response. It was the first time she had asked him a question rather than give him a command. Then he shook his head. 'No. They'll just say they're holding it for someone.'

'True.' Then she shook her head. 'But if we don't knock it, the package could disappear out of the back door. L.C. might even be in there right now.'

Arnie sighed. 'Call Bill?' he suggested.

But he should have known the effect the question would have. Katherine may be mellowing – but she was damned if she was going to lose control. 'No,' she said. 'We'll knock it now.'

Arnie shrugged. 'You're in charge.' Then he picked up his mobile, called Barry, and told him to stand by on his motorbike in case of action.

But there was no action beyond the receptionist's bafflement when Katherine, with Arnie in her wake, walked into the building, flashed her badge and stated who she was. 'City and South Investigation,' she added. 'I believe you have just taken delivery of a package?'

Totally bemused, the receptionist merely nodded and

pointed to the package, sitting beside the birthday cards on her desk.

Katherine nodded. 'We want to keep this friendly, but I may be arresting you on suspicion of importing obscene material.'

That was too much. The receptionist gaped, open-mouthed, at Katherine. Then she looked to her birthday cards, smiled, and turned back to Katherine. 'You're a singing telegram, aren't you?'

If Arnie needed any further proof that Katherine did indeed have a sense of humour, he got it; she laughed out loud.

He, too, laughed, until Katherine, after establishing the receptionist's complete and genuine ignorance of anything to do with what was in the package, deputed him to wait beside her until the mysterious L.C. made contact.

'How long d'you reckon that'll take?' he asked, realizing the stupidity of the question the minute he asked it.

'How long,' said Katherine in her most withering tone, 'is a piece of string?'

But the piece of string attached to the package was very short indeed. Twenty minutes after Katherine had left Arnie to his solitary vigil, the receptionist took the call they were all waiting for. He knew from her body language that this was the one. She went rigid as she listened and her voice when she replied was, as Arnie noted with alarm, tinged with wariness. 'For ... L.C.? Er ... yes, it's in.' Then she hung up and turned to Arnie. 'It was a man. He's coming to collect it in the morning.'

At the head office of City and South, Bill received the news with an enthusiasm that bordered on excitement. At last, he thought. Results. After replacing the receiver, he did something he hadn't done in years – he crossed his fingers. City and South desperately needed a major knock. With – as he knew from Alan Jackson – the unit's very existence in doubt, he needed to justify it; to boost his team's morale.

Thirty seconds later, he was obliged to uncross his fingers as the phone rang again.

'Yes?'

'Bill. Andreotti. I've just finished the run to France. And I've just seen a face from the past.' Then, because he was Andreotti, he paused for effect. 'Tommy Maddern.'

Eight

Diane Ralston was sitting opposite one of the least prepossessing individuals she had ever met. He was tall, skinny, unkempt, and sullen. That he was also extremely tired, none too clean and very nervous was, in part, her own fault for keeping him sweating for seven hours between his detention at customs and the interview with which she was now proceeding. She didn't normally wait that long, but Graham Marsh revolted her and she wanted him to know it. And that revulsion had nothing to do with his appearance: it was because of what he had tried to smuggle into the country.

Kevin Butcher, sitting impassively beside her, reflected that he had rarely seen her looking so coldly furious.

'This interview,' she began, taking Graham Marsh by surprise and switching on the tape recorder after a full three-minute silence, 'is being tape recorded and is an interview by Diane Ralston, Senior Officer, and Kevin Butcher, of Graham Marsh, 28 Alison Gardens, London NW10.' Then she paused and handed a printed leaflet to Marsh. 'Here's a notice which tells you what will happen to the tapes of this interview.'

Graham Marsh shrugged and didn't bother to read the notice.

'You have brought,' continued Diane, 'six phials of what are described as "a green coloured liquid" in from Kathmandu. Would you like to tell me what it is?'

Graham Marsh didn't like at all. He remained mute. A pity, thought Diane, that the phials were still being lab tested. She was positive about their contents. But she needed proof.

'Well,' she said with a grim smile, 'it's not washing-up liquid, is it? Are you going to tell me who gave it to you? No? OK Graham, I'm asking you these questions in a quiet, civilized way because I want to know, if we take you to court, whether I'll be telling the judge that you were helpful or not.'

Graham Marsh's prominent Adam's Apple quivered, yet he remained silent.

'Fine.' Diane's voice was like ice as she waved a piece of paper in Marsh's face. 'We found this address hidden in the lining of your pack. Two names: one Chinese, one probably British – and an address. Now, are you going to help me or aggravate me?'

Marsh's silence was answer enough.

'OK,' continued Diane as she glared across the table. 'We're sending the phials found on you for analysis. I'm letting you go. But when we've had the results, you'll be required to report back here. Understand,' she said as she got to her feet, 'this isn't over for you, Graham.'

Opposite her, Graham Marsh cringed. He wasn't so much scared by the possible ramifications of his actions as petrified of Diane.

Back in her office half an hour later, Diane stared at the opposite wall. Graham Marsh wasn't the only cause of her bad temper. Did he but know it, he had chosen one of the worst days of her life to make an appearance. She had a terrible hangover that had absolutely nothing to do with alcohol. The personal problems that she had been avoiding had, quite unexpectedly, hit her and Barry with full force the night before.

She had been lying down in the darkened bedroom when Barry had returned from work. Assuming that she was, as usual, still at Heathrow, he had sighed as he took in the empty flat and walked with a heavy tread into the bedroom. 'Jesus!' he had exclaimed, startled to find Diane lying, fully clothed on the bed. 'I thought you were out.'

'Headache.'

'You take anything?'

Diane shook her head. 'You know I hate taking pills.'

'Yeah. Prefer headaches.'

But Diane missed Barry's slightly sour note. 'I rubbed some oil on my temples.'

'Great. D'you want to eat?'

'No.' Diane gave a small, sheepish smile. 'There's ... er, not much in the fridge, I'm afraid.'

'Not much' proved to be an optimistic version. Barry found three eggs, a mouldy lemon, and some cheese that appeared to be enjoying a life of its own. More fed up than annoyed, he returned to the bedroom and sat on the end of the bed. While physically close to Diane, he felt as if he were miles away. What had happened, he wondered, to their tender conversations of yesteryear?

Diane's next words told him: they had been replaced by work discussions. 'I tried to call Bill again today ...'

'I'll phone for a pizza, shall I?'

But Diane wasn't listening. 'He's hardly ever there, Barry.'

And you, thought Barry, are hardly ever here. And when you are, your mind is somewhere else. He sighed. 'Yeah, well. You don't want anything at all to eat?'

'No.' Diane drew a weary hand over her eyes. 'Look, did you speak to Bill about . . .'

Barry stood up. 'Didn't have time, Diane. We're a little bit . . . you know . . . bit stretched.'

Barry's tetchiness registered with Diane. She propped herself up on her pillows and frowned at him. 'Why are you getting angry?'

'I'm not angry.'

For a moment they stared at each other in silence, staring across a chasm of lost intimacy. It was Barry who, with a deep and regretful sigh, broke that silence. 'You know, there are times when I think this is a bit of a game with you. The way you look at me, slightly confused, puckered brow,' – he did a passable imitation of Diane's expression – 'with that "why is this man getting so angry" expression. You're doing it now.'

'All I'm doing,' said Diane with more than a touch of frost, 'is lying here.'

Again an uneasy silence filled the room. Again it was Barry who broke it. 'How unhappy are you with me, Diane?'

Diane looked startled: then wary. 'What on earth brought this on?'

'Well, the last four months, actually.'

Diane looked away. 'We're . . . we're going through a difficult period.' She took a deep breath. 'I mean, it's probably my fault. I . . . er, I know I've been concentrating a lot on my work.' She tried a smile. 'With my review coming up and the rumours of changes I've got to work hard. Make sure I've still got a job.'

Barry just looked at her. Feeling distinctly uncomfortable, she went on. 'Trying to prove myself probably, and . . .'

But Barry had heard enough. 'Don't patronize me, Diane. You know exactly what you're worth so let's not . . .' searching for the right words, he turned his furrowed brow to his partner of the last four years. 'Look; work's important to a lot of people. So are their partners. This is about you and me, love, it's nothing to do with pressures of work.' He stabbed his chest and them pointed to Diane. 'You and me. Now let's be honest with each other and stop dancing around the problem. It's messing me up, Diane. I want the truth.'

He got it. Diane looked at him long and hard for a full thirty seconds. Then, in a flat, emotionless voice, she spoke the truth. 'I'm not in love with you any more. I'm sorry.'

Barry moved out two days later: the very day that the results on the phials Graham Marsh had been carrying came back from the lab. Already deeply upset by Barry's departure, Diane unwittingly took out her frustrations on the hapless Marsh. It wasn't difficult: the phials Marsh had smuggled into the country had contained the substance she had suspected from the very beginning.

'You were supposed to be here today at twelve,' she began. 'You're two hours late.'

'Sorry.'

'You would have been,' said Kevin Butcher from his position beside and slightly behind Diane, 'if we'd come and arrested you.' It had very nearly come to that. Whatever had been eating Diane for the past few days had begun to get to Kevin as well. Especially once she told him what was in the phials.

Diane's silent contempt was making Marsh feel distinctly uncomfortable. 'I said I was sorry,' he said as he squirmed in his seat. 'I live miles away.'

'Me too, but I was here.'

Marsh sighed. 'Is this going to be like school?'

Diane just glared and then switched on the tape recorder. After announcing the time, the place, and who was present, she addressed Marsh again. 'You do not have to say anything, but it may harm your defence if you do not mention when questioned something which you later rely on in court. We've had the analysis of the liquid you tried to bring into this country.' She paused and then, lip curling in disgust, looked Marsh in the eye. 'It's bear bile.'

Graham Marsh made absolutely no response.

'It sells,' continued Diane, 'as a very expensive medicine in the Far East and, if the address we found on you is anything to go by, here as well.'

Marsh looked genuinely surprised. 'I didn't know what it was.' Both Diane and Kevin believed him. Yet if he was expecting sympathy, he was in the wrong place. Diane leaned forward. 'But you knew you had something illegal or you wouldn't have hidden it in the lining of your rucksack.'

'I just didn't want it to get damaged.'

'Ah! So you knew it was worth something. Why else protect it from damage?'

Marsh didn't have an answer for that one.

'Bear bile,' continued Diane as she opened the file in front of her, 'is taken from the stomachs of young caged bears. I'll show you.' Extracting a photograph from the file, she held it in front of Marsh. He paled as he took in the image of a small, pathetic looking brown bear in a tiny bamboo cage. The only other object in the photograph was a metal pipe stuck in the animal's stomach. 'See the tap on the end?' Diane's voice was cool; deliberately dispassionate. It was the only way she could contain her utter horror at what she was explaining. 'The bears are kept just alive so that every two weeks, when that tap is turned, the fresh stomach bile can be extracted. It's sold,' she continued, fixing Marsh with a penetrating look, 'to pathetic old men who think drinking it will make them more virile. And when the bears finally die – or sometimes before they die – their paws are chopped off and sold to make a soup that sells for three hundred pounds a bowl. Can you imagine that, Graham?'

Graham couldn't.

'Somebody with a sharp knife,' continued Diane, 'drags out a half-conscious bear cub with a metal tube rammed in its stomach, and chops off its paws. What do you think of that degree of cruelty, Graham? I imagine,' she added, without giving the increasingly horrified man a chance to reply, 'that you're thinking "So what?". After all, you're helping the trade by bringing the stuff into the UK. Getting well paid, are you?'

But he wasn't looking at Diane. He was still staring, with a mixture of shock and disbelief, at the photograph.

'What did they give you, Graham? Fifty quid? Your air fare? Night with a girl before you left?'

'No.' The word was little more than a whisper.

Diane leaned back in her chair. 'Well, whatever you got probably wasn't enough. These phials will sell for anything up to seven thousand pounds.'

This time Graham Marsh's disbelief was directed at Diane.

'But,' she continued relentlessly, 'I suppose it's a bit of a giggle for you, watching someone torture a dumb animal to death. Have you made a lot of money from it?'

Looking the very picture of misery, Graham twisted his hands on the table in front of him. Gone was his earlier bolshiness. Now all he felt was misery – and a desperate need to redeem himself in Diane's eyes. 'I ... I'm not part of that,' he stammered. 'I just needed the money to get back home.'

'Then you shouldn't have damn well gone in the first place.'

'I didn't know what I was bringing in.'

'Yes you did, or you wouldn't have concealed it. Look at the photograph,' she spat. 'It's only an animal. What do you care. You'll be down the pub soon,' she scoffed, 'laughing with your mates. "Daft bitch who was banging on about bears". You're proud to be part of this, aren't you?' She fixed Graham with a penetrating, yet puzzled look. 'I'm just interested to know what kind of person you are.' But as she looked into his sad eyes, she realized that she knew exactly what sort of person Graham Marsh was: a pathetic, spineless individual who already regretted what he had done but hadn't the courage to admit it. In the silence that ensued, she reflected that her harshness towards him was due, in part, to her anger at herself. She was still hurting, badly, from the end of her relationship with Barry. She was wondering if she too was spineless, if she had lacked courage in her dealings with her ex-lover. And then, as she looked at the delivery address found on Graham Marsh, she realized something else about her relationship with Barry: it would have to continue on a professional level. The address was on City and South's patch. She would have to ask Barry's team to knock it. Life, she reflected with a sigh, was going to get more complicated, not less. Then she glared again at the man opposite her. He flinched under her gaze. A real ball-breaker, that one, he thought. Very beautiful and very deadly.

*

Two floors above the interview room, where Diane and Graham Marsh continued to stare at each other in mutual animosity, the phone rang in Diane's office. With Kevin Butcher also at the Marsh interview, there was only one member of staff in the office. And twenty-five year old Jake Munroe, the newest recruit to the Heathrow office, was heartily fed up with running the office single handed. So fed up that he had already forgotten his resolution to please the increasingly irritable Diane. So fed up that, after answering her phone, he forgot to write down the message left by the caller. And that was a pity, for the caller was someone intent on changing Diane's life yet again.

In sharp contrast to Diane's Heathrow office, Bill's headquarters at City and South was a hive of activity. Most of that activity emanated from one person; a sparky, good-humoured, sharp-tongued brunette in her late twenties. Jo Chadwick had returned.

'Jo!' Barry, who had been on the phone when she arrived, turned round and grinned broadly. 'How the hell are you?'

'Great.' She looked up from the mounds of paper that she had been throwing around her desk. 'Refreshed.'

'Done the computer thing?'

'Yep. Found the off switch, changed my life.' Then she looked pointedly at the desk opposite her own. It had been empty when she had left; now it was covered with unfamiliar clutter. 'New blood?'

Barry nodded. 'Katherine Roberts. You must have just passed her in the hallway.'

'Ah! By the front door, yes. Hint of a tint? What's she like?'

Barry thought for a moment. 'Not sure yet. The

smart money says she's a bit stuck up.' Then he grinned. 'She can't stand Andreotti.'

Jo grinned as well. 'Oh, she sounds great. Anyway,' she continued as she surveyed the empty office, 'fill me in on what's been happening. Everybody on holiday, I take it?'

'Dream on. Bill 'n' Andreotti are off on the trail of some bootleg booze ... remember Tommy Maddern?'

'Could I ever forget?' Jo, like the rest of her colleagues, had the names George Webster and Tommy Maddern imprinted on her brain. Not only were they the ones that had got away: they were responsible for Gerry Birch's downfall, and his death. Bill had phoned her while she was on the computer course to inform her of Gerry's suicide. 'Don't tell me,' she said, 'that Maddern's come back into our lives?'

Barry shrugged. 'I don't really know. Bill's not saying much.'

'Hmm. What else?'

'Well, Katherine and Arnie are investigating some bigwig about importing porn; snuff movies from Sweden, that sort of thing.'

'Yuk.' Jo wrinkled her nose in revulsion. 'What sort of bigwig?'

'The sort that goes by the name of Eric Short?'

'Eric Short? Footballer?'

'Ex-footballer.'

'Oh yeah, I remember. He's a high-roller in the fitness world. My sister's a member of one of his clubs. Says it's fantastic.'

'She might change her mind if she knew how it was being bankrolled.'

'Jesus! Can't wait to tell her.'

'Well don't. It's early days yet.' Barry looked at his watch. 'In fact, if all's going according to plan, they should be knocking one of their targets in about half an hour.'

'Good.' But Jo had lost interest. Back behind her desk, she was putting her new-found computer skills to creative, if not constructive use. She was designing graphics on her screen. So engrossed was she that she didn't notice Bill's arrival in the office and his stealthy approach to her.

'Ha! The prodigal returns. How are you?'

She nearly jumped out of her skin. To cover her shock, she instead jumped to her feet and, with an impish grin, saluted Bill. 'Ship shape and Bristol fashion, sir.'

'Good. Good.' With a grin, Bill nodded towards her computer. 'The course wasn't wasted, then.'

'Er...'

'Come on. Into my office. There's a lot for you to do.'

But Barry, who had again been called to the phone, delayed them. 'Bill,' he said, turning round. 'Target's picked up the package from Hold All. Arnie's had to go after him on foot. Katherine's just phoned: she's stuck in traffic – and now she can't raise Arnie. Thinks he might be on the Underground.'

'Hmm.' Bill looked slightly exasperated. 'Well, can't see how we can help them. Not a lot we can do from this end, is there?'

But half an hour later, Jo proved him wrong. By that time, Katherine and Arnie had reconvened and had also managed to trail their target to a street in the leafy suburb of Surbiton. The target, reflected Arnie, looked exactly like the sort of person who would live there. A nondescript man in his late fifties, he had 'suburbia' written all over him. Yet Arnie had been in the job long enough not to be surprised by the fact that the most ordinary looking people often indulged in the most extraordinary – and sometimes the most extraordinarily vile – private pursuits. It was while he was lost in those thoughts that he managed to lose the target. Somehow, after turning into the street, the man they knew only as L.C. had managed to disappear. In a panic, Arnie phoned the office on his mobile.

'City and South. How can I help you?' The chirpy, Northern voice was unmistakable.

'Jo! What the hell are you doing there!'

'I work here, remember.'

'Oh. Yeah. Listen, Jo, has Bill filled you in on the L.C. scenario?'

'Sure has.'

'Well, listen, I've lost our man, and the package he picked up is spiked. If it goes off before we find him he'll destroy the evidence and . . .'

'So where's the target?' Jo was already tapping away on her computer. 'Surbiton. Council Tax department'll have every name in the street.' As she spoke, her deft fingers were already typing out a request to access the information she needed. 'If there's an L.C., that might be him. Otherwise,' she added with a grin, 'just hang about and hope he doesn't open it.'

In the car parked at the end of the street in question, Katherine and Arnie surveyed the silent, empty houses in front of them. 'At least,' said Katherine, 'he hasn't opened it yet. Damned annoying to hear bleep-bleep and not know which house it's coming from.' Then she crossed her fingers. 'So far.'

Jo was back on the line in a matter of seconds. 'No names beginning with the initials L.C. There are, however, five C.L.s. Caroline Lane . . .'

'That's a woman.'

'Well spotted, Arnie.'

'But she could be the target's sister or mother or whatever.'

'Good point,' said Katherine, leaning over towards Arnie's phone.

'Who's that with you?' asked Jo, surprised at the unfamiliar voice.

'Katherine,' replied Arnie. 'Katherine Roberts. The new Senior Officer ...'

'Oh yeah.' Jo raised her voice. 'Pleased to meet you, Katherine.'

'You too,' shouted Katherine, leaning over again. 'Anything else for us?'

'Yeah, stacks. There's a Carl Lee at number 51, another Caroline, Caroline Lawrence at number 14 ... and a Cyril Lathem at ...'

'Forget it!' Arnie's voice was sharp, commanding. He had been watching the street, and in particular the progress of an elderly woman towards number 15. As soon as she had stopped outside the gate, a man emerged from the front door to help her inside. That man was their target; the man who had picked up the package from Hold All.

'Cyril Lathem,' continued Jo, irritated at being rudely interrupted. 'Lives at number 15.'

Katherine and Arnie looked at each other and nodded. Katherine was wild-eyed with excitement. 'We've got him, Arnie.'

Arnie nodded and then went back to the phone. 'Thanks Jo; we've got him.'

'Any time.' Jo's words were casual, yet her expression was triumphant. Not an hour back at work and she had already reaped rewards from the computer course about which her colleagues had been so scathing.

In the car, Katherine and Arnie waited with mounting impatience for the man they now knew as Cyril Lathem to open the package. 'Assuming,' said Katherine, 'that the old lady's his mother and he'll want to get her out of the way before he opens the package...'

'Unless she's involved as well.'

Katherine looked at Arnie in horror. 'Don't be disgusting. This whole thing's perverted enough without..' then she trailed into silence. It was perverted enough, a little voice told her, without her getting involved with Eric Short. Bill had been right to be furious about that. Yet what he didn't know was that she had seen him since their heated encounter: had had another rendezvous with the man who always left her feeling confused. If only...

'He's opened it!' Arnie jolted her out of her reverie. Alert again, Katherine looked at the gadget Arnie was holding. Sure enough, it was bleeping and the little red light was flashing: an indication that Lathem had opened the package.

Thirty seconds later the two customs officers were at the front door of number 15. It was Lathem himself who answered their ring. 'Mr Lathem?' Katherine smiled and flashed her identity badge at the unsuspecting man. 'Customs and Excise,' she continued. 'I have reason to believe you have in your possession suspected obscene material. I have the necessary authority to search your home for it.'

Beside her, Arnie watched the expression on Lathem's face change from polite interest to complete surprise – and then to terror. He stared open-mouthed at Katherine. Then he slumped against the open door. And when he finally responded to Katherine's words, he took both her and Arnie by surprise. He started to cry.

'Has Lathem made a full statement yet?'

Katherine nodded. 'Oh yes, he was a pushover.' She cast her mind back to yesterday's memorable knock at number 15. Terrified that his mother might find out who his callers were and what they were looking for, Lathem had bent over backwards to co-operate. Katherine, rather to Arnie's surprise, informed Lathem's mother that her son had witnessed a road accident and he was merely helping them with their enquiries. Mrs Lathem had seemed satisfied and had left them to their task. Had she stayed with them she would have discovered things about her son that would have probably killed her: the secret cupboard behind his wardrobe that contained a TV and a video, a stack of pornographic video cassettes and another one of particularly revolting magazines.

Katherine looked up at Bill with a grim smile. 'Felt almost sorry for him. Almost. Another "nonce" in jail for quite a while.'

Bill nodded. 'Hmm. But nothing to link him with Short?'

'No.' Katherine busied herself with the file on her knee. 'But Short ... er, wants to meet me on Friday – late, because he has some people to see beforehand.' She hurriedly extracted some photographs from the file. 'All the surveillance photographs we've got are of Friday night meetings at his office. We assume they're concerned with the copying and distributing of the material. I'm assuming this meeting's been called because of the dud videos delivered by the Swede.'

'Alternatively,' said Bill, 'it could just be an ordinary business meeting.'

Katherine shook her head and handed Bill a photograph. 'Apart from turning up at Short's office every third or fourth Friday, this woman has no connection with Short's business. Nor,' she said as she handed over another photograph, 'does this man.'

Bill studied the prints. Both had been taken at locations unfamiliar to him. 'Are these their homes in the background?'

Katherine nodded. 'Yes. Arnie tracked them both down. He's called Alex Britain but we still don't have a name for her. The only women involved in Short's official businesses are his two daughters. So why's this one turning up to so many "business" meetings?'

But Bill was still dwelling on Katherine's mention of Arnie. It was the first time she had ever given any indication that they were operating as a team. He raised an eyebrow. 'Arnie found them?'

The import of his words was not lost of Katherine. She caught Bill's eye and, with a self-deprecating smile, reminded him of their previous meeting. 'I'm not the Lone Star State, remember? The thing is, I want to get this case settled as quickly as possible.'

Surprised by her change of tune, Bill frowned over the desk. 'Eager to get Short behind bars, eh?'

Katherine looked away.

'Don't you think,' continued Bill, 'that you might be rushing it with him? You said the other day that . . .'

She brushed that one aside. 'But now we've got more. We've seen a courier deliver a package to him.'

'To the building, not Short's office. Katherine, we're still not certain Short is involved.' He cast his mind back to the Higson case; the failure that had so ironically coincided with her arrival at City and South. 'I really don't want us to lose in court again. We must be certain.'

Katherine left Bill's office feeling distinctly uncomfortable. She knew he was right; that she was rushing in while there was still a large element of uncertainty surrounding Short. Yet it was now extremely important to her to resolve the case as soon as possible – for reasons that she had not confided to Bill. On her return to her hotel the previous evening, Eric Short had surprised the life out of her. He had been waiting in reception.

'You work late,' he had said with a broad smile.

Wrong-footed and nonplussed, Katherine had blurted out a response that she immediately regretted. 'I've ... er, I've come from the estate agent. Found a flat.'

'That's great. Where is it?'

'It's ... it's not too far from here really.' Katherine looked up at Short and tried a smile. She found that as soon as she locked eyes with him, the smile broadened. Oh God, she thought. What a mess. I find him attractive. He likes me. And I've spent half the day trying to stick the label 'pornographer and criminal' onto him.

But Short seemed unaware of her inner turmoil. 'Terrific. Terrific.' Then he looked at his watch. 'You nearly missed me, actually. I was just about to leave.'

'But how did you know where I ...?'

Short grinned. 'You gave me the phone number. So I called.' Then he extracted a note from his coat pocket and handed it to her. 'I was leaving you this. Have to go to Italy for a few days. I'll be back on Tuesday. Thought we might do something. Supper?'

'Right.'

'Great. Give me the phone number of your flat and I'll call you.'

'There's no phone yet.'

'Oh. Well, I can lend you a mobile.' He grinned

again. His face was open, honest; his words friendly and sincere. Paralysed by her conflicting emotions, Katherine didn't reply. 'Where's the flat?' continued Short. 'Give me the address and I'll pick you up from there when I get back.'

Replaying the scene in her mind, Katherine walked slowly towards her desk. She couldn't tell Bill; she couldn't let on about the mess she had got herself into. He had only just recovered from his anger about her having contacted Short in the first place: as he had said only minutes before, he was resigned – albeit unwillingly – to let her continue the investigation in her unorthodox manner.

For a long moment she stared at the telephone on her desk. Beside it was the number of the estate agent from whom she was renting the flat. She could call them. She could say that she was sorry but she had changed her mind. There was still time to do so: no contracts had been exchanged. Then a little voice in her head told her that she would be running away; and that Katherine Roberts had never run away from anything in her life. Hadn't her father always told her – and hadn't she always believed – that difficult issues had to be faced head on?

Nine

George Webster was standing on a promontory looking out to sea. Behind him were the apartments he was in the process of building. Beside him was Tommy Maddern. 'Lounge area,' said George as he turned back and gestured towards the incomplete concrete low-rises. 'Double-glazed picture windows opening onto oval picture balcony. Three bedrooms, two bathrooms, one en-suite.' Grinning, he nudged Tommy in the ribs. 'How much? Go on, have a guess.'

Tommy sighed. George was doing this deliberately. Rubbing salt in the wound; letting Tommy know he was rolling in it – but not letting him know whether or not he was going to agree to Conny Devooght's plan. 'Look George, can we just talk about what I come for?'

Webster looked as if he hadn't heard. 'Hundred and forty three thousand sterling,' he said. 'You'd get nothing like this for that price in London. This lot's already sold. Got more on the drawing board for the next bay.'

Beside him, Tommy scowled. He had taken the point. George was rich and clever and he wasn't. Then he allowed himself a small smile. Perhaps George's behaviour was due to irritation, to annoyance that it was he, Tommy, who had the contact with Conny Devooght.

As if reading his mind, George turned once again to face the sea. 'Sure, let's talk about it. Sorry your friend couldn't stay.'

'You couldn't stand the sight of him, George.'

George roared with laughter. 'My face gives me away every time, doesn't it? What was he in, back in the old South Africa, exactly.'

'Branch of the police.'

'Hum. And he wants me to stump up three quarters of a million.'

Tommy nodded. 'You can trust him.'

'No I can't. I don't know him.'

'But you know me, George.'

At that, George turned and gave the other man a long, appraising look. A small smile crept across the battered face.

Disconcerted, Tommy looked away. 'Look, it was me wanted you in on this. Now, for old time's sake, stop pissing about and give me a yes or a no.'

George stroked his chin. 'Something went wrong for your mate last time he tried this. Went up in smoke, isn't that what he said? That's why he wants the money on the hurry-up.'

'Yeah, you said.' This wasn't the first time George had made that particular point. 'But that doesn't move us on, George.'

'No, but it puts us ... me, in a strong bargaining position.'

Tommy took a deep breath. This was too much. 'Look, you said you wanted to meet the other faces involved, then you change your mind, now you're ...'

'You have to appreciate,' interrupted George, 'that the three quarters of a million your mate's after is mine. I'm cautious because I don't want my dosh to vanish across the veld. Reasonable?'

'George, you stand to cop seven million! You don't get into something like that for nothing. Sure, it's a big punt, but something like this doesn't come along every day. It's one run, grab the profit and out. It's gotta be tempting!'

George wondered how much Conny Devooght had promised Tommy for his participation in the deal. A great deal more than he would eventually get, George suspected. Then he smiled again. Soon, if the plan he had already formulated came to fruition, he would know exactly how much Tommy would get. He would know exactly how much *everyone* would get. 'Of course it's tempting,' he mused. 'But I never dive in without knowing the water, Tommy. You should know that by now. And, OK, I'll come to Latvia with you. But we'll just put a toe in the water in case the sharks are about.'

But George, like Tommy, knew the exact location of the biggest shark in the game.

The contrast between Portugal and Latvia was extreme. Not only was the weather ten degrees colder in the latter, but the cars, the countryside and the people were all markedly different. Miserable, thought George as, with Tommy beside him and Conny Devooght in the front with the driver, they sped away from the lovely city of Riga into the barren, desolate countryside.

Devooght had been delighted that Tommy had managed to persuade George to come. Not the most astute of men, he was still labouring under the misapprehension that Tommy was a smooth operator who had the measure of George. And he still hadn't clicked that George couldn't stand the sight of him.

It was George who broke the silence that had descended at the same time as the rain clouds. He huddled further into his coat and grinned at the back of Conny's head. 'Conny, eh? How are you spelling that?'

Conny, beaming, turned round and told him. 'It's short for Conrad,' he finished.

'Hmm. I've got an Auntie Connie.'

Conny grinned uncertainly.

Silence reigned once more as the little car sped through the countryside. After ten minutes the driver prodded Conny's arm and pointed to his left, to what looked like a dilapidated heavy industrial complex. 'Ah!' Conny turned round. 'Our destination, gentlemen.'

Neither George nor Tommy had seen anything like it. The site was enormous, full of what looked like junk – and swarming with men carrying automatic rifles. As they turned and stopped at the huge gates, George realized that the place used to be a military base. The checkpoints; the observation towers and the Nissen huts dotted around the place told their own story. After their names were taken and their papers checked, they drove on and George, to his great interest, noticed that the equipment stacked around them was anything but junk. Sure, some of it was past its prime, but even a little bit of rust couldn't disguise military vehicles, tanks, field guns and MiG fighters. George sucked-in his breath. Impressive, he thought, making a mental note to remain impassive. It wouldn't do to let whoever was in charge of this operation think that he, George Webster, was awed by the sights before him.

The car slowed and finally stopped in front of a dingy complex of what looked like office buildings. Two men emerged from the nearest. One was a tall, Eastern European-looking man of about forty wearing a tracksuit and trainers. The other, slighter and younger man was Oriental.

Devooght, beaming as usual, made the introductions.

The man in the tracksuit, it was quickly apparent, was in charge. 'Mikolas Zenisek,' he said. 'George Webster.'

George accepted the proffered hand and smiled. 'Good afternoon.' He eyed Mikolas with interest. A confident, good-looking bugger, he concluded. His dark, B-movie-star looks were complemented by a pronounced Eastern European accent. 'Good trip?' he asked with an amused smile.

George grimaced. 'I've had better.'

Mikolas then indicated the other man. 'My associate, Cheung San.' Again hands were shaken. Cheung San, as instilled into him during his childhood in Vietnam, also bowed to the two newcomers. Tommy was very taken by that. He approved of people showing deference. 'OK,' said Mikolas, again addressing George. 'Mr Devooght tells me you're the new investor.'

'The *possible* new investor.'

Mikolas smiled and indicated the vast array of weapons all around them. 'Well, as you can see, we can supply most things. Anything from automatic rifles to MiGs.'

'I don't get much call for MiGs.'

Mikolas laughed. 'No, maybe not in London.' Then he held up a hand. 'We are the suppliers; Mr Devooght has the buyers and you, we are told, have the money. So we all need each other for something, OK? We require three quarters of a million, split into dollars and Deutschmarks. The goods will then be loaded onto a ship and sailed to their destination. On arrival they will be . . .'

'Hold it.' Now it was George who raised his hand. 'Just hold on a second.' Then he lowered his voice. 'Could you and I have a chat?'

Tommy and Conny, sensing power-play, looked at each other. Cheung San smiled politely. Mikolas merely shrugged. 'Sure. We'll go into my office.' Neither he nor George, as they walked inside, noticed the second, horrified look that passed between Tommy and Conny.

'Why,' said George as soon as they were alone in the small office, 'do you need three quarters of a million in cash?'

Mikolas laughed. 'You want me to take a cheque? No, no ... a joke. That was the price agreed with Devooght last time.'

George frowned. 'He was transporting Caesium, right?'

'Yes. Several kilos. In the one container.'

'Is it shipped as Caesium, or does he call it something else?'

'Calls it something else.'

'And what went wrong the last time?'

Mikolas, however, wasn't very interested in Conny Devooght's problems. 'I don't know. He paid; the goods were shipped ... they didn't arrive.'

'So now he has to start again.'

'Yes, he still has the buyers waiting.'

'And he can't move without my money?'

Mikolas merely shrugged. George looked him in the eye. 'And nor can you, I imagine.'

Mikolas's look was equally steely. 'Oh, I can always find a buyer.'

'Really.' George paced the room for a few seconds, mentally rechecking the plan he had hatched back in Portugal; the plan that would put him in the driving seat. 'Does a lot of money,' he asked suddenly, 'come and go from here?'

Bored by George's barrage of questions, Mikolas just shrugged again.

'I own property companies,' continued George. 'We

sell to people all over the world. A lot of cash deals. They pay us in yen, dollars, crowns. We don't ask how they got the money, we just give 'em a property for it.' He looked up at Mikolas and saw the beginnings of comprehension in the other man's eyes. 'I was thinking,' he continued, 'that instead of me giving you three quarters of a million pounds in cash, a better way might be for me to give you something that's *worth* three quarters of a million instead.'

Mikolas grinned. 'A . . . property?'

'A house. In Hampstead. London.'

Mikolas paused before replying. 'I think, George, that we'd better sit down, yes?'

They sat down and George immediately began to elaborate on the plan that had taken him many painstaking, and ultimately satisfying hours to formulate. 'What will happen,' he said, 'if you agree, is that I will give you a receipt, which will say that you have paid me three quarters of a million pounds sterling as part payment on the house in London.'

Mikolas nodded. 'But I pay you nothing.'

'Correct.'

'And you will give me a house.'

George smiled and leaned back in his chair. 'I will *almost* give you a house. Under English law, exchange of contracts – which is what my receipt will represent – means I can't back out of selling you the house. So the house will be yours – so long as our deal here goes well and we behave like honourable men.'

'And if things don't go well?'

'You'll have to tear up my receipt or find the remainder of the asking price.'

'Which is how much?'

George grinned across the table. 'The asking price is one and a half million pounds. If things don't go according to plan, you'll owe me three quarters of a million – which is what the place cost when I bought it. The worst that can happen to me,' he finished with a flourish, 'is that I get back exactly what I paid for it.'

Mikolas grinned from ear to ear. George wasn't stitching him up – just hedging his bets. He would have done exactly the same thing himself. As he had suspected, George was indeed a kindred spirit. He looked at him in admiration. 'Great insurance policy, George.'

'Not bad, is it?' Still smiling, George stood up. 'So that's agreed then?'

'Yes.'

'Good. Shall we go and rescue those boys from the cold?'

Outside, George was pleased to see that Tommy and Conny appeared to have run out of conversation. The latter was looking sullen and suspicious. The former, as soon as he saw George emerge from the building, leaped to his side. 'So? Are we on?'

George rubbed his hands together. 'Looking likely, Thomas, looking likely.'

'Great!'

'Thing is, I've restructured the deal a bit, that's all.'

Tommy looked confused. And, seeing the conspiratorial smile that passed between George and Mikolas, he became visibly uneasy. George patted him on the back. 'Don't worry about it, Tommy. It's all under control.' Then, at a sign from Mikolas, he made his way over to the shed where the Caesium was being prepared for shipment.

Still uneasy, Tommy looked at Conny. Conny looked back in disgust. 'I think we've just become the hired help, Tommy.'

*

At the same time, Bill Adams was sitting in his office at London City and South, peering at the monitor in front of him. The name he had logged into the computer was that of one George Webster; and the file beside him was the one relating to Webster's activities of two years ago.

But Bill was making absolutely no headway in his new, and strictly private, investigation. He told himself it was only curiosity, that he wasn't really conducting a new investigation: he had, nonetheless, just completed a search on George Webster's activities in Portugal. Hence his frown. Whatever Webster was doing in Portugal, it was obviously legitimate – or so swathed in secrecy and disguised under false names that there was no trace of Webster at all. Bill sighed, leaned back in his chair, and forced himself to contemplate two issues: one was that he had got his information about Webster being in Portugal from a casual encounter with an estate agent – hardly concrete evidence. The other was that if he caught a member of his staff embarking on a wild goose chase fuelled by a personal vendetta he would go ballistic. It was time, he told himself, to get a grip.

As if on cue, Alan Jackson chose that moment to phone him. Bill couldn't help grinning when he heard the familiar tones – despite the fact that he was still smarting from their 'little chat' the other day.

'So,' he said after exchanging greetings. 'What can I do for you, Alan? Tell you whether I'm taking the pension or not?'

Perhaps wisely, Alan chose to ignore the remark. 'Seen today's *Telegraph*?' was all he said.

Again Bill grinned. 'Not my paper, Alan.'

'Hmm. Well, they all read it here.'

I'm sure they do, thought Bill. Another good reason for not following in Alan's footsteps at York House.

'There's an article,' continued Alan, 'on bootlegging. *A new and profitable trade,*' he quoted, '*is now totally out of control, with Her Majesty's Customs and Excise seemingly unable to stem the tide of illegal alcohol and tobacco being brought into this country by organized criminal gangs*. I thought,' Alan added in aggrieved tones, 'that your lot were investigating something like this.'

Bill had to work hard to quell his instinctive, angry response. It was typical of Alan, he fumed, to equate the *Daily Telegraph* with the Gospel. 'I have all the resources at my disposal on it,' he replied stiffly. 'All one of him. Shall we go through our chat about manpower again? Or maybe get the Government to tax booze and tobacco at the same rate as they're taxed in France and we'd solve the problem overnight.'

Alan *had* forgotten about their chat about manpower. Realizing his phone call was, under the circumstances, less than reasonable, he backed off immediately with a humourless laugh and a remark along the lines of how pleased he was that Bill was still on the case. Bill only just managed to delay his snort of derision until he had replaced the receiver. Then he went in search of Andreotti.

He found him lurking by the coffee machine in the outer office.

'Not in the pub with the Peckham boys?' The remark was meant, but not taken, in good humour. Andreotti was now heartily fed up with hanging about in the dismal South London pub frequented by Eddie Davies and his mates. Worse, he was also becoming the butt of Chris Davies's jokes about how often and for how long he was in the pub. It wasn't so much the sneers about 'begging for work' that were starting to bother him: it was the gnawing fear that the longer he spent with Davies and his crew, the more likely he was to be rumbled as an imposter. And there was little he could do apart from frequent the pub: his first and only trip to France had taught him that the bootleggers were cautious people. A week after that trip, Chris Davies had gone on another one and Andreotti, at the time he was due back, had made a clandestine recce of the warehouse where they had dumped the alcohol on the previous trip. It had been empty. Each trip, evidently, involved a new location for storing the booze, and Andreotti knew he couldn't risk asking questions about things that, in his new identity as a Peckham boy, he 'didn't need to know'.

Realizing that he had said something wrong, Bill changed tack. 'Has Maddern shown up again?'

'No. But Davies and a few of his mob were missing from the pub all day yesterday and last night.' He grimaced and sipped his coffee. 'Mass exodus like that means there's either a plague coming on or they're fetching a load in.'

'They didn't offer you a drive?'

'No – and I didn't get too pushy or they'd start to wonder why.' Again the grimace. 'There's been a couple of awkward questions already, Bill.'

'What?' Alarm bells rang in Bill's head. The last thing he wanted – or would ever do – was keep a member of his team in the field with a blown cover.

But Andreotti allayed his fears. 'Nothing major. Things like "Remember the old fish shop? Remember old so-and-so?". Luckily, they think I'm none too bright so they're not altogether surprised that I'm a bit slow on the uptake.'

Bill suppressed a grin. 'So you don't think they suspect you?'

'No, but I wouldn't want to push my luck with 'em. If they offer me another drive, I reckon we should plan a knock round it.'

Bill considered that one. He knew Andreotti was right. And in the light of Alan Jackson's phone call, he knew that he was heading for serious trouble if they didn't knock the operation soon. But there was still that wild card that might come into play again...

'Tommy Maddern,' he mused, 'is Webster's man. Always has been. If Maddern's involved it means Webster's in the background somewhere. You ... er, you haven't mentioned any of this to anyone at the office?'

Surprised by the question, Andreotti shot Bill a peculiar look. 'No. I do think we should get a move on knocking Eddie Davies, though. Give him too much rope, he'll either retire stone rich, or find out who I'm really working with.'

Realizing just how uneasy Andreotti had become about the role he was playing, Bill sought to reassure him. 'Andreotti, I wouldn't ever put you or any of you at risk, but if you can just stay in place for a few more days, maybe Maddern will show again. We might even be able to find out where he lives.'

Andreotti stared after Bill as he walked back to his office. His boss had always been driven; ambitious for himself and his team. But now something other than professional pride seemed to be at work: something far less healthy and altogether more sinister. For the first time since he had started working for City and South, Andreotti found himself doubting Bill's words: the words about never putting any of his team at risk. Andreotti was at risk – and Bill knew it. Apart from the possibility of being tripped up on questions regarding his 'stamping ground' of Peckham, Andreotti was still driving around in the customs Transit van.

Later that afternoon, Andreotti was still in a quandary. What he wanted most was to throw in the towel regarding Tommy Maddern; to tell Bill he was on a wild goose chase that, in addition, was jeopardising the knock of the bootlegging operation. Yet Andreotti was neither blind nor deaf to the rumours spreading through City and South: rumours of amalgamation, of redundancy and even of Bill Adams's possible early retirement. Like the rest of his colleagues, he was feeling insecure about his job, and the last thing he needed was to be branded by Bill as 'unco-operative.'

It was the latter consideration – and Bill's *faux*-casual remark about finding Tommy Maddern's address – that led him back to the South London pub early that evening. The Davies clan, he knew, were on a run to France, but some of the other regulars may be able to shed light on a subject he had thus far avoided: that of Tommy Maddern.

He struck gold during a conversation with a man he knew only as Spider; a seedy, down-at-heel individual whom he had once observed talking to Chris Davies. As casually as he could, he asked Spider if he had seen Tommy recently.

'Tommy? Big Tommy?' Spider looked up from his pint. The expression on his face indicated that he was no fan of Big Tommy.

'Yeah. Big Tommy. How's he doing?'

Spider shrugged. 'Dunno. Been keeping a bit of a low profile lately. Car's still parked outside the lock-up, though. Must be around somewhere.' That thought clearly made Spider feel uneasy. He took refuge in another swig of his lager.

Andreotti thought quickly. He only had one more chance: any further questions and he would begin to arouse suspicions. 'Oh,' he said, hoping he sounded disinterested. 'Yeah. Eddie's lock-up. Bit of a mess nowadays, innit?'

Spider nodded. 'All that to-ing and fro-ing. Like bleeding Waterloo Station.'

Bingo! Andreotti sipped his own drink in a desperate attempt to hide the triumphant look in his eyes. His one, wild guess had proved correct: Tommy Maddern parked his car in the lane outside Eddie Davies's garage. The only problem was, so did a lot of other people. Thinking quickly, he looked at his watch, swore loudly and profusely, downed the rest of his drink and made his excuses with the dreaded words 'Interview at the Job Centre.'

Spider gave him a sympathetic look. He had been through similar experiences. Many times. 'Don't worry,' he said with a wink, 'they'll soon give up on you.'

Andreotti's sympathies, as he hurried out of the pub, were with the people at the Job Centre; making Spider look employable would be nothing short of a miracle. He headed for the nearest phone box. It was five o'clock. Jo Chadwick, he knew, was bound to be in the office at City and South. Katherine, Arnie and Barry were out in the field, following Diane Ralston's lead on something to do with strange green potions from the Far East. Bill, he knew, was simply 'out' that afternoon. But Jo, still catching up on paperwork, would be manning the phones. For a brief moment, Andreotti wondered how she would feel about being commanded by him to rush off to Eddie Davies's garage to take down the registration numbers of every car in the lane. She would probably be furious – not least because she was technically his field officer and therefore his senior.

But Jo wasn't furious; just curious. Andreotti's call interrupted her reading of his reports on the bootlegging case; a case about which she already had a strange feeling. Why, she asked herself as she turned to the last page, hadn't they already knocked it? And then, casting her mind back to her first day at work after the computer course, she remembered snippets of conversation with Andreotti. Conversation during which the name of Tommy Maddern had come up. Was that it, she wondered? And now Andreotti was asking her to drive half way across London to read out some licence plates to him. Why? The reports she had just read contained the names, addresses and vehicle licence numbers of everyone officially named in the bootlegging operation, yet Andreotti, in his brief but hurried phone call, had claimed he was still chasing up leads on that score. Jo didn't believe him.

She did, however, agree to his bidding. She drove to Catford, found the garage, and then, on her mobile, read out the numbers of the cars outside it to Andreotti. Then, after being dismissed with a 'Ta, Jo, You're a brick', she did something that caused her only a vague qualm of unease. She drove to the coffee shop where Andreotti had taken her call, waited for him to come out, and then followed him. To Deptford. She waited in her car while Andreotti, with a professionalism that impressed her, bluffed his way into a dismal, run-down block of flats and disappeared from sight. Ten minutes later he emerged – and ran straight into Jo.

He was so utterly surprised that Jo found herself laughing at his wide-eyed, open-mouthed, unwitting imitation of a rabbit caught in car headlights. 'Hi, Andreotti,' she said in the sort of nonchalant manner that suggested they were accustomed to bumping into each other outside run-down council blocks in darkest Deptford.

'Er ... hi.' Andreotti, not sure where to look, suddenly found the pavement extremely interesting.

'Andreotti, what's going on?'

This time he managed to look her in the eye. 'I'm supposed to report straight to Bill.'

Jo shook her head. Since when, she thought, had demarkation reared its ugly head at City and South. 'No. I'm your field officer – you tell me first. What the hell are you up to?'

Andreotti shrugged. 'OK, OK. But can we talk about it over a drink. I don't much feel like hanging around here.'

She looked up at the building in front of them, and at the rows of identical ones all around. They were most unprepossessing – and depressing in the extreme. And they were, if Andreotti's little recce was anything to go by, inhabited by at least one person worthy of investigation by customs. Not the sort of place to hang around.

By mutual accord, they drove several miles to a pub they both knew. 'You're buying,' said Jo as soon as they walked in.

'Oh! Ah ... yes. I was just about to order ...'

'A large gin and tonic for me.'

'Yes boss.' Andreotti hastened to the bar and, after he placed his order, looked back towards Jo. Was she, he wondered, really angry? Or was she just enjoying the fact that she had caught him on the hop? A bit of both, he suspected.

'So?' She looked up as he placed their drinks on the table. 'What gives?'

As soon as he started telling her, Andreotti experienced a welcome sensation of relief. He hadn't realized until now how stressful he had been finding the bootlegging investigation – and the burden of Bill's expectations that he had been carrying alone.

'It's about Tommy Maddern,' he said.

Jo allowed herself a small smile.

'He's in with this bootlegging mob. I found out he'd parked his car outside one of those lock-ups, but I didn't know which one it was. That's why I needed you to get the licence numbers of all of 'em. One came up trumps.'

'Evidently.'

Andreotti ignored the sardonic interruption. 'The Jag with the side panel banged in,' he continued, 'belongs to a bloke called Jack Foyle.' Suddenly Andreotti grinned. 'He's banged-up as well, as a matter of fact. That's his flat I was having a look at. Foyle's an old mate of Tommy Maddern.'

'And is Maddern using his flat?'

Andreotti frowned. 'Not sure. *Someone's* using it – but we'll need to get the phone number, and a copy of the bill ... er ... what's it ...?'

'Itemized.'

'Exactly.'

Jo paused to light a cigarette and, inhaling deeply, asked if Maddern was running the bootlegging racket. She hoped to God Andreotti's answer wasn't going to be a lie.

It wasn't. 'No.' Andreotti shook his head. 'Eddie Davies is. But Bill thinks George Webster might be involved somewhere.'

Oh shit. Jo grimaced. This was all becoming horribly

predictable. 'Has he any evidence for that?' she asked in slow, measured tones.

'Not so far. It's why we haven't knocked the job yet.'

'So Bill's hoping Webster'll put in an appearance?'

Although he shared her scepticism, Andreotti merely shrugged. She stubbed out her cigarette with a viciousness that surprised him. 'This is bloody silly! I'm going to have a word with Bill.'

'No!' Andreotti was appalled. 'Don't do that! I'll really be in it then . . .'

'Huh! You'll really be in it if we don't knock this mob soon.' She looked at her colleague and shook her head. 'You're driving round in a pool van when you should have had a clean, untraceable one bought for you . . .'

'Money's tight.' Suddenly Andreotti found himself defending Bill; negating the fears he himself had been experiencing.

Jo snorted and lit another cigarette. 'Cost 'em even more to bury you, wouldn't it? This job should have been wrapped up by now, Andreotti.' Then she articulated what they both knew were the reasons behind Bill's procrastination. 'It's because of Gerry, isn't it? Bill wants Webster at any price.'

Their eyes met over the table. Then Andreotti reached over for one of Jo's cigarettes. 'Yes,' he said. 'At any price.'

Jo went home and did some thinking. With her worst fears about Bill's obsession confirmed, she knew she had two options. One was to create the most almighty fuss and – even if it meant going over Bill's head to Alan Jackson – to demand that the tenuous Maddern/Webster link to the bootlegging operation be severed. After all, and as she knew from Andreotti's report, Tommy Maddern had appeared – once – during one of the runs to France. She knew that Bill's superiors would take an extremely dim view of his hunch that he would lead them to George Webster, a so-called crook who wasn't even on anybody's wanted list.

Jo dismissed that option almost as soon as she considered it. Nobody outside City and South would understand Bill's obsession: he would be laughed, or perhaps disgraced, out of his job. But Jo and her colleagues had lived through the dreadful tangled web that had ensnared and finally ruined Gerry Birch. They knew, as nobody else did, that George Webster and Tommy Maddern had a lot to answer for. They knew, although the law had decreed otherwise, that George Webster was a ruthless, unscrupulous criminal with no loyalty and no morals. And they knew that he deserved everything that came his way. So Jo thought some more and came up with an alternative course of action. It was a course that, until late into the night, she followed.

The next morning she requested to see Bill. Alone. Unsuspecting, Bill gave her an affable wave and invited her to sit down opposite him. 'Problem?' he asked with a friendly smile.

'Er ... I just needed a quiet word. Andreotti,' she continued, 'has told me about Tommy Maddern, and why tracing his flop seems to have taken priority over knocking this bootlegging team.'

Bill folded his hands on the desk. 'I see.' Then he lapsed into silence. He didn't really see. He knew from Andreotti's phone call late last night that Tommy Maddern's flop had been traced, but Andreotti had somehow neglected to tell him that Jo was in on the act. 'It hasn't,' he said more sternly than he meant, 'taken priority. I have every reason to believe ...'

'That George Webster may be involved, and that

you want to arrest him.' Anxious to deflect interruption, Jo held both hands in front of her. 'I understand that, but I'm very concerned about keeping an officer in the field longer than is absolutely necessary.' Then she looked at Bill with her familiar, cheeky grin. 'Even Andreotti.'

But Bill wasn't amused. 'I needed to know where Maddern lived. I thought it might lead us to Webster.' Why, he thought, am I being so defensive in front of an employee who is nearly twenty years my junior? But he knew why.

So did Jo. 'Aye, well,' she said. 'I think you may have been right. But whether that ties Webster to the bootlegging, I couldn't say. As I expect you know, Andreotti found Maddern's flop at six o'clock last night.' Much to Bill's surprise, she looked up and smiled. 'At ten o'clock I got the itemized bill for the ex-directory number there. There are several calls to Portugal.' She paused and, still smiling, watched Bill's reaction. He was, as Andreotti would say, gobsmacked. So, she thought, he already knows about Webster being in Portugal. 'Three of those calls,' she continued, extracting a notebook from her pocket, 'were to a bar and one to a house owned by a company called Apartmentos Marfin. It's registered on Jersey, so I went via Jersey customs. Apartmentos Marfin,' she said with a broad, triumphant grin, 'is owned by one Mr George Webster. And that,' she finished, handing a slip of paper to Bill, 'is his new phone number. For some reason he changed the old one a few weeks ago. Maddern's in touch with him, but why is anyone's guess.'

Bill was ecstatic. 'Jo, you are quite brilliant!'

'I know. But Bill,' she said on a more serious note, 'can we get on with knocking the bootlegging now, and get Andreotti out of the field? I may not like the little creep, but I don't want to have to scrape him off the pavement if Davies and his lads find out who he really is.'

Bill nodded. 'Sure. We'll nick Davies the next load he brings in.'

Neither Bill nor Jo could know that, elsewhere in London, Chris Davies was, at that very moment, talking to a friend who had a friend who knew someone who had contacts in the vehicle licensing department. 'It's a white Transit van,' he said down the phone. 'Belongs to a bloke I want checking out.' Then he proceeded to read out the licence number of the van that was beginning to cause Andreotti sleepless nights.

Ten

Katherine was facing her difficult issue head on. She was sitting in a hotel bar with Eric Short, sipping champagne and wondering, for the umpteenth time, what on earth she was doing. For reasons Short couldn't know, this meeting was vital to her. Flirting with him, however, was not. It had just become natural. Opposite her, Short smiled and waited for her reaction to the statement he had just made; a request to the waiter for another glass of champagne 'for my wife'.

Her only reaction was a cryptic smile.

'Do you mind?' he said at length.

'No.' Katherine smiled again. 'I don't mind games.'

This time it was Short who smiled.

'Tell me,' said Katherine as the waiter approached with her second glass, 'about your trip to Italy. Bring any dirty postcards back?'

Short laughed. 'They only sell postcards of popes and footballers over there.'

'A girl I was at school with brought back a whole collection of porn postcards from there once,' lied Katherine. 'She smuggled them in under her T-shirt.'

'Naughty nights in the dorm?'

Katherine laughed. 'It was quite funny really. Our first introduction to pornography.'

'Enjoy it?'

'Mmm ... did rather, yes.' Over the rim of her glass, Katherine studied her companion's face. There was not a flicker of alarm – nor any indication that they had touched on a subject of more than passing interest to him. 'It's not just men who enjoy looking,' she added.

'Really?' Short grinned even more broadly. Yet it was a playful, teasing grin rather than an indication of excitement. Then he leaned back in his chair. 'What'll we do after this? Eat something? Go somewhere else?'

Katherine made a face. 'You're going to hate me.'

He stared at her. In an attempt to ease the blow, she found herself leaning forward, curling into a kittenish posture and reaching out to stroke him on the knee. 'My mother,' she added with a grimace, 'has come to see the new flat.'

'Katherine...!'

'I'm sorry. I honestly didn't know. She was sitting outside when I got there this evening.'

'Really?' This time the word came out as sarcastic, barbed – and disbelieving. Again he stared at her for a long, uncomfortable moment. 'This isn't a wind-up, is it?'

'What do you mean?'

He shrugged. 'Dunno. The way we first ... er ... bumped into each other. A strong "come on" – but not a lot else.'

She could feel her heart beating faster. Was he suspicious – or just angry? She retreated from him, straightened her back and looked at him through eyes that were suddenly cold. 'I see,' she snapped. 'You just wanted a quick ...'

The ploy worked. Short looked horrified. 'That's not what I said. Not what I meant at all. It's just that ...'

'Look.' Katherine was suddenly contrite. 'Why don't we meet early evening tomorrow and ...'

Short shook his head. 'I told you. I have that meeting.'

Katherine hadn't forgotten. Tomorrow was Friday.

The only reason she was here today was to make absolutely sure the meeting was taking place. 'Eric,' she began, then stopped herself. This was the first time she had used his name. Flustered, she looked away. 'I don't want you to think I'm playing games.' Then, remembering their conversation of only moments ago, she turned back to him and grinned. 'I mean, I will when you want me to but ... Look, let's meet early tomorrow, you have your meeting and then we'll go wherever you want.'

Short looked her straight in the eye. 'I think you know where that is, Katherine.'

Katherine did know.

'But I can't meet you earlier,' he added. 'I would like to stay with you later.'

Katherine smiled and leaned towards him again. 'Friday night,' she whispered. 'We'll spend it together. I promise.' As she spoke, she felt a stab of sorrow. Then another emotion overcame her. It was fear. Tomorrow night she was going to betray Eric Short. She was going to knock him and his abhorrent importation racket. But, as she looked into his eyes, she realized that if she didn't get it right then Eric Short would start playing new games with her. Dangerous games.

Everything was now in place. The pieces of the jigsaw surrounding Eric Short had come together – mainly due to the efforts of Arnie. As per Bill's instructions, Barry was also supposed to be working on the Short case, but he was firing on only one cylinder. Earlier in the week he had told everyone why, had informed them about the end of his and Diane's relationship. Nobody was shocked, but they were all sorry – and slightly wary of mentioning Diane's name in the City and South office. Life was going to be awkward where co-operation with Heathrow was concerned.

Not as awkward as it was about to become for Eric Short and his colleagues. Two days before Katherine's Thursday rendezvous with Short, Arnie had identified the mystery woman in the surveillance photographs; the woman who always attended the Friday meetings.

'We now know how and why,' he had told Bill, 'she is connected to Eric Short.' Bill had smiled. If Katherine had been the one imparting the news, she would have said '*I* now know.' 'Her name is Pamela Harrison,' continued Arnie, 'and not only does she work at Goldwing Couriers, but she's on the board. And her husband Brian Harrison is on the board of Short's company ... Short's ailing company. He needs money as badly as Short does.'

'So we have a motive for their involvement.'

'Yes.'

'Let's just hope they'll be there tomorrow.'

The authorities in Sweden had also been busy. On intelligence provided by Katherine, they knew that another smuggling operation was due. And from information provided by the taciturn and now jailed Swedish seaman, they knew how to intercept the courier at their end. That they duly did – and put an undercover policeman in his place.

The undercover man followed the arrested courier's instructions to the letter. He took the ferry from Malmo to Ipswich, a train from there to Stratford East and then the tube to Eric Short's building. The journey from Ipswich to London took place on the Friday.

The only possible hitch, as far as City and South were concerned, could occur if someone from Short's end of the operation arranged a secret rendezvous and a transfer of the package *en route*. But that had never happened before: there was no reason for it to happen this time.

In the event, the only transfer that took place on Friday happened on the tube from Stratford East; and that was a swift, deft – and unobserved – exchange between Katherine and the undercover policeman. They had never met each other, and nor did they meet this time. Having identified each other from the photographs they had studied, they merely brushed against each other in the crowded carriage. Katherine left the tube at the next stop, carrying a package containing Swedish snuff movies.

The subsequent manoeuvre was the most tricky. Katherine left the tube station and ran hell-for-leather to a nearby parked Transit van. Inside, Arnie was waiting with two video recorders and several tapes. Working so quickly they barely had time to exchange a word, they positively – and with horror – identified the videos as pornography of the most explicit and perverted kind. As Katherine had said when Arnie had questioned the necessity of examining the tapes, 'We'd look bloody silly if we tried to arrest someone for importing *The Sound of Music*.'

Next they dummied-up an identical package with blank tapes and a bleeper that would go off when the package was opened. Then Katherine sped off again, but to a different tube station. She ran down the escalator and slowed down as she turned into the westbound tunnel. As casually as she could, she strolled along the platform and, with a sigh of relief, saw the undercover man sitting waiting for the next train. When it arrived a minute later both he and Katherine got on – and a minute later they repeated their earlier manoeuvre. The Swede then continued his journey to Short's building, carrying a package identical to the one with which he had left Sweden.

Barry was *in situ* outside Short's building long before the second exchange was made. He had established that Pamela Harrison and Alex Britain were already inside; and he had already relayed that information to Arnie, now parked nearby in the Transit van. A few minutes before the courier arrived, Katherine herself drove past and parked nearby. Everyone was ready; alert and on standby.

It was Katherine who saw him first. 'Tango 1 approaching building,' she whispered into her mobile. Arnie acted with alacrity. He jumped out of his van and followed the courier right into Short's building. Both men went up to the receptionist. She offered a bland smile to the courier, looked at the package he gave her, nodded her thanks and then deposited it in a tray marked 'E.S. Leisure'. Then, as the courier departed, she raised an eyebrow at Arnie. He made a show of examining the much smaller package that he had just extracted from his pocket. 'Er ... Clarion Printers. Do you ...?

Wordlessly, the receptionist pointed to her left. Arnie nodded, turned the corner, waited a few moments and then retraced his steps. All had gone according to plan. The package was definitely destined for Short.

As soon as he was outside the building he pulled his phone out of his pocket. 'Tango 1 delivered.' Then he went back to the van. All that was left to do was wait for Eric Short. If he arrived when expected, they would have to wait an hour.

*

Katherine wasn't very good at waiting. First she twiddled her thumbs. She ate a stale sandwich that she found in her glove compartment. And then she started to fret. A minute later she was on the phone to Arnie. 'Look, I'm going to try to get Short on the phone and get him to agree to see me earlier than arranged.'

'Why?' This was the last thing Arnie had expected. Everything had been planned to the last detail and timed to the last second. 'We all go in together...'

'Yes, but we can't afford to mistime it.' Her voice betrayed her increasing agitation. 'I need to be inside earlier. If not, we run the risk of them destroying what we're after.'

Arnie sighed down the phone. This really wasn't on – and she knew it. 'Katherine...' he began. But she had switched off her phone. 'Stupid bitch,' said Arnie under his breath. He had recently begun to warm to Katherine: he had begun to doubt her steely exterior, to suspect that it was just a protective cloak. Now he was beginning to doubt her brain. Unsure of where she had gone and unsure of what to do, he looked at his watch. Three quarters of an hour before Short was due to arrive; fifteen minutes before Bill was due to join them for the knock. With any luck, he would still be in the office.

He was – and he was furious when Arnie explained what Katherine was up to. 'She is not,' he said furiously, 'to try to gain access to Short's office before we're all ready to go in. You should have told her that.'

'Bill... she's my senior officer.'

'I don't care.'

'She does.'

Bill swore, loudly and inelegantly. Then he asked Arnie if the reinforcements had arrived.

'Yes. Barry just radioed through to say that the heavies are making their way up to the roof.'

'Good. At least something's going right.'

'So... er, what do we do now?'

'Wait.' Bill was still livid. 'I'll be there in five.'

Ten minutes later Bill drove into the surveillance area and parked his car round the corner from the office. His rage with Katherine had increased during the short journey from City and South. What the hell was the woman up to, he wondered? They had organized this knock with military precision. Nobody was to enter the premises until the package was opened and the bleeper went off. Barry and the heavies – in fact two other customs officers not much bigger than Andreotti – would use the roof entrance; Arnie would come in through the back entrance and Bill and Katherine would charge in through the front door. But now Katherine had developed some damn silly notion designed, he didn't doubt, to bring greater glory to herself. But where the hell was she?

She was in a phone box two blocks away and she was, as Bill fumed, dialling Eric Short's office number. Short, slightly out of breath, answered on the fourth ring.

'Darling!' Then he cocked his ear, frowning, as he listened to her request to come to his office. 'No. No, sweetheart, you can't. You *know* I've got this meeting...'

'*Please*.' Katherine hoped she wasn't overdoing the coquettish plea. 'I'll be very good. Very quiet.'

'It's a boring meeting. Look, I'll...'

'But I've been on my feet all day,' she whined. 'And in the West End all afternoon. I don't want to hang about in some wine bar all on my own and...'

'Oh all right.' Short couldn't help smiling. She sounded so pathetic. So eager to see him. But there was no way he was going to let her hang around in his office while he was having his meeting. 'Come here and I'll give you the key to my flat. You can wait for me there.'

'OK.' Katherine nearly fainted with relief. 'Er ... where ...?'

Short gave her the address. The address that had been engraved on her mind for weeks. She exclaimed with delight about how close it was, thanked him profusely, and told him she would be there in ten minutes.

Eight minutes after that she ran straight into Bill Adams outside Short's building. 'Where the hell,' he seethed, 'have you been?' Katherine didn't answer. Instead she skipped nimbly past him and rang the outside intercom of E.S. Leisure. 'What the blazes,' he whispered furiously, 'do you think you're up to? Get away from here!'

'Can't.' Katherine turned to face him. 'He's expecting me.'

Bill took a deep breath. 'He doesn't know it was you who pressed the bell. Now ...'

But it was too late. Eric Short's voice, clearly audible to both of them, came crackling through the intercom. 'Katherine?'

Katherine shot a defiant and, he thought, triumphant look at Bill. Then she leaned towards the intercom and identified herself. A moment later she was inside the building.

Bill had never been so angry in his life. Speechless with rage, he stared after her, at the door that had swung shut in his face. Then he turned on his heel and walked towards Arnie's van. Arnie, who had witnessed the scene, wished fervently that Bill was walking towards someone else.

'Bloody woman!' Bill wrenched open the passenger door and glared at Arnie. 'Gimme your radio!' He snatched the machine from the wide-eyed Arnie and punched a digit on the side. 'Barry!' he barked. 'Bravo 2 has just entered the premises.'

'What?' From his position on the roof of the adjacent building, Barry was unable to see what was happening outside the front door. He had anyway had his field glasses trained on Short's office. 'Why on earth's she done that? Any knowledge?'

'Negative! But she'd better have a bloody good reason.' Bill flicked the radio off and looked back at the building. Then he turned to Arnie. 'Better than just wanting to be the arresting officer. Jesus! If this goes wrong...' He shook his head and climbed into the van. 'You can just hear Short's QC now, can't you? "A Swedish customs officer brought the tape in, a female UK customs officer encouraged Short to view it and before he could see it he was arrested".' He shook his head in disbelief. 'The stupid idiot's providing him with a defence.'

But at that point the stupid idiot, ensconced in Short's office, was playing the weeping woman act. 'It was horrible coming along the street just now,' she said with a sniff. 'There was this ... this awful man, beery breath. He tried to grab me, stop me coming in here. I hope,' she finished with a pathetic look at Short, 'he's not still down there. Waiting.'

But Short had only half an ear on Katherine's ramblings. Her presence in his office was making him feel distinctly uncomfortable, especially as she had, on arrival, made her way towards the inner office; the office where the meeting was taking place. He had, gently but firmly, steered her away from it. He looked at Katherine and shook his head in reassurance. 'No, just some passing drunk. Look, here's the key to my flat. I'll call you a cab.'

'Couldn't I just . . . ?'

But her plea was interrupted by the sharp sound of the door buzzer. Short leaped towards it. 'Yes?'

Katherine couldn't hear the response, didn't hear the name of the visitor. But if today's meeting was anything like the previous ones she and Arnie had surveilled, she knew it would be Brian Harrison, Pamela's husband.

Short pressed the buzzer and let the visitor in. Then he looked at his watch. If they started without any further delay then he and Katherine . . . he looked over to her and smiled. 'OK. Why don't you sit in the office upstairs. I'll be about half an hour. Come on, I'll show you.'

On ground level, Bill was once again establishing radio contact with Barry. 'IC1 Male just entered premises. Nothing further. Bravo 6, have you eyeball on premises?'

Barry did indeed have the office in his sights. 'Yes,' he said with the beginnings of a smile. 'Tango 1 and Bravo 2. Top floor room at rear.'

'Oh God. I don't think I want to hear this . . .'

'He's settling her into the top floor office,' said Barry with a chuckle. 'Ah. Tango 1 giving her a kiss.'

Bill's response was a weary sigh, accompanied by an old-fashioned look at Arnie. 'Bravo 6,' he said after a moment. 'Get into position. Stay on Channel 2. Confirm when in position.'

'Tango 1 just kissed her again.'

'Oh get on with it!' Irritated, Bill clicked off the radio. Still highly amused by the fruits of his voyeurism, Barry turned to the other officers on the roof. It was time to make their way, via the fire escape, to the roof of Short's building. Time to get into position for the knock. Before he left the roof, he took one last look through the field glasses. Katherine was now alone in the top room. For a few moments she sat still, her posture indicating that she was listening for something or someone. Then she stood up and crept towards the stairwell leading down to Short's office and to the inner sanctum where the meeting was taking place.

She stopped at the top of the stairs and took her radio out of her pocket. When the package was opened in the office below, only Bill, who had the receiver, would hear the bleep. But all his colleagues would hear his immediate and urgent reaction as he spoke to them through his radio: the words 'That's it! It's knock, knock, knock!' And Katherine was closer to the scene of the action than any of them; she would be able to go in first.

Bill's instructions came through after three minutes. Everyone reacted like lightning. Barry and the heavies smashed their way through the fire door with weighty crowbars, and Bill and Arnie came pelting through the front door and up five flights of stairs to E.S. Leisure. But it was Katherine who was in the outer office when Short emerged from the other room, puzzled and alarmed by the sudden commotion. He looked blankly at her for a moment. 'Katherine! What...?'

Katherine pulled out her badge. 'Customs and Excise. Eric Short, I'm arresting you for...'

'No!' It was almost a scream. In a split second, Eric Short saw his world crumbling around him. He felt horror; he saw betrayal – yet he reacted like lightning. He rushed back towards the inner office. 'Pam!' he yelled. 'Customs.'

Pamela Harrison, too, reacted with astonishing speed. She slammed the door shut, locked it and, together with Brian and Alex, began to eject the tapes she had just loaded into the bank of video recorders; the fifty or so tapes onto which they had planned to copy the snuff movie.

Propelled by rage and disbelief, Short launched himself at Katherine, pushed her through the door leading to the hallway and tried to slam it shut behind her. His face was a mask of pure hatred.

But Barry and his team had arrived. Short was no match for them as they pushed from Katherine's side of the door, throwing her assailant backwards and onto the floor. Fighting for breath, Katherine turned to Barry and then pointed to the locked door. 'In there!' she gasped.

Barry ran forward, took a 'smart' key from his pocket and inserted it in the lock. A second later the door swung open, revealing the white faces of Pamela, Alex and Brian. Their arms were full of ejected tapes. 'Customs and Excise!' yelled Barry. 'Just keep still. Nobody do anything.'

Nobody did. The panic had been a reflex, instinctive reaction. Now, with the whole office full of customs officers, everyone was frozen into inertia. Only Katherine, smiling viciously, stepped forward. She went to one of the video recorders and ejected a tape. Then she held it between two of her long, elegant fingers and turned back to Short. 'Eric Short, I'm arresting you on suspicion of importing obscene material.'

Bill Adams, who had arrived just moments after

Barry, recognized the expression on Short's face as he stared at Katherine. Bill had seen that look once before – on the face of a once-sane man who had been driven to murder by a woman who had betrayed him.

Eleven

Two days previously Jo had proved yet again that her time spent on the much-derided computer course had not been wasted. Casting her mind back to her conversation with Bill about George Webster and Tommy Maddern, she concluded that, for the first time since she had started working for him, Bill's judgement was clouded by his ambition. He was, she felt, too intent on getting results and not concerned enough about the safety of his staff – and one member of that staff in particular.

Although Jo found Andreotti irritating and was constantly infuriated by his blatant sexism and his peculiar fascination with his hair, she was, deep down, genuinely fond of him. That she referred to him as a 'little creep' and teased him relentlessly was more an outlet for her exasperation than an indication of her real feelings. And, as far as this particular case was concerned, her feelings were for Andreotti's safety. She was concerned that, through no fault of his own, he was sailing far too close to the wind: the combination of his HM Customs registered van and his constant association with the bootleggers was too dangerous. Particularly because, as of yesterday, he had been asked by Eddie Davies to stand by to accompany them on another run. Sooner or later he would be rumbled. Unless Jo did something about it.

By sheer coincidence, she decided to do that something just hours before Chris Davies's contact came up with the information Chris had requested on Andreotti's vehicle. Tapping away at her keyboard, she logged into the vehicle licensing centre's database and, after trawling through various files, found what she wanted: the registration of Andreotti's vehicle. Then she did something that, prior to her computer course, she would have required both help and permission to achieve. She now had the knowledge to dispense with any help – but she still required permission. What she was doing was strictly illegal. Too bad, she thought, consoling herself with the thought that at least it wasn't irreversible. When the case was finished, she would replace what she was about to delete from the database: the registration of Andreotti's vehicle.

Five minutes after she had sat down at her computer, her task was completed. The white Transit van no longer existed. Nobody would be able to find it nor, more importantly, the fact that it was being driven by Andreotti and registered as belonging to Her Majesty's Customs.

Later, on the other side of London, Chris Davies greeted the news about Andreotti's vehicle with a snort of disbelief. 'Whaddya mean it doesn't exist?' he shouted down the phone.

His contact on the other end, who had spent hours trying to find some trace of the van, was by now thoroughly exasperated. 'I mean it doesn't bloody exist, that's all! There's no records – anywhere – of the geezer's van.'

'But . . .'

'You said he was a dodgy bastard. Now you know. He is.'

Chris put the phone down and turned to the man next to him in the small, cramped sitting-room of his flat. 'The little blighter's bent, I reckon,' he said. 'Looks like he stole his van and put a moody registration on it. And to think the bastard was worried that *we* were up to something. Of all the . . .'

The other man grinned. 'Aw, can it, will yer, Chris? Can't blame him for having more than one . . . one pan in the fire.'

'Iron.'

'S'what I said.' The other man shrugged. Normally he took offence at being corrected. But today he was in too good a mood to object. This afternoon Mikolas was flying over to look at George's house and he, Tommy, had been put in charge of showing him round. Suddenly being George's minion didn't seem so bad after all. Not with that big fat iron in the fire; the one that eclipsed the bootlegging operation and would net him, George had said, a hundred thousand big ones.

Tommy, however, was counting his chickens – hens, he called them – before they hatched. After ensuring Andreotti's cover couldn't be blown, Jo Chadwick occupied herself with the business of confirming whether or not Tommy was the mystery occupant of Jack Foyle's flat in Deptford. A few hours of surveillance was all it took to establish that he was indeed living there, but under the alias of Tommy Bennett. When she told Bill, he acceded to the request that she had now made more than once: that they knock the operation on the next run to France.

On the Monday after the episode at Eric Short's office, Jo and Andreotti met in a pub at lunchtime. Both had been out of the office in the morning – and neither was keen to return. They knew all about what had happened at E.S. Leisure, about Katherine's attempt to steal the glory and about Bill's fury. They rarely agreed on anything, but this time they concurred that Katherine Roberts was not only stuck up, but that she was a 'stupid cow' to boot.

'So,' said Jo once they had dealt with their colleague. 'It's all systems go for the bootlegging operation.'

'Yeah, but Chris Davies hasn't told me when it'll be yet.'

Jo shrugged. 'Doesn't matter – we're all set up.'

But Andreotti wasn't so sure, 'Look, Jo. That van.' He leaned forward, his brow furrowed with worry. 'Are you sure there's no trace of it? I mean, you can't just wipe it off every computer in the land.'

She looked smug. 'I can and I have. I promise you, however suspicious these guys get, they'll never be able to find anything to link that van to customs. It gave me a great deal of pleasure,' she added with a broad grin, 'to obliterate you and your little van.'

Andreotti made a clicking noise with his tongue and looked at Jo in mock sorrow. 'And to think,' he said with a shake of his head, 'I was just about to shock the living daylights out of you.'

'Oh?'

'Yeah. I was about to thank you.'

Up the road at City and South, there was not a lot of thanking taking place. Bill and Katherine were standing in the former's office, facing each other with undisguised antagonism. Two pink spots had appeared on Katherine's cheeks. Bill had just torn a strip off her for 'breaking the rules'.

'I broke no rules,' she snapped. 'I was conducting a surveillance operation.'

'So you keep telling us.' Bill cast his mind back to the interview with Short that had taken place immediately after they had knocked his premises. 'Short, as I recall, seems to think otherwise. He says you acted as an *agent provocateur*.'

She looked pained. That interview had been the worst of her life – but it and the scene in Short's office had at least cleared up one thing. Having seen Short in operation, having heard him yelling 'Pam! Customs!' had at last knocked some sense into her regarding her feelings for him. They were no longer ambivalent. And the look in his eyes as she had arrested him had sent a chill down her spine.

'He's threatening to say,' said Katherine, forcing her mind back to Bill's accusation, 'that I slept with him. I *didn't*.'

Bill believed her, but that didn't alter the fact of her mishandling of the knock. 'I asked you ... I *told* you to walk away before the arrest. You should not have gone into that building.'

'I was trying to make sure the team could get in fast and, hopefully, get myself into the room when the films were being copied. I was the senior officer.'

Doesn't she ever learn, thought Bill? We don't pull rank around here. Matching her *froideur*, he fixed her with his cold blue eyes. 'Then you should have behaved like one. All you were interested in was the arrest. Arnie didn't go in like a ...'

'Arnie wouldn't have got through the door! It was me Short wanted to see.'

'I'd play down that side of things if I were you.'

'But nothing happened.' Uncharacteristically, Katherine was beginning to show signs of real distress. She looked up at Bill with pleading eyes. 'What do you think I am?'

Bill sighed and shook his head. 'Look, I believe you – but I'm not Eric Short's barrister. He'll take you apart in court. Encouraging his client, suggestion of entrapment – a possibility of a sexual relationship. That,' he said ticking each category off on his fingers, 'is the ammunition you've given his defence. And none of that need have happened if you had stepped back and let other people make the arrest. Now you'll have to appear in court and talk chapter and verse about your "relationship" with Short. "Did she sleep with him or didn't she?" Christ, Katherine, if it's the attention you were after, you've certainly got it now.'

Katherine didn't reply. Weary and depressed after spending the whole weekend replaying the entire scenario in her mind, she no longer had the energy to defend herself. And she knew that Bill was right on two counts. She had been guilty of attention-seeking. But worse, far worse as far as she was concerned, she had made a mess of the whole Short business. His barrister *would* tear her apart in court; and she would have to relive both the relationship with Short and the awful interview after the knock. Seeing the hatred blazing out of his eyes as she read out the accusations against him had been a deeply unsettling experience. And his final words had horrified her. 'If I have any statement to make,' he had spat, 'it will include all those little things you'd like me to do to you.' And Katherine had no doubt he would make that statement in court.

After Katherine's departure, Bill forced his mind onto other things. Dwelling on the Short case depressed him: he suspected that the denouement would be another long drawn-out court case with, as was becoming increasingly common, a first-class barrister picking holes in every scrap of evidence that City and South had gathered. And there were a great many holes in the Short case.

Bill was heartily glad that he had other things to think about. First there was Tommy Maddern. Armed with Jo's information about his pseudonym, he had requested an all-ports alert for a certain Mr Tommy Bennett. If he ever left the country, Bill would know. And it was Bill's fervent hope that Tommy would leave the country for only one reason – to team up with George Webster.

But Maddern's other little interest in life worried Bill: the bootlegging operation. Although Andreotti had informed him that Tommy appeared to be a peripheral member of the Davies mob and was not always around, there was a distinct possibility that he would be present when City and South knocked the operation. If that proved to be the case, the trail to George Webster would go cold. So obsessed was Bill that he had quite forgotten that they weren't even supposed to be investigating Webster; that the files on him had been officially closed two years previously.

Three hours later Andreotti walked into Bill's office and confirmed his fears about losing the Webster link.

'It's on,' he said with a grin.

Bill looked up from his paperwork. 'What's on?'

'The next run to France. Two days' time.'

'Ah.' Bill leaned back in his chair. 'And we're still all set for knocking it, yes?' He hoped he sounded enthusiastic rather than disappointed.

'Too bloody right. I'm dead fed up with all this, Bill. And,' he added with a frown, 'I damn nearly got rumbled this afternoon. If it hadn't been for Jo, God knows what would have happened.'

'Jo?'

'Yeah. They asked about the van. She'd wiped it off the computer in the nick of time.'

Bill looked at Andreotti in concern. 'Are you telling me that the Davies mob investigated the van? How the hell could they have access to that sort of information?'

Andreotti shrugged. 'Dunno. Bent copper? Someone at the licensing centre taking backhanders?'

Bill was silent for a moment. Suddenly he was feeling guilty, irresponsible in his handling of his staff. He recalled his earlier conversation with Andreotti about never exposing anyone to risk. For a horrible, fleeting moment he wondered if he was losing it, if his obsession with Webster was clouding his judgement. His brow creased with worry, he looked at Andreotti. It took him a few seconds to realize that Andreotti was looking immensely pleased with himself. 'What on earth did you say to them,' he asked, 'about the van not existing? What did they say?'

Andreotti thought back to the conversation he had had with Chris Davies after he had left Jo and gone, as usual, to the Peckham pub. 'They were bloody suspicious. Caught me on the hop as well. I mean, there was only an outside chance that they would investigate me. Never thought it would actually happen.' Then he grinned. 'Told them it was two half vans welded together. Both nicked, and that the licence plate was bollocks.'

'What did they say to that?'

'Looked impressed and asked me where I'd had it done.'

Bill laughed. Then he looked serious again. 'But if they're still suspicious of you . . .'

'Nah. Reckon they're satisfied. Tommy Maddern certainly is.'

'Oh? He was there?'

'Yeah. Swaggering about, being pleased with himself.'

Bill could well imagine. Then, thinking of City and South's previous encounters with Tommy, he frowned again. 'So you're absolutely sure Maddern doesn't recognize you?'

'Absolutely. The only time we ever came near each other two years ago was in the dark. And I was, if you remember, in the back of a car.'

'Mmm. Is Maddern going on this next run, then?' Bill hoped his face didn't show that he hoped the answer would be 'no.'

'Yes.' Andreotti knew exactly what Bill was thinking. 'So we'll get him at last. But we won't get George Webster.'

Two days later Andreotti drove to Calais. It was, he hoped, the last time he would ever have to drive the wretched van that had caused him so much angst. And if everything went according to plan, tonight would also mark the end of his relationship with Eddie Davies and his cronies. Of that he was also glad; the strain of constantly lying about everything from his name to his background was beginning to tell. His liver was also suffering: he felt as if he had spent half his life downing pints in the Peckham pub. All in all, he badly needed a break.

Yet he was in a cheerful mood. The knowledge that the knock would happen when they got back to London kept his spirits up: and knowing that Bill, Jo, Barry and several back-up officers were already in place was an antidote to the feelings of vulnerability that, increasingly, had been gnawing at him.

The plan was to knock the vans as they deposited their loads at the London destination. Andreotti, still on a 'need to know' basis, hadn't been told where that was; he had been told only to go to France as part of a convoy and to follow Chris Davies's instructions to the letter. He was also following someone else's instructions: Bill's. Equipped with his mobile phone, he was to inform the team of every development during the evening and to relay the information to Bill at City and South; to Jo who was in a surveillance car at Dover, and to Barry in Peckham. With Barry watching Eddie Davies and the cronies who would meet the convoy and help unload the vans, it meant the City and South team would have a double-pronged attack on the bootleggers.

Everything went according to plan in Calais. The convoy went straight from the ferry to one of the enormous 'booze warehouses' on the outskirts of the town and bought more lager than Andreotti had ever seen in his life. Each van was loaded to the gunnels with crates of the alcohol and then they drove straight back to the ferry terminal for the return journey.

It was two hours later, when the vehicles started pouring off the ferry at Dover, that things started to go wrong. The van in front of Andreotti's suddenly ground to a halt. Chris Davies, leading the convoy in the van in front, noticed the stoppage through his wing mirror. 'Bugger it!' he swore under his breath. This was all they needed: a breakdown slap bang in the middle of Dover customs. And the last thing he wanted was for one of the customs officers to come over to help. Not even the smooth-talking Chris would be able to convince the authorities that the thousands of pounds worth of lager packed into the five vans was for 'personal consumption' and therefore exempt from duty. He waited for a moment to see if the van would start again. It didn't. Wrenching the steering wheel of his own van, he moved the vehicle out of the way and, with his ever-present cigarette dangling from his lips, leaped out to see what the problem was. At the same time he yelled to Andreotti and the others to help. Chas, the driver of the crippled van, was desperately trying to fire the engine into life. He looked up as Chris approached. "'S done this before, mate. Sorry. We're gonna have to clutch-start it.'

'Jesus! Now you tell me. Fine fucking time for this to happen.' Chris leered at the hapless Chas. 'Go on then, shove it into second and we'll push. C'mon,' he added to Andreotti and the other men who had now gathered round. 'We'll soon get the bastard moving again.' But as he walked round to the back of the van, he saw that Andreotti's vehicle was too close to give them enough leeway to push. 'Stupid fucker,' he fumed, blaming Andreotti for something that was patently not his fault. He looked behind him. Andreotti was still at the front of the other van, talking to Chas. Chris shrugged and, seeing that Andreotti's door was open and the key still in the ignition, jumped in. Then he swore again as ash fell from his cigarette onto his lap. Turning the key with one hand, he reached for the ashtray with the other and opened it. A crumpled piece of paper with a distinctive logo caught his eye just before he stubbed out his cigarette. Intrigued, he pulled it out of the ashtray and unfolded it. His heart raced and he swore again under his breath as he realized what it was: a Crown Licence, a tax disc bearing the insignia of Her Majesty's Customs and Excise. He had been right; the little bastard was a viper in their midst, a customs officer or a policeman or something.

As panic threatened to overtake him, two things happened at once: the van in front roared into life and the little bastard himself appeared, looking pleased with himself. The look vanished as he saw Chris in the cab of his van. 'What're you . . .'

'Was gonna reverse it, wasn't I?' replied Chris, quickly stuffing the paper back into the ashtray and shutting it.

'Oh. Well, no need. I got it started. If he keeps revving it, should stay alive.'

Chris descended from the cab. 'Yeah,' he said, avoiding Andreotti's eye. 'Right.' There was nothing, he realized, that they could do about this now: the place was awash with customs officers. Whatever the little bastard was up to, it looked like he was going to wait until they got to London to do it.

Andreotti, did Chris but know it, had been equally alarmed to see the other man in his van: an alarm that vanished as soon he patted the breast pocket of his leather jacket. Thank God, he thought, I remembered to take the phone out. The phone was his only method of keeping in touch with Bill and the team, and it would undoubtedly have aroused Chris's suspicions. Impoverished, unemployed odd-job men did not normally own one of the world's most sophisticated cellular phones.

Andreotti breathed a sigh of relief as the convoy moved off again. Then he grinned as he recalled Chris's panic about the customs officers at Dover. No doubt he had been terrified they would intervene and discover what they were up to. Little did he know that, on instructions from Bill, Dover had been warned that under no circumstances were they to stop the convoy.

His high spirits restored, Andreotti reached for his phone and called Jo. He dialled, keeping the phone in his lap: the last thing he wanted was for Chas in front or Jim behind to see, via their mirrors, what he was doing.

When Jo answered he had to shout down towards his lap. 'Jo. It's me. I can't risk picking the phone up in case they see me. We've just left Dover. Target destination is still unknown. I've been told just to follow. I'm keeping this line open.'

'Understood.' Then Jo chuckled over the line. 'This'll be the longest conversation we've ever had.'

'That'll be nice.'

Two vehicles in front, Chris Davies was also making a phone call. 'Dad!' he shouted over the roar of his engine. 'We've got a problem. That geezer with the van? I think he's old bill or customs or something. You'd better get somebody to meet us halfway and unload him. Send Tommy...'

For the next hour the Kent countryside buzzed with phone conversations. Had anyone been able to eavesdrop, they would have made little sense of what was being said. Bill's officers, in constant communication with each other, were keeping tabs on the convoy as it moved towards London and into the Dartford tunnel.

'Bravo 3. All Tango wheels cleared tunnel.'

'Back-up, are you in position?'

'Yes, yes.'

'Eyeball to you, Foxtrot 3.'

'Foxtrot 3 has eyeball. Two for cover. Speed forty and decreasing. Approaching roundabout. Foxtrot 4 in position.' Then, shortly after the convoy cleared the tunnel, one of the back-up officers called down the line with a new urgency in his voice. 'All vehicles hang back! Vehicle Gulf India Oscar 551 Sierra slowing. It's stopped. Stop, stop! Eyeball over-shooting.'

'Shit!' In his own car, now speeding through South London, Bill glared at the phone in his hand. What the hell was happening? Why had the vehicle in front of Andreotti's pulled over and stopped? A moment later he learned that the entire convoy had pulled over. But a minute after that the convoy was on the move again – minus Andreotti's vehicle. None of Bill's team, however, was close enough to see exactly what had happened.

Then Jo's voice, high-pitched with worry, came over the line.

'Our man's been burned! His phone line was open to me then he went off the air.'

'Shit!' Bill thought quickly. This was the last thing they needed. With three vehicles now following Eddie Davies and his cronies, recently departed from the pub and heading south, and another three following the convoy, there was little manpower to spare. 'Send Bravo...'

'Our man's vehicle on the move again! Proceeding towards river down Foxtrot Road.'

'Send Bravo 6!' yelled Bill. This was Jo's vehicle. 'Bravo 6, I have no spare back-up for you. Keep your channel open, we'll get back-up as it comes available. Acknowledge, Bravo 6.'

Jo acknowledged. Her lips set in a thin, worried line, she gunned her engine and sped after Andreotti's vehicle. Down to the river, she thought. Please God don't let anything awful happen to him...

The convoy, still closely monitored by Bill's team, headed into Deptford Industrial Park and towards the empty unit where Eddie Davies and his pals were already waiting. So, sitting silently in their darkened cars behind the next block of units, were Barry and the officers who had driven from Peckham. As the convoy neared its destination, the other vehicles converged, like birds coming home to roost, on the bleak industrial site.

Inside the empty unit, Eddie Davies paced up and

down, looking at his watch every five seconds. The business about the imposter had put him on edge. And Chris's last phone call hadn't allayed his fears. Chris could be a real moron sometimes. Imagine thinking they had time to send someone down from London to deal the with the bloke with the van! Eddie's own idea had been far better: to stop the convoy, transfer three of the heavies from the rear van to the little bastard's van and get him the hell away from the others. And, of course, to beat the living daylights out of him and then dispose of him. Permanently.

But what worried Eddie was Chris's information, imparted when he confirmed that the plan had worked, that they had found a mobile phone in the alien van. If the little bastard had been in touch with the old bill or ...

His thoughts were violently and noisily interrupted by the arrival of Chris's van. Galvanized into action, Eddie guided him to the back of the unit and then, after the other vehicles appeared, ran forward and pulled the front doors closed.

Chris jumped down from his van. 'I think we're OK,' he shouted over to his father. 'He's being dealt with and no one followed us here.'

'Well get a bloody move on anyway! I want us to be out of here as soon as possible.' Still nervous, Eddie gestured to the men who had arrived with him. 'C'mon. We'll unload the hooch into our vans and be away in two shakes.'

Her Majesty's Customs and Excise thought otherwise. One shattering, dramatic second later the front doors of the industrial unit splintered into a thousand pieces as a black Jeep, headlights blazing, smashed into the warehouse unit. Bill Adams was at the wheel.

'Shit a . . .' Chris turned, disbelieving, as the vehicle advanced towards him. 'Jesus . . .!'

Hot on its tail came the other vehicles, and, as they screeched to a halt, what seemed like an army descended from them. 'Cover the doors!' shouted Bill. 'Get 'em into a corner.' Then he swivelled round and locked eyes with Eddie Davies, standing, shocked into immobility, to his left. 'Davies!' he barked. 'Customs and Excise! I'm arresting you on suspicion of being concerned in the fraudulent evasion of duty.' Then he marched up to Davies with murder in his eyes. 'Now, where have you taken my officer?'

Bill's officer was in a derelict building site on the banks of the Thames. He had been driven there in the van that had ultimately caused his downfall: the van that he now feared would cause his death. Andreotti, lying on the ground, was fighting for his life.

It was a very one-sided fight. The three men who had driven him to the dark, abandoned site knew that no one could hear his screams as they kicked him repeatedly with their steel-capped boots. In between blows, they verbally vented their anger on their victim. 'Bastard!' snarled the tallest man. 'Plod, are you? Customs?' He kicked again: viciously, and in the kidneys. Then he laughed. 'We all know about your lot. Don't waste much on funerals, do they?'

The man who had driven Andreotti's van to the building site laughed as well. 'Might not even be a bleeding funeral. Your grave's over there, chum. In the water.'

'Yeah. Happen they won't find your body – or what's left of it.'

All three men laughed out loud. Then they set about their task with renewed vigour. Andreotti, curled up in the foetal position, desperately trying to avoid their blows, felt something in the pit of his stomach that had nothing to do with pain. It was raw, naked terror. This time, he knew, there would be no escape. He had started this case alone: he would end it, conclusively, the same way.

But Andreotti and his attackers had reckoned without another solo operator. Propelled by fury and horror at what she knew would happen to Andreotti, Jo had driven hell-for-leather down the deserted road to the site. The back-up customs vehicles and the police car sent by Bill were close behind her. But not close enough. Headlights blazing, she rounded the corner leading to the river and screeched to a halt. In a split second, she decided she wasn't going to wait for her back-up. She leaped out of her car. Appalled by the sight of a bleeding Andreotti lying on the ground, and by the fact that his assailants, after a brief moment of panic, were making a bee-line for her, she pounced with savage glee on a scaffolding pole at her feet and went into the fray.

It was fortunate for her that Davies's men had chosen to fight rather than run away. Otherwise, the four policemen right behind her would have had something to say about the way she swung the pole and, in a manner that would have appalled her hockey mistress at school, clubbed the nearest man in the midriff. With an agonized roar, he doubled up and fell to the ground. Seeing that the customs and police officers were tackling the other men, Jo then rushed over to Andreotti. He, too, was doubled up in agony. His face was covered in blood and his eyes clouded with pain. He did, however, manage a smile as she knelt at his side.

'Keep still!' she urged.

Andreotti moaned. 'Where the hell,' he gasped, 'd'you think I'm planning to go?'

Jo grinned with relief. Then she reached out and touched him gently on the head. 'They haven't ruined your hair. Hasn't moved an inch. What do you do – just cement and go?'

Andreotti's eyes flickered. He was beyond witty banter. 'It was that pool van,' he sighed. 'Some prat had left the Crown sticker in the ashtray.' Then he opened his eyes again and stared, pleading, at Jo, 'D'you think I could go to hospital, please?'

'Your wish,' replied Jo as she beckoned to the officers behind her, 'is my command.'

One of the back-up customs vehicles took Andreotti to hospital. The police cars departed with Eddie Davies's thugs in the back. And Jo, suddenly exhausted, trudged back to her own car. It was from there that she phoned Bill to tell him what had happened. He, supervising the rounding-up of the men at the Deptford warehouse, was greatly distressed to learn of Andreotti's savage beating. 'It could have been worse,' said Jo with an edge to her voice. 'He could have been killed.'

'I know. If you hadn't got there when you did, God knows what would have happened. That animal Maddern . . .'

'Maddern?'

'Yes. He was one of the ones beating him up, wasn't he?'

'No.' Maddern's face was imprinted on Jo's mind. He had most definitely not been there.

'Oh.' Baffled, Bill scratched his head. They hadn't arrested Maddern with the rest of the Davies mob. He wasn't one of the three who had attacked Andreotti. So much for him being on this evening's run to France. The man, thought Bill, had the luck of the devil. And, as soon as he learned that the Davies mob had been arrested, he would no doubt vanish into thin air again. So near, thought Bill with a sad shake of his head, yet so far. He left the warehouse with a heavy heart, swallowing the bitter pill that tonight had brought failure as well as success.

Twenty miles away, at Heathrow airport, a young check-in clerk handed a ticket to the man at her desk. 'Enjoy your flight, Mr Bennett,' she said with a smile. The smile was even more forced than usual. Mr Bennett, her computer told her, was a wanted man. As soon as she had entered the name Tommy Bennett, a small red light had started to flicker. For a moment she watched his broad back as he sauntered over to the departure gate. Then she reached for the telephone beside her.

Twelve

Things hadn't been going too well for Tommy Maddern, alias Bennett, since he had shown Mikolas round George Webster's Hampstead house. George, for some reason, seemed to have gone cold on him. And Mikolas, well . . . it wasn't Tommy's fault, was it?

Mikolas had suddenly demanded twenty thousand pounds in cash for what he described as 'extra backhanders' for export staff. George hadn't liked that at all, but had agreed to stumping up ten grand in advance and the balance when the cargo was at sea. Then Mikolas had discovered, through a lawyer, that the deal over the house in Hampstead was more complicated than George had made it appear. Tommy was unsure of the details, but Mikolas had told him there was something called a 'charge' placed on the property at the Land Registry Office. It meant, so Mikolas said, that there was money owed on the property and that the owner couldn't sell until that money had been paid. Tommy, however, didn't care. It was nothing to do with him.

But Tommy should have cared. If he had paid more attention to the argument that ensued between Mikolas and Webster, he would have gleaned some inkling of just how devious George was being. The money owed on the property was, by unlikely coincidence, exactly three quarters of a million pounds. Mikolas had demanded that George clear the debt or the deal was off.

'I can't,' had been George's succinct answer. 'I haven't got the money. I will have when our cargo is delivered and our profits start to roll in.' Then he had gone on to explain, in no uncertain terms, just what sort of position Mikolas was in. 'I had to advise the UK Land Registry. It's the law. So, if something were to happen to me, they wouldn't release the house to you until that money had been paid. The only way for you to get the house for nothing, my friend, is if I'm alive and well and in profit. Otherwise it'll cost you what it cost me.'

'Three quarters of a million.'

'Right. But if our deal goes through and I get the profits I'm expecting, the debt on the property will magically vanish and you'll get this place. Any other scenario ... we all get bugger all. Except,' he had added with a disingenuous smile, 'I keep the house.'

Mikolas had been livid. His initial admiration of George had given way to annoyance and not a little suspicion. If George didn't trust him, why should he trust George? 'To whom,' he had asked in his impeccable English, 'do you owe the money?'

George shrugged. 'A company called Apartmentos Marfin.'

'Who owns it?'

'Dunno.'

Tommy, listening to the conversation with half an ear, hadn't picked up on the reference to the Portuguese company. The name meant nothing to him. Good old George, was all he thought. Being cautious as hell.

Tommy's admiration vanished and was replaced by fear when, the following day, George unexpectedly turned on him with murder in his eyes. Since his arrival in London three days previously, George had not been idle. Aside from his machinations to wind Mikolas round his little finger, he had been doing a spot of background research into Tommy's activities in the bootlegging trade. His findings had appalled him.

'Why the hell,' he shouted at Tommy, 'didn't you tell me about the bloke you shot? Eh?'

'What . . .?' Tommy's surprise had been total, and terrified. How did George know about the little Indian? 'Who . . .' he stammered, 'who says I shot . . .?'

'Don't you lie to me again! I wouldn't have touched you with a barge pole if I'd known. I want you out of the country today.'

'I can't! I'm doing something with Eddie tonight . . .'

'Bootlegging.' George's distaste – and disdain – was palpable. 'You're working for me, Tommy. You got me into this deal; you can keep an eye on it for me.' He jabbed a finger in Tommy's face. 'You're going back to make sure what I've paid for gets loaded on that ship.'

'What! To bloody Latvia?'

'You'd prefer to stay here and get pulled for a shooting, would you?' Something in George's eyes told Tommy that, if he disobeyed, the police would miraculously be given a lead on the shooting of Arjun Malhotra. 'This,' continued George, 'is the last time I deal with you. The last time ever.'

Tommy's opinion of George changed yet again. He stared after the man, hating him. And then he prepared to fly to Latvia.

The information that one Tommy Bennett had checked in on a flight to Riga was swiftly relayed to Diane Ralston in her office at Heathrow. 'Why,' she asked Kevin Butcher, 'if he's a wanted man, haven't we been given instructions to pick him up?'

'Search me. Maybe someone thinks he's going to lead us to George Webster.'

'Oh goody,' said Diane, dripping sarcasm. 'As if we didn't have enough on our plates.' Then she looked up again. 'Anything else?'

Kevin looked at Diane. She had been trying, over the past few days, to pretend that nothing was wrong, to soldier on as if the collapse of a relationship that had, at one point, been a mere whisker from marriage, had not affected her in the slightest. Kevin knew better. The bags under her eyes, the recent lack of enthusiasm with which she had tackled the job she purportedly loved, pointed to an underlying and deep unhappiness. He wondered if the next piece of news would cheer her up. 'Er . . . Andrew Ryan, QC phoned.'

'What about?' snapped Diane.

'Um . . . meeting up for a drink or something.'

Diane put her head in her hands. 'Oh God, that's all I need.'

'Are you OK, Diane?'

'Of course I am. I'm fine.'

Kevin shook his head. 'You're always fine.'

'Fortunate, aren't I?'

Kevin shrugged and turned back to his own desk. Oh well, at least he'd tried.

As he sat down and contemplated the mountain of work in front of him, he was visited by a sudden and unexpected *déjà vu*. 'God . . . I've just thought. Ryan.' He looked over to Diane, wrinkling his brow as he fought to retrieve a memory. 'The girl near the carousel . . . she was in court . . .'

'Kevin, what on earth are you talking about? What girl?'

'Well, you know the suitcase that came in today from the Kingston flight? Unclaimed?'

Diane knew. After twenty minutes of going round and round the baggage carousel, it had been collected by her team and opened. Inside they found seven kilos of cocaine hidden amongst a fairly nondescript collection of clothes. There had been nothing, however, pointing to the identity of the owner. Under Diane's orders, it was put back on the carousel. Someone, she hoped, would come to claim it.

Wondering what he had done to deserve such a thrilling life, Kevin had spent the next hour watching the suitcase going round and round again. On several occasions, the carousel was swamped with luggage from more incoming flights and he nearly lost sight of it – but it still remained unclaimed. At one point, a young, concerned-looking female had appeared and, he had thought at the time, looked as if she was going to pick it up. But after a few moments she had disappeared, leaving Kevin to conclude that her quizzical looks at the case had been nothing more than wishful thinking on his part.

Now he wasn't so sure. The name Andrew Ryan had jogged something in his memory; an association that hadn't registered at the time. On the receiving end of Kevin's somewhat vacant look, Diane sighed and prompted him to continue. 'The suitcase, Kevin. What about it?'

'Well, there was a girl, white girl, she hung around. I saw her on the monitor. I thought I'd seen her before but I couldn't place her. Now I can.' He looked eagerly at Diane. 'She was in court when Ryan defended Nadine Charles. She could be part of that Rufus Teague thing that Barry worked on, y'know, the bastard who did Nadine in and then escaped.'

'Good God, yes! I was hoping we hadn't seen the last of him. I wonder,' she continued with a frown, 'if Barry knows anything about the girl . . .'

Diane reached for her telephone and then, as her

hand hovered over the instrument, looked sheepishly at Kevin. 'Um ... actually, would you mind calling him?'

Kevin shrugged. He wondered if Diane knew just how awkward her split with Barry was making relations between Heathrow and City and South. This wasn't the first time that he had had to tread lightly round the issue: the follow-up and subsequent knocking of the bear bile smuggling had seen them all treading on eggshells around Barry and Diane. Then, registering the uncustomary, pleading look on Diane's face, he phoned Barry. But Barry wasn't there: he was in a warehouse in Deptford. Kevin left a message.

Rufus Teague may have escaped the attentions of Her Majesty's Customs and Excise, but he hadn't forgotten about them. Furious about losing the cocaine that Nadine Charles had smuggled in (but not overly concerned about killing Nadine), he had spent the next few weeks setting up another smuggling operation. But that, too, had gone wrong. The bloody courier had got cold feet and scarpered at Heathrow, leaving seven kilos of cocaine going round and round the carousel. When the courier hadn't shown, Rufus had despatched his girlfriend to the airport to see if she could claim the case. She had nimbly bluffed her way through to the baggage reclaim area, but had decided against picking up the case because, she said, it had remained unclaimed for nearly two hours and she was frightened that someone might have noticed it.

'And who would that someone be?' Rufus had asked in an ominously casual voice.

'Dunno. Customs?'

Rufus had walloped her in the face. 'But you don't fucking know, do you? It's just an ordinary bleedin' suitcase. No reason for customs to open it, is there? You stupid cow!' he had yelled, landing another, even harder blow in her stomach. 'I'm not going to kiss goodbye to seven kilos of coke just like that. You'll have to go back for it.'

Rufus knew that the airport wouldn't leave the case on the carousel for ever: they would take it away and put it in an unclaimed baggage room to await its owner. But he – the owner – wasn't going anywhere near it. Oh no. Someone else would have to do that. Worried that he was in effect kissing goodbye to his cocaine, he phoned the airport and said that someone would arrive to collect it on Monday. A pity he would have to wait until then, but he had a very busy weekend ahead of him. Very busy indeed. He hadn't recovered from his last brush with customs and had spent a great deal of time putting plans in motion to teach them a lesson.

The customs officer of particular interest to Rufus was Barry Christie. He would never forget the sight of Barry, eyes blazing with fury, racing up the stairs of the block of flats where Nadine had met her gory end. Barry was the one who needed to be taught; who needed to realize that no one interfered in Rufus Teague's affairs without getting badly burned. So, many days before the second episode at Heathrow, Rufus despatched two of his heavies to do a little background research into Barry Christie. They came up with the interesting information that Barry had a sister. A very pretty sister.

Barry's sister was going to be dealt with at the weekend, on Saturday. It was particularly ironic that Saturday was also the day Barry informed Charmian that her friends the Malhotras could rest easy in their beds; that the bootlegging operation had been cracked the night before.

On Saturday night, Charmian had arranged to go out with Indra Malhotra and, at seven o'clock, was making her way from the flat that her brother now shared with her to Indra's house. It was a journey she had made many times before. The only part of it that caused her any concern in the dark was the little alley which led from the bus stop to Indra's street. Yet as she walked down it on Saturday, fear was the last thing on her mind; she was smiling and thinking how overjoyed Indra would be to hear about the end of the bootlegging racket.

The attack took place halfway down the alley and was so unexpected that Charmian didn't even offer any resistance. All she could remember about it afterwards were the words 'Say hello to your brother, bitch,' and the searing pain as the knife sliced into her throat.

Thirteen

Alan Jackson looked at Bill Adams over the rim of his half-moons and wondered, not for the first time, if the man was losing his touch. He had certainly lost Alan's respect and, if the rumours were true, that of several of his own staff.

From the other side of the table, Bill eyed Alan with a mixture of weariness and suspicion. He had spent a miserable weekend, castigating himself for what had happened to Andreotti. Even Libby, ever faithful and rarely critical, had not demurred when he had, during a walk in the park on Sunday, blamed himself for putting the life of one of his staff in jeopardy. Yet now, on a bleak Monday morning, Bill was on the defensive. He had not forgotten his last 'chat' with Alan and the unwelcome realization that his job was anything but secure. In an even weaker position now, he was nevertheless determined to fight his corner.

Alan Jackson scanned the piece of paper in front of him and, with a weary sigh, resumed the uneasy conversation. 'Three smashed ribs,' he said, waving the paper in Bill's face, 'and I've just received an overtime bill that could have been five man days shorter. George Andreotti was in the field far longer than he should have been, Bill.'

'Which are you most concerned about? The bill or the injuries?'

It was the wrong thing to say. Alan glared. 'It's what *you* were most concerned about that worries me. You could have knocked that mob two weeks earlier, and you know it.'

'No. I had no way of knowing when they'd make their next run. I needed to be sure I had sufficient evidence...'

'Bollocks. You hung on because you thought George Webster was the finance behind it. True?'

Bill opened his mouth to deny the accusation, then closed it again. It was true. He just couldn't bring himself to admit it. Alan's smile, as he registered Bill's expression, held little warmth. 'You still don't like being wrong, do you?' he said softly.

'I'm not wrong in the opinion that George Webster and Tommy Maddern are involved in some illegal activity.'

'But you weren't investigating "some illegal activity", Bill. You were supposed to be nicking a bootlegging firm.'

'And we did.' Adopting a challenging posture, Bill leaned forward in his chair. 'Look ... Tommy Maddern, using the name Bennett, was flagged taking a flight from Heathrow Airport to Malmo in Sweden. Swedish customs reported him taking a flight on to Riga in Latvia.'

Alan waved that aside with a shrug and a 'so what?' expression.

'Well,' continued Bill, 'it's hardly the sort of place Tommy Maddern would take his holidays.'

'OK – so why wasn't he arrested when he was seen? There's a ticket still out on him, isn't there? Bill, if you're letting active, arrestable villains wander about because you have some private agenda, I'd warn you to seriously reconsider...'

'I'll defend my actions if and when I have to.'

Alan twirled his pen in his hands for a moment and

then stared Bill straight in the eye. 'You might have to.'

But Bill was determined to press home his point. If he was going to be hanged, it might as well be for a sheep as for a lamb. 'Two days before Maddern left the country,' he said, 'George Webster flew in.'

'And?'

'Bit of a coincidence, isn't it?'

'I don't know – is it? Webster still here?'

Bill shook his head. 'No. He flew back to his home in Portugal. His retirement home.'

But Alan had heard enough. 'Flew in, flew out. Clearly guilty as hell. Forget it, Bill. We've enough that's current to worry about without fighting battles from the past. This "snuff" investigation,' he said, waving another sheet of paper at Bill. 'Eric Short. We're not going ahead with the prosecution.'

'What!

Alan shrugged again. 'Apparently the others you arrested are going to make statements that will clear him of any involvement.'

Bill couldn't believe what he was hearing. Another villain getting off scot free. 'But he was there when we knocked the place!'

'He wasn't actually in the room where the films were being copied.' Alan paused and then delivered another glancing blow to Bill's professional pride. 'You should have waited and nicked him when he was.'

Bill glared across the table. It took all his self-control not to start another, more serious argument. Instead, he knocked Alan Jackson sideways by asking him a favour.

'You're doing what?' Andreotti's start of surprise was such that he hit himself, most unwisely, in the ribs. 'Ow! Christ . . .'

'Sorry.'

Bill grinned and took a sip of his pint. 'Didn't know it'd have such a dramatic effect.' Then, his face creased with concern over Andreotti's evident pain, he asked how he was. 'Sore.' Yet Andreotti was grinning. 'And happy. More to the point, how are you?'

Bill looked away. His whole demeanour was answer enough. He was clearly extremely unhappy.

'Well,' continued Andreotti, thinking back to the remark that had so surprised him. 'Taking a break'll do you good.' Bill rarely took breaks – and never at this time of year. 'Taking the family?'

'No. Going on my own. Take stock. Look, I might as well tell you, Andreotti, they'll ... they'll be amalgamating our collection with Thames-side in a couple of months.'

'Oh.' Another surprise. And, judging by Bill's expression, an unwelcome one. 'What's that going to mean for us.'

Bill shrugged. 'Probably a new Surveyor. Super-boss, you know.'

'Will you be ... er ... you know?'

Bill smiled, touched by Andreotti's concern. Then he shook his head and looked, unseeing, across the bar. 'No. No, I doubt it'll be me.'

Bill's period of leave was effective as of that afternoon. He would, he explained to Andreotti as they left the pub, spend the next day and a half 'tying up a few loose ends' at home and would be contactable there. Otherwise, he was leaving the team to get on with it. 'Any problems,' he said with a grin, 'and Katherine'll deal with them.'

Andreotti didn't grin back. The thought of Katherine in charge was enough to give him a relapse.

Later that afternoon, Jo walked into the office and was stunned to see Katherine sitting in Bill's office, at his desk, looking for all the world as if she owned the place. Unaware of Bill's abrupt departure, Jo looked to her colleagues for explanation. Seeing her bafflement, Andreotti grinned and nodded in Katherine's direction. 'There's been a coup,' he explained. 'She shot Bill at eight o'clock this morning and she's holding us hostage.' Then he lowered his voice to a desperate, imploring whisper. 'Get help!'

'Oh very funny.' Jo stalked off towards her own desk. 'Bill off sick or something? Unlike him.'

Arnie, at his desk opposite Jo, replied. 'Gone on leave.'

'What? Just like that?'

'Just like that. But he's at home today and tomorrow in case we need him.'

'Oh.' Jo was extremely surprised. It was even more out of character for Bill to take sudden leave than to be ill. Life, she reflected, must really be getting to him. 'Where's he going, then?'

Again it was Arnie, looking wistful, who replied. 'Lake District.'

'Lovely.'

'Mmm. Coleridge took a lot of drugs, you know.'

Jo looked at Arnie as if he had gone mad. Then she looked at Andreotti and Barry for enlightenment. Equally confused, they returned her questioning look. Andreotti whispered the word 'barking'.

'No,' said Arnie, obviously still miles away. 'I was just thinking. Lake District. Wordsworth . . . Coleridge. Odd to think the revenue wasn't interested in drugs in those days.'

'Or in lager, probably,' retorted Jo as she sat down. Sometimes she wondered about Arnie.

Arnie looked at Jo. Sometimes he really wondered about her.

An uncustomary silence descended in the outer office as the four officers applied themselves to the paperwork that had built up over the days when they had all been busy either with Eric Short or with the bootlegging operation. Only Barry had difficulty concentrating on his work. He found it difficult to think of anything other than Charmian; his beautiful, innocent sister now lying in a hospital bed with a heavily-bandaged throat.

Charmian had told him, in the soft, hoarse whisper that was all she could manage, what her assailant had said. Then she had described him as best she could. At first it made no sense to Barry – until he remembered Rufus Teague. And then, when he had received Kevin's message over the weekend, he knew that Teague was behind the attack. It was just the sort of vicious, cowardly act a man like that would order one of his heavies to perform. Barry hadn't told Charmian about Teague. He told her that he had no idea who had attacked her, or why. She had reacted by turning her large, soulful eyes on him and pleading with him not to tell their mother. Barry had smiled. 'Not telling mother' was part of the *modus operandi* in the Christie family: it had taken Barry all his courage to tell his mother about the end of his relationship with Diane. She had, as he had known she would, taken the news extremely badly. The sound of wedding bells had been ringing in her ears for years. Diane, she had tearfully wailed, was like a daughter to her. That, Barry knew, wasn't strictly true. His mother found Diane rather intimidating; she found the combination of Diane's beauty, her confidence and her 'class' rather alarming. But she did genuinely like her, and was pleased that Diane and Charmian were such friends. 'Like sisters,' she told her friends. That *was* true: Diane and Charmian were great friends and, as Charmian lay in her hospital bed looking up at her brother and wondering if he really did know who had attacked her, she asked if he had told Diane about what had happened. Barry had. Old habits died hard and, in moments of crisis, it was still to Diane that he directed his thoughts. And anyway, this crisis was of real concern to Diane. He leaned closer to his sister and told her that she was on her way to visit as they spoke.

In the hospital, out of Charmian's earshot, Barry told Diane of his strong suspicions regarding Rufus Teague. 'If I get a sniff of where he is, I tell you, Diane, I'll kill the guy.'

Diane looked at her ex-lover, concern written all over her face. 'I know, I know. But just remember what they did to Nadine Charles.'

'Yeah. Brave, aren't they? Kill her, now they try to maim my sister.'

'Barry ... think. Look, don't do anything. When she's discharged, I'll look after her. She can stay at my ...' Then she faltered and looked away. 'My place,' she was about to say. How strange that sounded, and how different from 'our place'.

Barry smiled at her. 'At your place,' he said totally without malice, 'That's nice of you.' Then they parted, both thinking, with sadness, of the way things used to be.

Barry was still thinking of the way things used to be when the silence in the City and South office was shattered by Katherine, in a towering rage, coming thundering out of the inner office. 'God in heaven!' she shouted. 'He was there. He set the whole thing up. I mean ... *twice*!' she squeaked. 'We saw him receive them twice!' Seemingly unaware of her colleagues' astonishment she glared at each one of them in turn. 'Why wasn't I consulted about this?' she thundered.

'Er ... Katherine.' Jo offered an apologetic smile at the furious woman. 'We haven't a clue what you're talking about.'

A fax was waved furiously. 'This. I'm simply not accepting it. I'm going to speak to Alan Jackson.'

'About what?' Barry, like the others, was still in the dark, and was now looking at her with more than a hint of amusement. There was something endearingly childlike about her anger.

'Bloody Eric Short, that's what! He's guilty of importing snuff movies and I'm going to ... Oh!' She banged the door panel in impotent rage. 'I just can't believe our people caved in.'

'Ah.' Arnie, like Jo and Andreotti, now realized that Katherine had somehow missed the news about Short. Being the last to know the denouement of her own case was obviously doing nothing to improve her temper. 'We ... we thought you knew.'

Katherine slumped in the nearest chair. 'Well I didn't.' Suddenly she looked small, lost and vulnerable. 'If Eric Short walks, I'm going to look ridiculous.'

No one could think of a reply to that, beyond an obvious 'Yes, you are.' Yet the looks her colleagues gave her were uniformly sympathetic. None of them liked to be made to appear idiotic, and they all suspected that, behind her brittle façade, Katherine would hurt more than most.

Yet as she sat, staring numbly into space, Katherine was struck by another, far more alarming thought. Eric Short was now a free man. He hated her with a vengeance. And he knew where she lived.

*

Katherine was unable to banish Eric Short from her mind. At intermittent periods throughout the day, he flashed back into her consciousness. And each time he appeared, his expression was increasingly murderous. It was with a jolt that she was forced to contemplate the unfamiliar sensation of being very scared.

By six o'clock, only she and Barry were left in the office. At ten past six Katherine's phone rang and, her fear temporarily forgotten, she reached out and, without even looking up from her paperwork, picked up the receiver. 'City and South,' she said without much enthusiasm. 'Katherine Roberts speaking.'

'Hello Katherine.'

She froze. Her entire body was suddenly paralysed: no words would come as she sat, open-mouthed in horror, with the receiver pressed against her ear. Then she felt an awful, churning sensation in the pit of her stomach. Fighting off the nausea, she gasped for breath and clung even more tightly to the telephone.

Her shock and fear communicated themselves to Eric Short at the other end of the line. He chuckled. 'What a little Miss Surprise you turned out to be.' Then his voice turned icy cold. 'I've got a long memory, Katherine. Nothing may happen for months. But I know where you work ... and where you live. Be careful.' Then the line went dead.

She had no idea how long she sat, frozen into immobility, with the phone still in her hand. Barry, looking through the glass partition at her white face and blank expression, reckoned it must have been a full thirty seconds. Worried, he got up from his desk and put his head round the door of Bill's office. 'You OK?'

Katherine nearly jumped out of her skin. 'Oh!' she said, slamming the receiver back into its cradle. 'You startled me.' Then she flushed. 'Yes, yes ... I'm fine. Just thinking.'

Although not entirely convinced, Barry smiled and then looked at his watch. 'Well, it's far too late to be doing things like that. If you're sure you're OK, I'll leave you to it.' He looked at his watch again. 'Off to see my sister.'

Katherine looked uneasy. The last thing she wanted to be reminded of was of a young, attractive girl who had been badly beaten in a vicious, vindictive attack. The thought sent another chill down her spine. Forcing herself to concentrate on Barry, she smiled in sympathy. 'How is she?'

Barry shrugged. 'Oh ... well, you know. I think it will only hit her when the bandages come off and she sees the scar she'll have for the rest of her life.'

'Poor girl. Arnie ... er, said you were pretty sure you knew who'd done it.'

'No doubt in my mind.' Barry's eyes narrowed. 'Rufus Teague – or one of his henchmen. I'm just waiting for him to put his head above ground.' Then, frowning, he peered more closely at Katherine. She really didn't look at all well. 'You sure you're OK?'

'Fine.' Katherine offered him a bright smile and stood up. 'But you're right; it's been a long day. I think I'll leave with you.'

The street outside was dark and empty. Katherine huddled into her coat and, quite unconsciously, brushed against Barry as they walked down the street. At the intersection with Wardour Street, Barry stopped and pointed in the direction of the tube. 'Well, I'm going this way.'

'Right.' Katherine nodded. 'I ... I hope she's OK.'

'Thanks.' Still concerned, Barry asked her if she had her car with her.

'Yes. It's in the multi-storey. Did ... um, did Arnie go off to the pub?' Katherine knew the question sounded peculiar; but she was unable to stop herself asking it.

'I dunno.' Barry scratched his head and looked at the pub opposite. 'Andreotti was wittering on about going, so I guess he might have.' Then he put his hands in his pockets and made to leave. 'Oh ... oh *shit*,' he suddenly exclaimed.

'What?'

He made a face. 'I've forgotten my bloody filofax. Bugger it. Look, I'll have to dash back to the office. See ya!'

Worried that he was going to be late, he dashed off back the way he had come, leaving Katherine to continue her journey alone. The street seemed suddenly quieter and darker and she felt a chill that had nothing to do with the weather. For a moment she contemplated waiting for him to return, but dismissed that thought almost as soon as it had occurred to her. He would think she was completely off her trolley. And anyway they were going in different directions.

Clutching her briefcase so tightly that her knuckles turned white, she hurried on – at the same time as a man appeared at the other end of the street. He was wearing a long, dark coat and he was looking straight at her. Katherine stiffened and stopped in her tracks. Then, telling herself not to be so ridiculous, she raised herself to her full height, tried to adopt an expression that was both brave and haughty, and took one step forwards. One step was all she managed. Abruptly, she turned on her heel and hurried back towards the pub.

Andreotti saw her the minute she came through the door. Grinning, he turned to his companions. 'Quick!

Start digging the tunnel – Commandant Roberts has found us.'

Jo laughed. Arnie, however, looked both superior and disapproving. 'Don't be so down on her, Andreotti.'

Andreotti grimaced. 'Should think that'll be the last thing I'll ever be with her.'

At that, the fourth member of their party howled with laughter. A pretty, though heavily made-up girl in her late twenties, she had just returned to the table with the round she had bought and had squeezed herself onto the banquette beside Andreotti. He seemed thrilled by her proximity.

Jo, however, noticed that Katherine was hanging back, smiling uncertainly at them. 'Come and join us!' she shouted with a smile. The smile was genuine: Jo had found herself warming to Katherine after her outburst in the office and, if she was at last making the effort to socialize with her colleagues, it could only be a good sign.

Katherine looked immensely relieved, and beamed. Arnie was on his feet in a flash. 'Drink?'

'Please. Tomato juice.'

As Arnie went off to the bar, Andreotti did the introductions. 'Katherine, this is Mandy. Mandy, Katherine.'

Katherine smiled and shook the proffered hand. She thought she rather liked the look of Mandy. The girl had an open, honest face and a friendly smile. 'Hi Mandy. Are you in the service as well?' Mandy roared with laughter. Unsure as to what was so funny about her innocent question, Katherine looked to Andreotti for enlightenment. He grinned. 'Well, I s'ppose our Mand is in *a* service. She's on the game.'

Katherine went pink.

Mandy, however, was a stranger to embarrassment and, between sips of her gin and tonic, prattled on about her job. Katherine found herself becoming more and more intrigued; she had never met a prostitute before, and Mandy defied the stereotype she had always envisaged – especially when she started talking about becoming VAT registered. At that point, Katherine offered to buy the next round. She felt she needed something a little stronger than a tomato juice and, having taken the orders, went to the bar. When she returned, it was with a large shot of vodka in her own drink.

Mandy looked up and smiled. 'Thanks, Katherine. Cheers!' Then she turned back to Andreotti and resumed her conversation. 'But I don't know whether I could do it. I mean I might need an accountant or something.'

Andreotti looked pensive. 'Mmm. Why don't you talk to Bill? What that man doesn't know about VAT...'

'Well, I think I *should* be registered,' interrupted Mandy with conviction. 'A therapeutic masseuse is a proper job, after all.' Katherine looked covertly at her colleagues. None of them were smiling. She quickly rearranged her features and, like Jo, nodded in agreement.

'After all,' continued Mandy, warming to her theme, 'I've got outlay. Oils ... stuff. Things, you know,' she added, suddenly looking rather vague.

'Yeah.' Andreotti swigged his pint and then wiped the foam off his mouth with the back of his hand. 'Whack 'em in the input tax column.'

Katherine leaned forward and smiled at Mandy. 'Actually, I really think you should be able to register your ... your professional services for VAT. I think anything that gives people in your line of work – men or women – protection under the law is to be welcomed.'

Andreotti, for the first time since he had met her, looked at Katherine with something approaching admiration. Jo, grinning, noted his expression and shot him a 'told you so' look. And, delighted that Jo and now Andreotti were following his lead in deciding that Katherine was, after all, a good egg, Arnie beamed at her.

Never happiest with silence, Mandy then proceeded to regale them with her plan to use any money she saved to do nightclasses – 'well, perhaps dayclasses' – in French.

Did Katherine but know it, her initial plan to wait for Barry would have seen her standing in the street for more than the few moments she had envisaged. For Barry was delayed at the City and South offices – and not by a forgotten filofax.

As he switched on the office lights, the phone started ringing. 'Jesus!' he said to himself. 'I knew it.' Although tempted to ignore it, he was impelled by his ingrained sense of duty to answer. 'City and South,' he said in a flat, disinterested monotone.

There was a chuckle on the other end of the line. 'Glad somebody works late.'

'Bill!' Barry sat down and cradled the phone to his ear. 'Where are you? Not in the Lake District already?'

'Not exactly.' Suddenly all traces of humour vanished. 'Listen, Barry, I want you to do something for me. I want you to contact the Customs Investigation Branch in Faro, Portugal. I want you to tell them that a UK officer will be contacting them and would appreciate some assistance with his investigation.'

This, thought Barry, is all extremely strange. 'Er ... who's going to Portugal?'

'I am.' Bill's voice was defiant. Then, in conspiratorial tones, he asked Barry to keep that information to himself. Barry felt suddenly cold: a vague premonition drifted into his mind. A premonition that he couldn't identify.

'You still there?'

'Yes.' Confused, Barry struggled to find words. 'What are we ...? I mean, why keep it to myself?'

'Because,' said Bill, 'I'm taking a flyer, and if I'm wrong I'm going to have a very long way to fall without a net.'

Barry stared wordlessly at the telephone in his hand. Again he felt the cold premonition, but this time he knew why.

Fourteen

'This Webster has been very smart.' Zavier Febrer gestured towards the building site and the large, brash sign sporting the legend 'Apartmentos Marfin'. 'Building regulations only allow you to build up three floors, so the skyline remains unspoiled. Webster scoops out the cliffs and builds apartment blocks down into them.' His dark, almost Oriental face lit up as he grinned at Bill and pointed again to the opposite shore. 'More apartments, more profit – and he doesn't break the building laws.'

Typical, thought Bill. George Webster; sailing close to the wind but never going adrift. 'But you have nothing on him here?' he asked.

Zavier shook his head. 'No. He's a respectable businessman.' Bill sighed and, with the tall, amiable Portuguese customs officer at his side, walked back to the car. He had been in Portugal for two days now and had discovered absolutely nothing that indicated Webster was up to his old tricks; nothing that suggested he was on anything other than a wild goose chase. The only positive element thus far was the co-operation of the young, enthusiastic Zavier Febrer. Barry, as Bill had hoped, had acceded to his request. And Bill knew it would have been against his better judgement. God knows, he said to himself, what my staff are thinking of me. First I endanger Andreotti's life; now I'm making Barry bend the rules and keep my secrets.

After dropping Zavier off at his office, Bill went back to his hotel. The punishing midday heat was getting to him, making him tired, hot and extremely irritable. After showering, he lay on the bed and studied, for the umpteenth time, the notes he had made regarding his investigation. He knew now that Tommy Maddern had travelled yet again to Latvia via Malmo the previous Friday. Surely, he thought, that *must* mean he's up to no good. Tommy Maddern, as he had said to the uninterested Alan Jackson, was not the sort of man to holiday – especially twice in quick succession – in a cold climate where English was barely spoken. Yet that information didn't help Bill much. What he needed was more information on Webster, something to connect him to Maddern. He hoped Zavier would be able to come up trumps in that direction.

He was unaware that he had drifted off to sleep until the bedside phone woke him. Unsure, for a few seconds, of where he was, he blinked at the sunlit room, at the dazzling white buildings visible through the french windows and at the sea beyond. Wasn't he supposed to be in the Lake District? Wasn't that what he'd told Libby and his colleagues? Then he remembered where he was, and why, and, with a pang of guilt, reached for the telephone.

It was Zavier. 'Hi, Bill,' he said in his perfect though heavily-accented English. 'Didn't wake you up, did I?'

'Er . . . no. No, you didn't.'

Zavier laughed. 'Well, just phoning to say that I checked Webster's recent travel for you. In Portugal we still require to see passports so it's easy.' After a rustle of papers clearly audible to Bill, Zavier continued, as if reading from a report. 'He made a journey to the UK on the 19th of last month and a journey to Malmo in Sweden in the 7th of this one. He was out of Portugal forty-eight hours only. Probably a business trip. Is that,' he finished with a hint of anxiety, 'of any help to you?'

Bill was suddenly wide awake – and smiling. 'Yes,' he said. 'Very. Thank you. Thank you very much.'

At the other end, Zavier replaced the receiver with a sigh of relief. He was worried about this. The man on the phone from UK customs had been evasive about Bill's exact position and purpose, yet the confident authority emanating from Bill indicated that he must be a senior officer on extremely important business. Zavier wanted to keep him sweet, and it looked, at last, like he had succeeded.

In his hotel room, Bill realized his heart was racing with excitement. He picked up his notepad and, under the name Webster, wrote the word 'Malmo' underneath it. Then he looked at the dates of Tommy Maddern's trip to the same destination and realized, with glee, that they were identical. Then he picked up the phone again.

'City and South,' said the familiar voice at the other end. 'How can I help ... oh! Er ... hello ...' Barry faltered and lapsed into silence as Bill's urgent, commanding voice interrupted his greeting.

'Don't let on it's me!' he barked. Then, more quietly, he told Barry that he wanted another favour. 'Maddern and Webster were both in Malmo,' he said, not leaving Barry an opportunity to object, 'on the same day. We know Maddern flew on to Riga. It's likely Webster did the same. Webster,' he continued, 'is using a phone in a bar here to receive his so-called business calls. I want you to speak to the Portuguese again and ask for a wire tap.'

Barry was horrified. 'On what grounds? Anyway, that's the province of the Investigation Departm—'

'I can't do it from here,' interrupted Bill. 'Believe

me, Barry, this is important – and it's got to sound very official from that end. Try, Barry,' he urged. 'Be vague but insistent. It's very important.'

Conscious that both Andreotti and Katherine could hear his side of the conversation, Barry didn't feel he could continue. Trying to sound as official as he could, he asked Bill to give him the number. Then, after writing it down, he replaced the phone and, frowning, bent to continue his work.

But Katherine's sharp antennae never missed a trick. 'What was that,' she called over his desk, 'about Investigation?'

Barry looked up with a shrug. 'Oh, just ... wrong department, you know.' As he averted his gaze once more, he caught Andreotti's eye. The expression left Barry in no doubt that Andreotti knew he had been talking to Bill. They had worked together for long enough to identify the nuances in each other's voices and the way they spoke to different people – and especially to Bill.

Making the movement as casual as possible, Andreotti walked over to Barry's desk a minute later and, with a nod towards the door, asked quietly if they could have a little chat. Barry didn't feel he could refuse.

'That was Bill, wasn't it?' he said as soon as they reached the hallway.

'Um...' Barry didn't know what to say. He desperately wanted to explain his predicament to Andreotti, but he was also mindful of his promise of secrecy to Bill.

Andreotti made it easy for him. 'Look,' he said with a sympathetic smile. 'I had this with Bill on the bootlegging job. Jo was the field officer, but he was telling me to report direct to him. It's about George Webster, isn't it?'

Relieved, Barry nodded. 'Yes. The thing is, he's in Portugal.'

'Yes. I know.'

'No, *Bill's* in Portugal.'

'What! Bill?'

Barry nodded miserably. 'He reckons he's got something on Maddern and Webster. He's gone out there freelance. Wants me to ask Portuguese customs for a phone tap.'

'But you can't!' Andreotti was appalled. Phone tapping, even for customs officers, was hardly a run-of-the-mill business. 'You do that,' he said, pointing upwards, 'and somebody upstairs is gonna want to know why, and Bill'll be in deep how's-your-father. Look, Barry, I'm as loyal to Bill as anybody, but this is ... you know.' To illustrate his point, Andreotti put his forefinger to his temple and swivelled it round. 'He's going a bit ...'

'But what can I do?' wailed Barry in anguish. 'I can't say I won't help him.'

Andreotti didn't envy Barry's predicament. It was far worse than anything Bill had landed *him* in, yet there was that wretched question of loyalty ... 'If you do help,' he said unnecessarily, 'you could be in serious trouble, man.'

'Yeah.' Barry looked torn, miserable. 'Well, I'll have to think about it. Look,' he added with a glance at his watch, 'I've got to go. I'll be back later.'

Barry phoned Bill in Portugal that afternoon, choosing a time when he was alone in the office. He swallowed hard. He knew he had to steel himself for a stream of invective from the other end. Bill was not going to be at all happy. 'Er . . . Bill . . . I can't phone Portugal and ask for a wire tap for you.'

Barry would have been extremely surprised to see the expression on Bill's face as he heard the news. He was smiling. Almost as soon as he had put the phone down on Barry that morning, he had felt crippled with guilt. Why, he asked himself, am I doing this? I pushed Andreotti too far and nearly got him killed; now I'm forcing Barry to put his job on the line for me. It simply isn't on.

And that was why he greeted Barry's news with relief. 'I know,' he said quietly. 'I know you can't. I shouldn't have asked you. It was wrong of me. It's enough that one of us is bending the rules. You're right, Barry. Forget about it.'

Barry, too, was immensely relieved. Yet, like Bill earlier, he felt guilty. 'I'm sorry, Bill, I . . .'

'Don't be. You're doing the right thing. We'll talk soon. Bye.' After replacing the receiver, Bill walked out onto the balcony of his room and stared out to sea. His time was up: he had told Libby he would be back from 'the Lake District' tomorrow. There was nothing more he could do here. He had failed in his quest to find out what George Webster was up to. Oblivious to the beauty of the view and the warm, inviting sunshine, he found himself contemplating his future. He knew he would have to come clean to Libby about where he had been; he suspected to would end up telling Alan Jackson. He knew he couldn't live with the lies he had spun round his activities of the past few days. But he didn't know if, when City and South was reorganized, HM Customs and Excise would want to live with him. He suspected not.

Depressed, he wandered back into his room. The

mini-bar caught his eye. Drowning his sorrows seemed, under the circumstances, the only sensible thing to do.

He was still on his first whisky when the thought hit him. Initially he dismissed it as preposterous. It was too risky – dangerous, even – and could kill his investigation stone dead. He took another sip of his drink. The investigation, he reminded himself was already dead. Playing this last card could resurrect it. And it carried with it an irony that amused him: an irony that, if all went well, would not be lost on George Webster. Smiling to himself, Bill put down his whisky and picked up the phone.

'My name,' he said a moment later, 'is Jack Turnbull. I'm interested in one of your new properties. Yes, that's right – Apartmentos Marfin. Would it be possible to arrange an appointment with Mr Webster?'

'Mr Turnbull?'

Bill held out his hand. 'Mr Webster?' He hoped his dark glasses hid the searching look in his eyes: the search of Webster's expression for any sign of recognition.

To his dismay, Webster frowned slightly and held on to his hand longer than was necessary. 'Haven't we met before?'

'Er . . . you know, I think we have.' Heart racing, Bill forced a smile. 'I bumped into you. In a bar. Er . . . oh, the name escapes me. On the front,' he said, gesturing towards the sea. 'Mind you,' he added with a laugh, 'you could've seen me all over the place. I've been dashing about from the day I arrived.'

The moment passed. Bill's explanation seemed to satisfy Webster. 'Hmm. I've been told,' he said, 'that you're interested in buying one of these.' He turned, as did Bill, to face the apartments.

'Yes,' replied Bill, his relief giving him a new confidence. 'Good of you to see me at such short notice.'

'We have a brochure, you know,' said Webster. 'Everything you need to know about them is in there. Unless . . .?' he turned to Bill and smiled.

For a moment Bill sensed danger. Then he recognized the look on Webster's face for what it was: an invitation to consider 'a deal'.

'Well,' replied Bill. 'I have a couple of questions about payment.'

Webster smiled. 'Yes?'

'Will you take cash, and would I get a discount?'

Webster feigned disapproval. This, his expression indicated, was the last thing he expected to hear. He said after a short pause, 'It's not something we do as a rule. This is a very sought after spot, you know.'

Bill looked deflated. 'Should have known.' Then, warming to his theme, he laughed. 'I try to run everything like my fruit and veg stall.'

'Oh! That your line?

'Yes. Well – was. I've just taken early retirement. Sold up.' And there, thought Bill as he smiled at Webster, is another potential irony. A vision of a smiling Alan Jackson flashed through his head.

Webster, however, seemed delighted. 'Small world,' he said. 'My dad sold fruit and veg. Commercial Road. Twenty-six years. Come hail, wind or rain, day in, day out, he was always there.'

'Really?' Bill grinned. 'Hope you've fixed him up with one of these places.'

''Fraid not.' Webster looked genuinely upset. 'All those freezing cold mornings finally caught up with him. Bronchial pneumonia. He died when I was thirteen – broke and unnoticed. 'Cept by me,' he added with a wistful sigh. Then he shrugged and, forcing his mind back to the matter in hand, gestured towards the buildings. 'Which apartment had you in mind?'

Bill had seen the brochure and had a ready answer to that one. 'One of those,' he said, pointing.

Webster looked surprised. 'Must've sold a lot of fruit and veg.'

'Yeah.' Bill grinned. 'Y'know how it is – with cash businesses.'

Webster laughed. 'Well, you'd better come inside. Inspect the goods.'

The apartment, like all the others, was still an empty shell. Once inside, Bill made the requisite admiring noises and, apologizing for behaving like a tourist, took endless photographs of the interior of the apartment as well as the view. 'For the wife,' he explained. Webster wasn't very interested in the wife, or in Bill's photographs. He wandered out onto the balcony, unaware, as he did so, that Bill had him in the frame of the camera.

'I'll give you,' said Bill as he joined him outside, 'a hundred and forty-two thousand for it.'

Webster had been waiting for that one. 'Hmm,' he mused. 'Twelve per cent less than the asking price.'

Silence reigned for a moment. It was Webster who broke it. 'A hundred and forty-eight,' he said, 'you got a deal.'

Bill was beginning to enjoy himself. This was like playing Monopoly. 'Hundred and forty-five. Then I'll have got a four bedroom one for the price of the two.'

Webster grinned. That was exactly the price he had decided on. Jack Turnbull, he thought with amusement, knew his onions – as well he should. 'Done,' he said, holding out his hand.

Bill shook it. 'So long,' he said as they clinched the

deal, 'as my wife likes it. I'm fetching her out here next week. I'd like her to see it – and to meet you.'

Webster looked pleased. He was all for the personal touch. Then, remembering, he shook his head. 'Sorry, won't be here next week. I'll arrange for one of the boys in the office to show...'

'That's a shame,' said Bill with feeling. 'I'd like you to meet my wife. Will you be gone long?' As he asked the question, Bill's pulse quickened. His entire investigation hinged on the answer.

'I'll be away,' said Webster, blissfully unaware of the importance of his words, 'from the thirteenth to the seventeenth.'

'Oh, right. Well, maybe I'll see you after that.' Bill felt like leaping in the air with joy. He'd got him: he knew when he was leaving – and Zavier Febrer, presented with that information, would be able to find out where he was going. Unless, of course ... Bill looked away, ostensibly at the view. 'Going anywhere nice?' His heart was thumping so loudly he feared Webster might hear it

Webster didn't – but nor did he answer the question. Instead he joined Bill in admiring the view. 'Where,' he asked with a sweeping gesture, 'could be nicer than here?'

An hour after Bill had departed – professing himself delighted, pleased, chuffed, and 'looking forward to meeting you again' – George was sitting in the sun, thinking about how much he was enjoying himself. Selling an apartment for cash was always good news. George liked cash: it stayed in pockets; didn't have to do boring things like go through the books or to the bank. And Jack Turnbull's cash, wherever it came from, was as good as anyone's.

George hadn't believed the story about the fruit and veg stall. He had been momentarily carried away by memories of his own father, of life in the dingy slum in Commercial Road. His memories had supplanted his doubts about Jack Turnbull's story. But George knew a dodgy bastard when he saw one – and there was definitely more to Jack Turnbull than met the eye. He was positive, for one thing, that he had seen the man in London. Somewhere in the dim and distant past, their paths had crossed. George sipped his beer and tried, for a few moments, to place the man. He failed. Then, grinning to himself, he dismissed him from his mind. What did he care? As long as Turnbull came up with the goods, he was welcome to the apartment.

The morning's sale wasn't the only reason why George was in a good mood. He had spent the last few days indulging in one of his favourite pursuits: playing people off against each other. He had, he thought, dealt rather nicely with Mikolas; a man he in fact quite liked, but who needed to be treated with caution. George recognized a kindred spirit when he saw one. Mikolas's demand of an extra twenty thousand as backhanders for 'export officials' had, of course, been irritating, but he had paid half as promised. After all, he had Mikolas well and truly in his palm as regards the house in Hampstead.

It wasn't Mikolas who worried him most: it was Conny Devooght. George disliked Conny intensely and distrusted him even more. He had absolutely no faith in him and had no doubt that Conny would try to stitch him up. That was why he had hatched a new plan. One that he was extremely satisfied with. One that, as he sat in 'his' bar in the bright sunshine, he was happy to share with Mikolas.

Mikolas was impressed. 'Can your man at the container port really do what he claims?'

'I sincerely hope so. Otherwise I might be saying goodbye to my investment.'

Mikolas took a swig of his beer and smiled across the table. He had just had an idea. 'To get my captain to help,' he said, 'will cost you something, George.'

George grinned. 'When I get paid, he'll get paid. He's putting into Rotterdam anyway, isn't he? He's not exactly going out of his way to help me.'

Mikolas had to laugh. 'My God!' he exclaimed. 'You are about to make maybe seven million profit and still you won't pay anyone up front. You're a monster, George. I must never,' he mused, 'do a deal for nerve gas with you. You'll have it diverted all over the world to make sure you get paid.'

George was glad he was wearing dark glasses. Mikolas, he was sure, couldn't see the sudden shock that registered in his eyes. Nerve gas? That really was the big time. 'You ... you actually deal in that?' He hoped he sounded only politely interested. Mikolas waved a dismissive hand. They might as well have been discussing dealing in doughnuts. 'Sure. Tabun nerve gas. I have done, yeah. Eight hundred kilos; fifteen thousand dollars. Sarin gas's about the same.'

George just stared.

'Are you shocked?' laughed the other man. 'You can't be. I mean, you're transporting Caesium.'

Alarm bells rang in George's head. 'What're you telling me? Caesium's not a nerve gas?'

'No, no, no. Caesium is for ... you know ... boosting the delivery capability of strategic weapons.' He leaned forward across the table. 'If it goes to Iraq, say, they can use it to hit Israel. If,' he added hastily, 'that's where it's going. I don't know where this lot's going. Did Devooght tell you?'

This time George couldn't disguise his horror. He hadn't known ... not really. What had that creep Devooght called Caesium? An earth metal or something? Nobody had told him exactly what it was capable of doing.

Registering George's expression, Mikolas sought to assuage his conscience. 'Don't worry, George,' he said with a bright smile. 'If we don't do it, somebody else will. And, as you keep saying to me, we just take the money and run.'

'Er ... yes.' For once, George Webster couldn't think of anything to say. He sat in silence, clutching his beer as the full implications of what he was doing finally sank in.

A few minutes and another beer later, he began to cheer up. Mikolas was right: *somebody* had to do it – so it might as well be him. And if he was going to do it, he was going to do it his way.

The plan he had just outlined to Mikolas was simple, and designed simply to prevent Conny Devooght from pulling a fast one. Conny had told George he would get his millions when the Caesium reached its final destination: a destination that, as he and Mikolas both knew, was Guinea. George didn't like that idea. Guinea was too far away; the ship would take too long to get there and, as he well knew, there was many a slip twixt cup and lip. Unless, of course, George arranged for the Caesium container to be kidnapped in Rotterdam and held to ransom until Conny Devooght paid him three million in advance. George would fly to London, collect the money, and then instruct Tommy to let the Caesium continue on its voyage. Poor old Tommy; always got the bum deal. He was, at this very moment, supervising the loading of the Caesium onto the ship that would carry it to Rotterdam. George supposed that, later in the afternoon, he ought to phone Tommy to inform him of the change of plan in Rotterdam. But first a few more beers. Mikolas was fun to be with and life was good. It would be even better with another seven million pounds.

Conny Devooght, when he had joined Tommy in Latvia the second time, had warned him that George would try to pull a fast one. Tommy had told him not to be so ridiculous, had said that George was hypercautious and just took a lot of precautions. Conny wasn't convinced: the way he had got Mikolas into a stranglehold over the Hampstead house had aroused his suspicions.

Tommy, for his part, didn't tell Conny that he himself was in something of a pickle because of George. George had made it quite clear that, if Tommy didn't do exactly as he was told, he would shop him to the police about the shooting of Arjun Malhotra. Tommy knew George well enough to take that threat extremely seriously. Yet he also knew something that George did not: that Conny had hatched a plan that would deprive George of every penny of the seven million he had been promised. Tommy was torn: not out of loyalty to either man but because he couldn't decide whether or not Conny's plan would actually succeed.

His mind was made up for him during George's next phone call from Portugal. He listened, appalled, to what George told him and, still reeling from shock, relayed the news to Conny.

'He's done us,' he fumed.

'Eh?'

Tommy clenched and unclenched his fists in impotent anger. 'Webster. I've just talked to him. The container.

It's not staying on the ship till it gets to Guinea. It's coming off at Rotterdam. He says,' he added with an accusatory look, 'that it's staying there till he gets half the purchase price.'

'What! He wants three million for not delivering. The devious ... Jesus!' Lost for words and in a towering rage, Conny paced up and down the hotel room, cursing Webster in his head. Suddenly he stopped. 'Right, if that's the way Webster wants to play it, that's fine. We'll just make sure the container doesn't reach Rotterdam.' He looked at his watch. 'When does the ship sail?'

'It's already gone. An hour ago.'

'Bloody hell!' Conny turned on Tommy. 'I told you he'd try to do us, didn't I?' Then, eyes narrowed in suspicion, he went up to Tommy and grabbed him by the lapels. 'Are you involved in this?'

'How'd you mean?'

'With Webster. I thought you were with me on this?'

'I am, Conny, I am. This,' added Tommy, shaking Conny off and looking extremely pained, 'is as much a surprise to me as it is to you. He's just told me about it. He's a cunning bastard. I told you that.'

'No. *I* told *you* that. Jesus!'

'We should,' said Tommy as he contemplated their new, unenviable position, 'have had the Caesium flown to Guinea. The container's pretty small. None of this would have happened then.'

But that only served to fuel Conny's rage. 'Don't be so fucking stupid!' he thundered. 'You can't ship Caesium by air!'

'Why not?'

'Because it'll fucking explode, that's why! It's extremely dangerous. And so,' he added, 'am I when

I've lost my rag. Where's the fucking telephone? I'm gonna speak to Webster. Now!'

But it was to no avail. No matter how much Conny ranted, raved, swore and threatened, George was adamant. He also made it perfectly clear that he had hired someone to organize the unloading of the Caesium at Rotterdam. Someone whom neither Conny nor Tommy knew. Someone who, waving a fistful of official papers, would prevent them indulging in any 'funny business'.

'But what,' said Conny in a last ditch attempt to foil Webster, 'if my principals can't get hold of the money so quickly?'

George had been expecting that one. 'They were expecting to pay for the load you didn't deliver three weeks ago. What they do – spend the money? No, no, Conny, they'll have the money.'

Conny had to admit defeat. But as soon as he put the phone down, having promised to deliver the money as agreed, he turned to the scowling Tommy. He was, much to Tommy's surprise, smiling. 'The container port in Rotterdam,' he said. 'When the load is checked I think Webster should be there.'

'Why?'

'So that we can bury him at sea.'

Fifteen

'A bag off the Kingston flight the other day. Friend of mine's sister lost it. I don't know much about it but they've asked me to get it back. How's that done?'

'No problem, sir. Happens all the time. Bring the young lady's ticket stub to the BA desk and ... in fact, to save time, gimme the number now and I'll let you know if we've got the bag.'

A few moments passed while the caller searched for, and then read out the flight number. Kevin Butcher replied that yes, they had the bag and that it would be no problem for the caller to collect it on Monday.

'I bet,' said Diane who had been listening on an extension, 'he's too smart to show up himself. He'll send the girl.'

'Yes,' replied Kevin. 'They usually do.'

'Mmm.' Diane seemed to suddenly find her fingernails extremely interesting. 'Perhaps you ought to call Barry? Tell him to be on the alert for Teague.'

Why the hell, thought Kevin, can't you call him? And then he remembered why. Casting a covert look at his boss, he wondered if her reluctance to speak to Barry had more to do with the latest development in her personal life than the collapse of her previous relationship. Diane, he knew, had been on the phone to Andrew Ryan. More than once.

Barry wasn't in the office first thing on Monday morning. Nor, although he was due back from 'the Lake

District' that day, was Bill. Katherine, however, was – and she was extremely interested in Kevin's call. She had heard a lot about her colleagues at Heathrow but had never met them. In her inimitable manner, her first thought was to impress them, not to get on with them.

'Speak to me,' she commanded in response to Kevin's request for Barry. 'I'm the senior officer here.'

'Er ... it's about something he's worked on and I'd like his opinion.'

'That's fine,' said Katherine, her tone contradicting her words, 'but could you just explain to me what it's about?'

'Well ... I'd prefer to speak to Barry ...'

'Look, I'm in charge here.'

At the Heathrow end, Kevin rolled his eyes and looked over to Diane. He covered the mouthpiece of the phone with his hand and whispered, 'It's Boadicea. They were right – takes no prisoners.'

Diane laughed and signalled for him to hand the phone to her. 'Hello. Katherine Roberts? Hi. This is Diane Ralston.' The sub-text was clear: don't try to pull rank with me.

Wrong-footed by the quiet authority of Diane's voice, Katherine paused a moment before replying. 'Ah. Yes. Hello. What's this about?'

'We have a case containing seven kilos of cocaine. We think it might have been on its way to Rufus Teague: City and South has surveillance photographs and addresses. Barry ... er, Barry Christie ran a previous investigation so he'll know.'

On the other end of the line, Katherine pursed her lips.

Diane continued, 'The package was supposed to be collected the other day but no one showed up. We've been given permission to run live with the package, but we may be running over your patch.'

Katherine was delighted. Here was a chance to salvage her reputation; to redeem herself after the Eric Short fiasco.

'Fine, we'll be glad to help. Any idea when you might need us?'

'No – nor even if. We've got a man on the BA desk, but Teague may play safe and leave the stuff where it is. We'll either get a big arrest or get nothing. It all depends on whether someone shows up for that suitcase.'

'Well, let us know,' said Katherine, her mind already clicking into overdrive. 'I'll get things moving at this end in case anything happens.'

She moved very quickly indeed. She gathered the troops – Jo, Arnie and Andreotti – around her and alerted them to the possibility that they could be knocking Rufus Teague that very day. 'What about Barry?' asked Andreotti. 'Shouldn't he be in on this?'

'Barry's not here.'

Andreotti took a deep breath. No, he thought, Barry's not here: he's visiting his sister in hospital – the sister who was attacked by one of Teague's men. He was going to be livid when he found out that Katherine was running away with his case.

'We need,' continued Katherine as she looked at the addresses they had for Teague, 'at least three surveillance cars.' Then she looked pointedly at Andreotti. 'And we need to check their tax discs. No more Crown Licence mistakes.'

Andreotti almost hit her. ''Scuse me,' he said with admirable self-control. 'That wasn't my mistake.'

'No, I know. All I'm saying is that we don't want it happening again. A Crown Licence in your windscreen is fine if you want to double park outside Sainsbury's, but not for the surveillance of a suspect.'

'Jesus!' fumed Andreotti as Katherine went back into Bill's office a moment later. 'Cruella DeVille or what?' He glared at the blameless Arnie. 'Barry's gonna be real revved up when he comes back and hears about this. It's his case by rights.'

Arnie shrugged uncomfortably. Katherine was, he had to admit, being more than a little tactless, but that was only a cover for her nervousness. She had told him as much the other night when they had gone back to her flat after drinks with Mandy in the pub. He had seen a completely different side of Katherine that night: the soft, vulnerable side. But perhaps now wasn't the time to tell that to Andreotti.

Barry arrived an hour later and as predicted was not at all pleased that Katherine had hijacked the operation. Flying into a temper wasn't, however, his style. 'It's actually my case,' he said to her with cold fury.

But she didn't notice his anger. 'Well, it's not really. It's actually Senior Officer Ralston's. It's starting from Heathrow.'

Barry glared at her. 'Rufus Teague tried to kill me. Then he had my sister's throat slashed. What do you mean, it's not my case!'

Belatedly registering that Barry was livid, Katherine softened and offered him what she hoped was a conciliatory smile. 'I do understand, Barry. But SO Ralston and I will be running this. I . . . er . . . wouldn't want what Teague did to your sister to . . . you know . . .'

'Cloud my judgement?' snarled Barry. 'Well, I certainly won't let Teague know where I live so that he can phone me at night!'

Katherine recoiled as if she had been hit. 'How . . . ?'

she began – but Barry had turned on his heel and was already out of the door. Feeling sick, Katherine stood staring into space as Barry's words reverberated in her head. It wasn't so much the remark as his ability to make it that shocked her. How had he known? She hadn't told anyone about Short's phone calls, about the time he had phoned her at the office or, more threateningly, about the call that had come in the middle of the night. And then she remembered. She had told Arnie. In confidence. So much for his sweet words that night; so much for his promises to keep her secret. Arnie was as bad as the rest of them; not to be trusted.

Still fuming, Barry stomped over to his desk, grabbed his phone and dialled the number that was engraved on his memory. He used to dial the number with a fond smile and, sometimes, in pleasurable anticipation. This time he dialled in a rage.

'Why didn't you call me,' he thundered in response to Diane's hello, 'when you got something on Rufus Teague? I should be running it. Instead I have to listen to a woman with an ego the size of Birmingham telling me how we're going to go after the guy! She didn't even know the guy existed before you called her.'

'Barry.' Surprised and not a little shocked by such an uncharacteristic display of temper, Diane had to hold the phone away from her ear for a moment. Then, angry herself at his unfair accusations, she railed back. 'For God's sake, Barry, don't you think we didn't try to call you? You weren't bloody well there! What were we supposed to do? Risk letting Teague escape again so as not to offend you? Look,' she added, taking a deep breath. 'I *know* it was your case. Now it's *our* case, OK? It's unlike you,' she finished in a soft, concerned voice, 'to be so dog in the manger.'

'I know, I know.' Barry sighed heavily, expelling the last of his anger. 'I guess I'm just upset about this whole thing, specially about Charmian.'

'How is she?'

Barry smiled into the phone. 'Better. Looking forward to going to stay with you.'

'Good. What about you, Barry. Are you OK?'

'Yeah, yeah, I'm fine. While Charmian's with you I'm going to look for a new flat for us. She's none too happy about staying where she was.'

'No. I can understand that.' Not sure what to say next, but eager to fill the silence, Diane said she'd 'keep her ear to the ground' and let him know if she heard of anything.

'That would be nice. Thanks.' It was a full minute after Barry replaced the receiver that he realized he was still smiling. He knew he and Diane were finished, but now he knew that, in time – and probably soon – they would be friends again.

He looked through the glass partition at Katherine, beavering away in Bill's office. Was she ever going to fit in, he wondered? And were things ever going to be the same again at City and South?

The atmosphere had definitely changed over the past few days. Arnie was being protective of Katherine, looking down his nose at the rest of the team whenever her name came up. He had made it quite clear that he liked her, that he found her intelligent, well informed and cultured. The others had taken offence at that, assuming that Arnie took them to be philistines.

Later that morning, when Arnie went into Bill's office to have a 'chat' with Katherine behind closed doors, Jo beckoned Andreotti and Barry over to her computer.

'What gives?' asked Barry.

'Bill.'

Both men suddenly adopted an impassive 'I know nothing' stance. Jo giggled. 'Don't look at me like I'm daft,' she scoffed. 'I know about Bill being in Portugal. You know,' she said, turning to Barry, 'I know. Andreotti knows. It's only . . .'

'Cruella and her handsome prince who don't.' Andreotti nodded in the direction of Bill's office. 'Hey! D'you think there's something going on there?'

'Nah!' Barry was scathing. 'Look at them. They're having an argument.'

'Lovers' tiff.'

Frowning, Andreotti looked back at Jo. 'How the hell did you find out about Bill, then?'

Jo gave him an old-fashioned look. 'Take me for an idiot, do you? All that whispered boy's talk. Little words like "Bill" and "Portugal".' She fixed Barry with a particularly penetrating stare. 'I s'ppose you're going to tell me that you were phoning that bar in Portugal to order tapas?'

'How the hell . . .?'

'I know everything,' said Jo darkly.

Barry, glancing again into the inner office, looked worried. Despite the fact that Katherine had really riled him earlier in the day, he was concerned about the ever-widening chasm between the three of them and Arnie and Katherine. 'Look, I know she can be ghastly, but don't you think . . .'

'No!' Andreotti's lip curled. 'It's not like we're one big happy family, is it? If she finds out, she'll tell somebody and Bill'll be in for the high jump.'

Sensing that they had embarked on a conversation that was likely to become heated, Jo drew both men's attention to the screen in front of her. 'Look, this is what I wanted to show you. That house in Hampstead...'

'What house in Hampstead?'

'The house, Andreotti, to which I followed Tommy Maddern before he decamped to Latvia. It's Queen Anne, I think. A lot nicer than that dump in Deptford where...'

'Oh get on with it!'

'OK, OK.' Jo was enjoying herself. 'The house,' she explained with a smug smile, 'is owned by a company called Apartmentos Marfin, aka George Webster. It was rented out, furnished, until a couple of months ago. Rent paid to an off-shore company.'

'So?' Andreotti was deeply unimpressed. 'Where does that get us?'

'To the fact that Webster hasn't paid any income tax on the earnings.' Jo leaned back and put her hands behind her head. 'It may not be much – but it *is* how they got Al Capone in the end.'

At the same time as Jo imparted her potentially explosive information to her colleagues at City and South, Kevin Butcher rushed into Diane's Heathrow office, brandishing his mobile phone. 'She's turned up!'

'Who?'

'Teague's girl. The one from court. You were right. She's on her way to the BA desk now. And she's bloody nervous.'

'Great!' Diane jumped to her feet. 'Get City and South, tell them we're off. And tell Jake to delay the girl until I'm in position.'

Jake Munro, in a British Airways ground staff uniform and manning the airline's baggage counter, had, moments before, called Kevin to tell him the girl was heading his way. Now, heart pounding, he was watching her from under his lashes. She was, he thought, really scared; so scared that for a moment he doubted if she would dare complete her mission. But maybe, he thought as he recalled the photograph of Teague, she was more scared of her boyfriend than she was of the task in front of her.

When she finally appeared in front of him at the desk, he concluded that that was indeed the case. Her heavy make-up failed to disguise the black eye she was sporting. Jake smiled. 'Good morning. How can I help you?'

He knew, of course, exactly how to help her. More importantly, he knew how to help Kevin and Diane. He had to give the latter time to get to her car and the former, who was watching from a distance, the opportunity to alert the undercover officers they had summoned to help them. Accordingly, he fiddled about with bits of paper, clicked his tongue now and again and, after several muttered apologies and an admission that it was his 'first day on the job', located the girl's suitcase. She didn't smile once during his performance and didn't even thank him when he offered to escort her through the green channel. Kevin, monitoring their progress, flicked his mobile phone. 'IC1 female,' he said to the officer on the airport's land-side. 'Blonde hair. Blue jacket, carrying suitcase. Victor 2 will be with you in . . .'

'Victor 2 in position now!' Victor 2, alias Diane, had just reached her car and was, as she said over the air, ready and waiting. So were the City and South team. Alerted moments before by Diane, they were ready for whatever Heathrow may throw at them. Barry and Katherine, their differences forgotten now that the operation was under way, were in one car, travelling westwards towards Heathrow, while Andreotti and Jo, in the latter's vehicle, were at the ready in Central London. Only Arnie, left behind to man the phones, was absent.

Nobody met Teague's girlfriend at Heathrow. Tailing her on foot, Kevin saw with a sinking heart that she was making for the Underground. 'Tango hasn't been met,' he informed his waiting colleagues. 'She's on foot, making for the tube.'

Diane had allowed for that eventuality in her rapidly-executed plans: she had stationed an undercover officer below ground. He took over the surveillance and followed her onto the next train. It now seemed definite that she was heading into City and South's territory. 'We'll follow the tube route,' said Barry to Katherine as he swung the car round. 'See if she gets off.' But twenty minutes later she was still on the train. 'Tango still on board,' they heard from the undercover officer. 'Possible destination South London. Advise line changes.'

'Damn!' said Katherine under her breath. Things could get complicated now. She wondered if Teague had advised the girl to take a complex, convoluted route to her destination in order to thwart any possible pursuers. She knew that's what she would have done. Cradling her phone under her jaw, she consulted the tube map on her knees. 'Possible change at Hammersmith, Barons Court, Earls Court, Gloucester Road, South Kensington . . .'

'It's Hammersmith! Tango standing up. Tango exiting.' From his vantage point in the carriage adjacent to Teague's girlfriend, the undercover officer watched as the train slowed, halted and the girl got out. He, too, alighted, and watched as the girl took the escalator and, rather than changing to the District Line, carried on upwards towards the exit. 'Tango leaving Underground! Foxtrot 3. Tango leaving...'

'Foxtrot 3 in position,' replied Andreotti excitedly. The minute he and Jo heard the word Hammersmith, they drove hell for leather in that direction to take over the surveillance. 'She's all ours!' shouted Andreotti to Jo as, mere seconds after their arrival, they saw the girl emerge from the Underground at Hammersmith Broadway. But Jo wasn't so sure that they had her. The girl, after glancing at her watch, cast an expectant look around her. So did Jo. And so did the black man who emerged from a blue Mercedes waiting on the double yellow line at the entrance to the tube. As soon as he saw Teague's girlfriend, he ran towards her and she, evidently relieved, passed the suitcase on to him. As he sprinted back to the car, she headed in the opposite direction – followed by the undercover officer.

'Tango has passed bag to IC3, male, black leather coat, twenty-five to thirty years old, driving blue Mercedes, Alpha Delta Golf 134 Whisky.' Andreotti hesitated and looked at the vehicle as it pulled out into the traffic. 'Heading,' he continued into his phone, 'North... no... heading... which is it, Jo?'

Desperately trying to follow the Mercedes in the heavy traffic, Jo raised her eyes heavenwards. 'It's Hammersmith – one bloody great roundabout. No! Wait... heading west,' she added as the Mercedes took the left turn towards the M4. 'Back towards Heathrow.'

Jo looked at her passenger and grinned. 'Whaddya' know. They're feeling guilty. They're going to take it back.'

The Mercedes did, in fact, go a long way down the motorway towards the airport – a bonus as far as its pursuers were concerned. It gave all the vehicles an opportunity to regroup more closely. It also suggested that the car's destination was Teague's house not far from Heathrow. Diane, in her earlier conversation with the police, had already informed them of that possibility.

Katherine's car was eyeballing the target when, three miles from the airport, it turned into a suburban street and stopped with a screech of brakes outside an unprepossessing, run-down house.

Barry consulted the notes in his lap. 'Yeah,' he said with a nod. 'One of Teague's addresses. You'd think he could afford something a little nicer.' Then, as the driver of the Mercedes opened his door and exited from the vehicle, Barry's face became taut with anger. He was recalling Charmian's description of the man who had attacked her. 'If that's who I think it is,' he said to Katherine, 'he's the one who slashed my sister's face.'

Alarmed by Barry's tone, Katherine looked sideways at him. She saw murder in his eyes. 'We're only here,' she said gently, 'to arrest them, Barry.'

But the look on Barry's face didn't change.

Five minutes after the driver of the Mercedes went into the house and closed the door behind him, a battered old van cruised into the street, rattled past Katherine's car, turned left at the bottom where Jo's car was now in position and then stopped round the corner.

Katherine looked at Barry. 'Here we go.'

The van, driven by a tired-looking, scruffily-dressed young woman, may have looked unassuming, but its contents were not. There were eight heavily armed policemen huddled in the back.

In the next street another, smarter van drew to a halt. Diane Ralston was one of the three people in the front seat. She turned round and looked into the back. Behind her were two television monitors which were flashing into life, one showing the front and the other the rear of Teague's flat. The customs surveillance expert monitoring the screens returned her smile.

Then she turned to the man beside her. 'Katherine Roberts will join us here, Superintendent.'

The policeman nodded. Diane grinned to herself. She had never met Katherine and, looking at her surroundings, reflected that this was an extremely odd place to be introduced.

Katherine thought the same thing. When she arrived she looked at the attractive woman she took to be Diane and grinned. 'Interesting place to meet, Diane.'

'Too right.' Diane smiled, shook Katherine's proffered hand and then turned to her companion. 'Superintendent Blair, Katherine Roberts.'

Blair nodded and shook hands. These two, he thought to himself, look as if they'd be more at home at a cocktail party than at a highly dangerous knock. 'Well,' he said, hoping his eyes didn't betray his opinions. 'You two are in charge. What do you want to do?'

Diane began, 'We haven't got any sound in the building, but we do know there are at least two of them in there—'

'Nobody move!' The urgent command rang into Diane's phone, taking them all by surprise. It was Barry's voice. 'IC1 female approaching premises. It's Teague's girl. Entering premises,' he added after a pause.

Diane and her companions looked at the TV monitors. The minuscule cameras capturing the pictures had been installed in lamp-posts that morning – as had cameras at all five of Teague's addresses. An expensive operation, but one that looked as if it would pay dividends. The screen showing the front of the house displayed a picture of a man letting the girl into the house. 'Damn,' said Diane. 'He wasn't the one driving the Merc. That means there's at least four of 'em inside.'

'Teague,' said Blair, 'is definitely inside.'

Diane didn't reply: she was looking in alarm at the flak vests the policeman was pulling on. 'Two?'

'Mm. And two for each of you.'

'Will these stop bullets from an Uzi?'

'By the time you go in he won't have one.'

Katherine and Diane exchanged an uneasy look. 'Time,' said the former, trying to regain the initiative, 'to seal off the streets.'

Ten minutes later there were more policemen and customs officers in the area than there were residents. All of them, however, remained out of sight. The team from City and South, along with Kevin Butcher and Jake Munro and two undercover officers, had moved their vehicles to a parking lot nearby and were standing watching as the armed policemen moved swiftly to take up their positions near Teague's house. 'Odd,' observed Jo, 'to think that two hundred years ago it was the customs who were armed to the teeth and the police who only had cudgels.'

'Guess that's progress,' replied Barry. The look on his face indicated it was a progress he could well do without. He would have given anything to approach Teague with a gun.

'Look,' said Andreotti as a white car approached and stopped behind them. 'Thelma and Louise have arrived.' Jo giggled as Diane and Katherine, trying to look nonchalant in their flak vests, emerged from the back seat.

'Morning,' said Diane. 'The police are ready.'

'They know who they're aiming at, do they?'

'Don't worry, Andreotti,' she replied with a grin. 'We'll be behind them.'

'That's what I'm worried about. Safest place is usually in front with some of this mob.'

Diane ignored the remark. She had just spotted Barry. Suddenly she felt awkward; vulnerable. 'When the police have secured the premises,' she said to the assembled officers, 'SO Roberts and myself will go in at the front door. Jo, Kevin and Jake – you'll be with us. Andreotti and Barry ... er ... you'll cover the back of the premises. You'll have five armed police officers with you. Well,' she added with a confidence she didn't feel, 'we'd better get on with it.'

They made their move as soon as the house was confirmed as secure. Radios crackled into life; the words 'Armed police' rang throughout the entire street; officers brandishing weapons smashed their way into the house and screams were heard from within. But Superintendent Blair had been misinformed about Rufus Teague's whereabouts. As all hell broke loose in the house, he emerged at a run from the back of the house next door. And he was armed with an Uzi.

'Hold it!' yelled a voice through the radio. 'He's out the back! He's out the back!'

So was Barry. 'He's there!' he shouted to the officer beside him. 'Making for the next garden!'

'Get down!' screamed the officer.

Then Teague fired.

'Somebody's down!' Diane and Katherine, looking at each other in horror, heard the words through their radios at the front of the house.

'What's happened?' panted Katherine.

But Diane was already on her way round the back.

'No!' she said to herself under her breath. 'Please God, no!' Then she turned the corner and ran straight into Barry.

'It was Teague,' he said. 'They shot him.'

'Oh.' At once breathless, angry, confused and relieved, Diane just stared. 'But I thought . . .'

'I know.' Barry smiled at her. 'It's OK.'

Feeling suddenly shy, Diane held his gaze for a moment. She didn't know what to say to him. They continued looking at each other until Diane turned abruptly away. Eyes blazing, she rounded on Superintendent Blair. 'Which total dick-head,' she screamed, 'said the place was secured? I have unarmed officers here! Our men were put at risk because of your bloody stupid . . .' Then, as her anger outpaced her vocabulary, she lapsed into a furious silence and stood, arms waving impotently at her sides glaring at Blair.

Behind her, Barry started to laugh. Some things about Diane never changed.

Sixteen

'Hello. I'm back.' Bill slammed the front door behind him and waited for Libby's greeting. It didn't come. Shrugging, he bent down to pick up his suitcase. Libby appeared from the drawing room just as he was about to lug it upstairs.

'Hello,' she said, without smiling. 'Did you bring any Kendal mint cake with you?'

Bill sensed immediately that something was wrong. She knew. 'Er . . . look, I have something to tell you.'

'I think,' replied Libby with a nod towards the room she had just left, 'I already know.'

Frowning, Bill stepped forward into the room.

'Hello, Bill,' said Alan Jackson. He gestured towards the man on the sofa. 'I think you already know Assistant Chief Investigation Officer Scudamore.'

Stunned into immobility, Bill paled under the tan he had tried hard to avoid. He looked back at Libby. He looked at the two men. Alan Jackson had never seen him looking so shocked in his life.

Jim Scudamore stood up. 'Hello Bill. It's been a long time.' Like Alan and Libby before him, he seemed only grimly satisfied to see Bill.

'I think,' said Alan Jackson, stepping forward to fill the heavy silence, 'we need to have rather a serious chat with you, Bill.'

Still Bill stared. This was worse – far worse – than anything he had envisaged. It had indeed been a long time since he and Jim Scudamore had met. Two years.

'Perhaps,' said Jim, smiling for the first time, but at Libby, not at Bill, 'we ought to go to York House, eh? We've imposed on you for long enough, Mrs Adams.'

Libby nodded. 'I've got to go out to pick the girls up, anyway.' She was speaking to Jim, but her eyes never left her husband. 'They'll be wondering where I am. It seems,' she added with sadness rather than anger, 'to be becoming something of a habit in this family.' Then she turned to leave the room and added, over her shoulder, 'I'll see you later, will I, Bill?'

'Yes, Libby. Yes, you will. And then I'll . . .'

'Explain,' said Libby. 'Yes. That would be nice.' Then she left the room.

'Sit down, Bill.' Alan Jackson indicated the chair opposite him.

Bill sat and took a deep breath. 'So,' he asked, eyeing the two men. 'Is this where we stop being pals and the serious questions start?'

Jim Scudamore leaned forward. 'Bill, we came to your home because we wanted to keep things very quiet. Very quiet indeed.'

Bill shrugged. 'Is this formal? Am I up for disciplinary action for . . .'

'No.' Jim stalled him with an authoritative hand. 'Not so far, at least. Look Bill, we know you like to play things close to your chest, but . . . er . . . is there anything from your personal investigation into the activities of George Webster that you haven't told us?'

Again Bill stared. What the hell was going on? He looked at the man he hadn't seen for two years: the severe-looking senior investigation officer who had come into his life at the same time as Gerry Birch, unbeknownst to Bill, had first been corrupted by George Webster. Jim was only called in when something very serious was happening within the service. Something internal – or something so sensitive that it had to be treated with kid gloves and dealt with at the highest of levels.

As he looked across the table, Bill felt a strange elation replacing the awful, mind-numbing depression that had descended on him the minute he had seen the two men in his house. They had not come because of him: they were here because of George Webster.

Yet still he was cautious. 'Well,' he said at length, 'if you'd tell me exactly what you're after, I might have a clearer idea of how I can help.'

'We know,' said Jim, 'that Webster and Tommy Maddern went to Latvia. Is there . . .'

Seeing red, Bill interrupted and turned to Alan Jackson. '*I* told *you* that!'

'Yes. And Alan passed it on to my department.'

Bill leaned back in his chair. 'I see. So Webster is involved in something big. Must be if your lot are involved. Well,' he added, dripping sarcasm, 'life goes on as usual. I give you information about Webster and Maddern, you tell me I'm wasting my time – then you take the case over.'

Jim didn't bat an eyelid. 'That's your job.'

'*I* put you onto Webster.'

'You *stumbled* across him, Bill. You've wanted to nick him for something ever since he corrupted your officer Gerry Birch.'

Bill didn't reply: he couldn't deny it – but he didn't want to admit it.

'This,' said Jim as he stared across the table, 'is too big to stay personal.'

'So what is it? Come on, you're making me feel like the damned office boy.'

Jim Scudamore and Alan Jackson stared at each other. Slowly, Jim nodded. Then he turned back to Bill.

'Remember a couple of months ago, an explosion at a container port? A female customs officer was killed?'

Bill wrinkled his brow, casting his mind back. Young woman. Left a young kid behind. Whole thing was hushed up. 'Yes,' he said. 'I remember.'

'Well, the explosion was caused by a badly packaged load of Caesium 133. It had,' he added pointedly, 'come in from Latvia. What we don't know is where it was eventually going. Iran? Iraq, maybe? We hadn't got very far in our investigation until you stumbled across your pal George Webster and mentioned he'd travelled to Latvia. Explosion. Caesium. Webster. Latvia.' Jim smiled. 'Suddenly we had a connection.'

But, thought Bill, you didn't bother telling me about it. I'm just the office boy.

Not noticing Bill's miffed expression, Jim opened a file in front of him and extracted a clutch of surveillance photographs. 'Philip Player,' he said, handing one over to Bill. 'English. Nicely connected.' Bill looked at the nicely connected Englishman. Distinguished and middle-aged, he was also nicely dressed and nice looking, and was standing outside the Hyde Park Hotel in Knightsbridge. 'He puts the overseas rich in bed with our indigenous influentials for a fee,' continued Jim. 'He made a fortune selling weapons to the Burmese junta.' Jim grimaced. 'Smug sod. I followed him all one night last summer. He ate at the Connaught. I couldn't get in; didn't have a tie. Had a McDonald's outside the place.' A slow smile spread across Bill's face. Jim Scudamore was thawing.

Seemingly regretting his brief moment of levity, Jim frowned and handed Bill another photograph. 'A few days ago, he met this bloke, Conrad Devooght. He was suspected of trying to smuggle Caesium from Dakota a year ago. The FBI went after him too early and his lawyer had him out in twenty-four hours.' Jim's expression revealed exactly what he thought of the FBI. It also, as Bill looked up at him, gave some indication of why this whole operation was so secret. Bill knew the extreme dangers of Caesium: any leaks to the public would be disastrous and would, he knew, lead to mass hysteria in the tabloids. Bill frowned and tapped the photograph of Devooght. 'Don't know the man.'

'He was spotted at Faro Airport in Portugal.'

Bill raised an eyebrow. 'Seeing Webster?'

'I hoped,' said Jim with a sigh, 'that you might know. He also went to Latvia via Malmo. So, it's either a huge coincidence or he's doing business with Webster.' He gave Bill another, sharp, loaded look. 'Now he's in London.'

'Ah.'

'Problem is, we can watch and we can follow 'em, but unless we can link them to an illegal shipment of Caesium to a proscribed country – assuming there is a shipment – we're ... well, we're outside the Connaught eating a McDonald's. What we need,' he finished, 'is for Webster to turn up.'

Andreotti looked at his watch and grinned. 'Hey! What time do you call this? Still in holiday mode are we?'

'No.' Bill looked, inscrutably he hoped, at the other man. 'I had an appointment.' Then his expression changed to one of concern. 'How are you? How's the ribs?'

'Only hurt when I laugh. You got a tan?' he asked with a cheeky grin.

Bill glared at him. But his eyes were smiling. 'From the Lake District? Don't be ridiculous.' So, he thought; he knows. I suppose everyone knows. Then he cast his mind back to the end of his conversation with Jim

Scudamore and Alan Jackson. 'I don't know what Webster is involved in, but I do know when he'll be on the move,' he had said, silently congratulating himself for playing that last risky card in Portugal. 'He'll be out of Portugal between the thirteenth and the sixteenth of this month. I was going to arrange an all-ports alert and have him watched.'

'We'll do that,' Scudamore had said. 'Do we have any recent surveillance pictures of him?' The question had been addressed to Alan Jackson, but it had been Bill who replied.

'I do. From my trip to Portugal.'

'Ah ... so maybe it was worth you going there after all.'

'So ... er ...' Thoughts of disciplinary action suddenly assailed Bill. 'What are you ... y'know. Disciplinary action and ...?'

Jim had looked across the table, wide-eyed and innocent. 'I don't know what you're talking about. It's none of my business where you go on holiday.'

Bringing his mind back to the present, Bill looked around him and frowned. 'Where *is* everybody?'

Andreotti shrugged. 'Dunno. Recovering?'

'From what?' Visions of all-night parties and day-long hangovers shot into Bill's suddenly suspicious mind. Andreotti, looking smug, soon put him right and told him about yesterday's massive operation and the death of Rufus Teague.

Bill was delighted. 'That's fantastic. And, Katherine ... did she ... you know...?' he left the question hanging in the air: did she go power-crazy?

Andreotti grinned. 'Nah. Cruella came up trumps in the end. I think maybe Diane sort of made her think. Y'know ... you can be a woman in charge without lopping the balls off the men.' Bill smiled and nodded in approval. Thank God for that. 'And, talking of which,' continued Andreotti, 'the smart money says there's something going on between her and Arnie.'

'No!'

'Yes.'

Bill looked at the empty desks. 'Is that . . .?'

'No. I dunno where Arnie is, but Katherine 'n' Barry'll be in any minute. She's been showing him round her flat.'

'Eh?'

'Mmm. Apparently she's gone off the place she rented. Barry and his sister are looking for something and so . . .' Andreotti waved his arms in an expansive, 'all's well that ends well' gesture. 'A regular little happy family, then.' But Bill was smiling as he said the words. Life was definitely looking up.

'Jo,' said Andreotti, remembering, 'has found out something a bit interesting about George Webster.'

'Funnily enough, so have I. I was hoping . . .' Bill looked at the empty room.

'S'all right. Jo's just out getting sandwiches. Back in a minute.'

'Good. D'you think you could ask everyone to come into my office when they're back?'

Half an hour later, the entire City and South team was sitting in a semicircle opposite Bill listening to Jo relating her findings on Webster. They had just heard from Bill about his own discoveries – and those of Jim Scudamore. The only thing Bill kept back from his team was the possibility of Caesium being involved. Jim didn't want anyone – 'and I mean *anyone*, Bill' – to know about it. Bill had reluctantly agreed to keep quiet about it.

Only Arnie and Katherine were surprised about

232

Webster – and only Katherine had started to make an objection about 'not being informed'. But halfway through her complaint she had suddenly, and with a sheepish grin, lapsed into silence. This, she had realized, was about far more than the events of the last few days: it was about things that had happened two years ago, before her time. Things that had affected her colleagues deeply. She had no business interfering in the past. Arnie, realizing what she was thinking, had been delighted.

'The house Webster owns in Hampstead,' Jo was saying, 'was bought from somebody who'd gone skint. Cost him half a million. But he's claiming there's a loan of three quarters of a million outstanding on it.'

'Who's the money owed to?'

Jo grinned over at Bill. 'He owes it to himself. One of his companies owes it to another of his companies. Plus, he hasn't paid any income tax on the money he's been earning from it in rent. We could do worse,' she finished, 'than talk to the Inland Revenue.'

'Mmm. But I'm convinced that George Webster is up to a lot more than avoiding paying his tax.' Bill smiled at the intent faces opposite him. 'Two men we have reason to believe are involved with him are in London at the moment. And Webster is leaving Portugal on the 13th.'

'For London?'

Bill smiled at Jo. 'That's for George Webster to know – and us to find out. Which I'm hoping we will. I've requested an all-ports alert for him.'

Bill hardly slept that night. After he had given Libby a full explanation and a fulsome apology for deceiving her as well as everyone else, the two of them went out to dinner to celebrate his homecoming – and his retention of his job. 'If we can nail Webster,' said Bill over brandy, 'then I reckon Scudamore'll wipe my slate completely clean.'

Libby had sent up a silent prayer that they would indeed nail the wretched man. She hated to see her husband so obsessed; she loathed the fact that he had put his job on the line and she was, above all, heartily sick of hearing about Webster. As far as she was concerned, the sooner he was behind bars the better for all concerned.

But Bill was more obsessed than ever and spent most of the night – and much of the following day – worrying that the man who had eluded them for so long would continue to do so.

Two days later, on the thirteenth, his worse fears were confirmed. Cradling a phone under his chin, Arnie called over to him. 'Bill? It's a call for you from Portugal. It's on three.'

Bill leaped up and grabbed his phone. 'Hello? Yes, it is. Zavier, yes. How are you?'

Then his smile vanished as Zavier Febrer explained why he was calling.

'Why on earth didn't you...? Oh, I see. No,' he added with a sigh. 'It's ... er ... thanks for calling me. Yes. Bye. Hell and damnation!' he shouted as he hung up. 'George bloody Webster left Faro for London on an Air Portugal flight three hours ago!'

In the outer office, everyone's face fell. 'I thought,' said Katherine, 'customs there were supposed to inform you the minute he went through passport control.'

'So did I. They forgot, apparently.' Bill looked at his watch. 'Still, the flight maybe hasn't landed yet, and if it has ...' his face creased with worry, Bill picked up the phone again and dialled Diane's office at Heathrow.

'I'm praying,' he said to Diane after he had imparted

the news to her, 'that his baggage has been delayed or something.'

But neither Webster nor his baggage were delayed. Webster, in fact, didn't have any luggage – and he didn't go through immigration. Instead, he went straight into Transit and to the boarding gate for a flight to Dublin.

'Bugger!' snarled Bill as soon as Diane phoned with the news. He couldn't – wouldn't – let Webster evade his clutches. With a heavy heart, wishing he had good news, he then phoned Jim Scudamore. Although not pleased, Jim reacted with admirable alacrity. 'I'll phone Dublin and tell them what this is all about,' he said. 'Can you send Webster's mugshot down the photophone to them? Let's pray the flight's late. We're cutting things a bit fine.'

Bill didn't need to be told that. Nor, half an hour later, did he want to hear the news from Dublin. 'We've lost him. In fact, we never found him. He must've had no luggage, gone straight through.'

'Brilliant. Absolutely brilliant!' The trail had gone dead.

George Webster was feeling extremely pleased with himself. Extremely pleased, as well, with the late and, as far as he was concerned, not much lamented Gerry Birch. Thanks to Gerry, George knew how to keep customs men on their toes. Ever since his involvement with Gerry had begun, he had taken precautions when flying into Britain. Not, he was sure, that anyone would be interested in him. Still, it was best to play safe. In the back of the Dublin taxi, he looked at his watch. A cup of coffee, perhaps, at the best hotel. Then back to the airport. If immigration had been alerted, it would have been to his arrival from London – not departure for that city. Especially his departure under a different name and with a new passport.

He was particularly pleased with the name on the new passport and kept grinning to himself as he looked at it. James Riddel, it said. Jimmy Riddle, of course, to his friends.

In London, George went to stay with Henry Mitchell. Henry was a good sort, always willing to help out his old mates – as illustrated by the news he had given George about Tommy's activities with guns and Indian shopkeepers. And his two strapping sons, Leslie and Warren, were always willing to act as bodyguards. George wanted protection; Conny Devooght was a slimy bastard if ever there was one.

Conny Devooght was worried. Webster's point-blank refusal to go to Rotterdam to see the container unloaded had annoyed him, but not unduly. A burial at sea would have been amusing and appropriate, but it wasn't strictly necessary. Murder was easy and he envisaged no problem in killing Webster in London, after he had handed the grasping bastard his three million. But what *did* worry Conny was that Webster seemed to have disappeared. He hadn't made contact in London and he hadn't phoned Tommy in Rotterdam.

Tommy, phoning from Rotterdam that morning to say that the ship had arrived and the container would be unloaded the next day, was also worried about George.

'Maybe he doesn't trust us,' he had said. 'No bad judge, is he?'

'Forget about him,' Conny replied. 'He's history. Couple of days you'll be spending money he thought was coming to him. You'll be worth three million. And all you have to do,' he added with a smile, 'is leave Webster to me.' As he said the words, Conny made a mental note to arrange for Tommy's demise as well. Couldn't have the man waltzing off with three million. Wouldn't know what to do with it, anyway.

After putting the phone down on Tommy, Conny Devooght had phoned Philip Player with the news that the ship had docked in Rotterdam.

'Good. Let's get this over with as quickly as we can and get it on its way. And get rid of this Webster character before he becomes a real liability.'

The Webster character would have been interested, but not unduly alarmed, to hear Conny's conversations. Anything Conny could do, he could do better. He would thwart any of Conny's amateurish plans to kill him by only accepting the money in a public place, and in the presence of his bodyguards. But what pleased him most was what would happen next in Rotterdam, after the Caesium was unloaded from the ship. That really would destroy Conny.

Sitting in Henry Mitchell's outrageously ostentatious living room, nursing a small whisky and watching the football, George decided that it was probably time to phone Tommy. The idiot was no doubt wetting himself by now.

Five minutes later and on the other end of the phone, Tommy did indeed sound as if he was panicking. 'George! Where the hell have you *been*?'

'Oh, you know, here and there. Anything to tell me?'

'Yes. Your ship's come in, George.'

Oh good, thought George. That means yours has as well. Two minutes later, George made another call to Rotterdam, to the man he had sent to execute the next, most brilliant part of the plan.

'Everything in place?' he asked.

'Yes.' The other man laughed. 'Or out of place, more to the point.'

George laughed as well. Life was getting better and better.

Bill hadn't given up hope. They had lost Webster the day before, but they still had some cards on the board. And one in particular, marked 'Latvia', had been preoccupying him all morning. 'Jo,' he said, wandering into the outer office just before lunchtime. 'If you suspected an illegal load being moved by container ship, what would you do? How would you go about finding it?'

'Depends where it was coming from.'

'Latvia.'

'Ah. No problem. I'd use via techniques and the Anna-Capa.'

'The Anna-Capa computer program?'

'Yeah.'

'Can you run it from here or do we need to ... er, plug into a network or something?'

Jo grinned. It was nice to know that Bill no longer regarded her computer course as a waste of time. It would be even nicer, however, if he could bring himself to say so. 'No,' she replied. 'I can do it from my desk.'

'Great. I want to know the destination of every container that's left a Latvian port in the past three weeks.'

'Is that all? Why not plot the world trade routes as well.'

'Jo...'

'Yeah, yeah, OK.' She began to tap at her keyboard. 'Actually, it's not that difficult. We can plot it, see? It's just a matter of feeding in the dates. What they were carrying and where their containers are being delivered all comes up automatically via the cargo manifest. Course, I can't tell you what's actually in the containers. If it's heroin being carried,' she said with a shrug, 'it'll likely be marked down as furniture or something.'

'But you can have a go?'

'Sure. But it would help if I knew where it was supposed to be going.'

'Mmm.' Bill stroked his chin. He didn't know where an illegal load of Caesium would be bound. But he could have a damned good guess. 'OK, what we're after is a container from a Latvian port that's say, taken north for eventual delivery south. Something that seems to have lost its sense of direction, but has an interesting destination. Like, for instance, a proscribed country that shouldn't have chemical or nuclear weapons.'

Jo, eyes narrowed with suspicion, looked round at her boss. 'Latvia. This is about Webster, isn't it?'

'Yes.'

'You reckon he's involved in the weapons trade? Why didn't you tell us that yesterday?'

Bill put a finger to his lips and pointed upwards. 'Investigation Department,' he whispered.

'Ah. We're not supposed to know?'

'Got it in one.' Bill knew he shouldn't be telling Jo what they suspected Webster of being involved in – but he had had enough of lying to his staff. It hadn't paid very many dividends in the past. Besides, he strongly suspected Jim Scudamore of trying to steal all the thunder. No doubt he and his Investigation mob were already playing with the Anna-Capa programe. He just hoped that Jo could play better.

She certainly played well. She accessed the program

and, after typing 'Latvia' and the relevant dates, hit the 'return' key. The numbers on the screen vanished and were replaced by a map of Northern Europe. Pinpointing Latvia itself, she then hit another key, giving her a grid-map, criss-crossed with lines representing the movement of ships. Then she isolated the ships coming from Latvia. Some of them, represented by thick lines on her screen, were destined for Northern European ports like Rotterdam and Felixstowe. The thinner lines represented cargoes going further afield, cargoes that might interest Bill. One of them extended to the bottom of her screen. Jo pressed the scroll bar on her keyboard and accessed the large map of Europe again. But still the line went further. Pressing the scroll bar again, she extended the map to take in West Africa. The line she had been following went straight to Guinea and stopped there.

Jo stared at the screen. Then she followed the line back and traced it to Latvia, via Rotterdam.

'Bill! I think I've found something.'

Bill came running over and looked, puzzled, at the screen. It was all gobbledegook as far as he was concerned. Jo grinned at his expression then pointed at the screen. 'See this line? It represents a cargo going from Latvia to Rotterdam and then to Guinea. It's ... hey!' As she spoke, there was a bleep from the screen and a large section of the line disappeared: the section going from Rotterdam to Guinea.

Half-amused and half-intrigued, Jo looked at Bill. 'Well, whaddya know? They've changed their plans. They've unloaded the cargo at Rotterdam.'

Bill ran back to his office and phoned Jim Scudamore. Grinning, he leaned back in his chair as he waited for Jim to answer. Who, he wondered, had got there first?

Jim had – and he was shocked that Bill had got there as well. 'You cunning old . . . how did you know?'

'Well,' said Bill, fighting the irritation he felt. 'It's what I would have done if I was leading the investigation.'

At the other end of the line, Jim found himself smiling. Good old Bill, he thought. Never gives up. Determined to win this one. 'Mmm, so you've done it anyway, even though you're not leading it.'

Bill didn't reply.

'OK.' Jim had to concede defeat – and complete co-operation. 'We're getting the Dutch to put the cargo under observation. We can't know for certain whether it's connected to our enquiry, but we're not taking any chances. I'll . . . er, keep you informed.'

'Yes. I'd appreciate that. And I'll keep you informed as well.'

The two men had information to exchange sooner than either expected. Jim's news was not good. 'Bill. The container. They had it on their screen in Rotterdam as being booked in and stored.'

'Yes?'

'Then it flashed up "booked out". It's disappeared.'

'Disappeared? How can a sixteen-ton container disappear?'

'I don't know. But it has.'

Bill's news came an hour later. It was good, it came from Diane, and it also concerned Rotterdam.

'Bill,' Diane said. 'This Tommy Bennett, or Maddern or whatever he calls himself.'

'Mmm?' Bill sat bolt upright.

'Well, I've just done a ticket check on him.'

'Yes?' Bill's heart started racing.

'He flew from Malmo to Amsterdam four days ago.'

*

The information about Tommy Maddern being in Holland was enough for Jim Scudamore. They had lost the container – but they had found one of their men. 'We're still working in ifs and maybes,' he said to the two customs officers he summoned later that day, 'but it's our only hope. If Maddern shows up in Rotterdam, then so might the missing container.' Addressing the shorter of the two men, he waved a cautionary finger. 'You keep well out of the way if Maddern does show up. You're just there to identify him. My men and the Dutch will do the rest.'

The taller man – Jim's officer – nodded. The other man looked relieved. 'I'll be delighted,' said Andreotti with feeling, 'to keep out of Maddern's way any day.'

'Right.' Jim dismissed them. 'Off you go to Heathrow.' Then he turned back into his office. There was much to do in London, including stepping-up the surveillance on Conny Devooght and Philip Player. The combination of circumstances was too great to ignore. The disappearance of the container; Tommy Maddern being in Holland and two of their suspects having recently arrived in London invited the strong speculation that both Webster and the container were about to reappear.

Later that evening, Philip Player and Conny Devooght met at the Hyde Park Hotel. Jim Scudamore heard the news with a sinking sense of *déjà vu*: visions of eating his McDonalds' outside the Connaught came back to haunt him. He looked at his deputy, grinned, and told him to hand over his tie. Then he phoned Bill. 'Our two suspects have met at the Hyde Park Hotel. I'm on my way there.'

'Any sign of George Webster?'

'None.' Jim held the receiver under his chin and

began to tie his newly-acquired tie. 'But if he does arrive, even though we've got your snap of him, I'd prefer someone to identify him. Just to be certain.'

Bill didn't hesitate. Nothing would give him greater pleasure than to be present at the arrest of George Webster.

They missed his arrival at the hotel. While Conny Devooght, watched by Scudamore's men, had entered from the front, Webster, accompanied by his two minders, sneaked through a service entrance. He was grinning when he arrived in Philip Player's room on the fifth floor. Player and Devooght were not. They had just discovered from Tommy Maddern that the container had gone missing.

'What's going on?' said Conny in a low, threatening voice. 'The container isn't there.'

Still smiling pleasantly, George looked around him. 'Nor's the money by the look of it. First things first, eh?'

'I hope,' said Player in his deceptively lazy, upper-class drawl, 'you're not playing silly buggers with us.' Then he produced a suitcase from under the bed. 'Here's your money,' he said with a grimace. 'Three and a half million in fifties.'

George peered into the case and selected two notes at random. Then he turned to Leslie Mitchell. 'Go downstairs and ask reception to check these under one of them machines they have near the till. I'd hate,' he added with a smile at Conny, 'for them to be forged.'

Mitchell, flexing his muscles, did as he was bid.

And I'll do a rough count up,' continued George as he extracted several bundles from the case. 'Then I'll tell you where the container's parked.'

Conny looked thunderous. 'Why isn't it where it should be?'

'Because I'm cautious. In fact,' he added, 'I'm so

cautious that I think we ought to exchange cash for information in a rather more public place, don't you?' George's smile was more of a condescending leer now. 'That way I know I'll leave in one piece.'

A minute later they went down to reception and through to the bar. After they had passed through the foyer, a man who had been loitering out of sight behind one of the jewellery showcases nodded to the man standing at reception. It was a confirmation from Bill to Jim that Webster was now in their midst. Jim then followed Webster's party into the bar. Conny Devooght, he noted, was speaking into a mobile phone. In a perfect world, thought Jim as he went up to the bar and ordered an orange juice, Devooght would be talking to someone in Rotterdam, checking on the missing container.

Did Jim but know it, the world was, at that moment, absolutely perfect. Devooght was speaking to his man at the container port in Rotterdam, telling him where to find the container. Happy with his money, George had just told him where it was hidden. 'He'll call me back,' said Conny as he retracted the phone's aerial. 'He'll have to open the crate to verify the contents.'

'Fine.' George nodded. The Caesium was in the container, packed into airtight cylinders. Conny's man would be satisfied. He tried to envisage the scene at the container port: his own man, the man who had organised the disappearance of the container in the first place, would be looking over Conny's man's shoulder. So would Tommy. Poor old Tommy. George smiled to himself. He would miss Tommy in a way. Such a buffoon – but always good for a tease. Conny's man he didn't know. Still, he would be company for Tommy in his burial at sea. That, if all went according to plan, would happen shortly after the contents of the container were verified; only moments after George walked out of the Hyde Park Hotel with a suitcase full of money.

Yet what George didn't and couldn't envisage about the scene in Rotterdam was the little band of Dutch undercover customs officers watching the activity at the container port through nightsight field glasses. All of them were holding their breath as they saw the container being opened. All of them were armed.

In the foyer of the Hyde Park Hotel, Bill paced up and down, careful to stay away from the bar, torturing himself with visions of things going wrong. The Dutch *had* to knock the operation at their end before Scudamore could arrest Webster: the whole knock was contingent on perfect timing. And there were so many things that could go wrong.

He needn't have worried. As he paced, the pager in his pocket started to bleep. Bill stopped in his tracks. For a moment he thought his heart might stop as well. The bleep was the signal that a flare had gone up in Rotterdam, that the Dutch were swarming all over the container port. It was also the signal that heralded the arrival of ten undercover officers at the Hyde Park Hotel – and it was a signal that also reached Jim Scudamore's pager.

Bill walked to the door of the bar at the same time as a party of five armed policemen, posing as businessmen, somehow managed to block the only entrance: at just the same time as Jim Scudamore reached into his breast pocket for his identity card and walked over to George Webster's table.

Seventeen

'I am telling you, here and now, that I had no idea what that man was up to.'

Jim glared across the table. 'You didn't know that Conrad Devooght was shipping Caesium?'

'Never heard of Caesium. What's it do?'

Jim sighed and leaned back in his chair. It was late, he was tired, and the interview room was depressing. So, thus far, was the interview. It had been two hours since Webster's arrest, an hour and a half since they had arrived at York House, and fifteen minutes since he had started questioning Webster. And still the man was saying that there had been a mistake.

'I want to see my lawyer,' said Webster suddenly.

'It doesn't work like that at this level, Mr Webster. Your main problem, you see, is that Devooght is looking to make a deal with us.' Jim cast his mind back to the previous interview. He had been sure that half of what Devooght had said was complete rubbish – but he had, all the same, given them a lot of rope to play with. Jim leaned forward again and smiled without warmth. 'He's put you at the centre of this racket. He's saying you put up the money and therefore stood to gain the most. He's also suggesting you were involved in a previous shipment . . .'

'I was not.'

'. . . which exploded, killing a female customs officer.' Jim stared into Webster's icy cold eyes. 'We could be looking at a charge of murder as well.'

'I swear on my mother's life, I had no idea.'

'It wouldn't appear that you value your mother's life very highly, Mr Webster.'

George Webster swung round at the sound of the new voice. As he did so, the colour drained from his face and, for the first time in his life, words failed him. 'Jack Turnbull' was standing in front of him. Momentarily confused, George just sat and stared. Then his confusion gave way to horrified recognition. The distant memory, jolted by the shock of the man's appearance, was distant no longer. He had indeed seen Turnbull before. In London. In a room not dissimilar to this one. And in an identical situation. Turnbull wasn't Turnbull at all.

With a supreme effort of will, Webster regained his voice. 'Bill Adams,' he said in a barely-audible monotone. Then, overcome by humiliation, anger and defeat, he reverted to silence.

This was the moment Bill had been waiting for: the wish he had long cherished had come true. He smiled down at his victim and then began to quote from the sheet of paper he held in front of him. '"I swear on my mother's life",' he read, '"I had no idea Gerry Birch was sleeping with my wife, or that they were involved in smuggling gold into the UK".' Bill put the paper down and smiled, predator-like, at the man before him. 'You're gonna go this time, Mr Webster.'

George Webster's trial, and that of his accomplices in London and Rotterdam, took place six months after his arrest. It was a six-month period during which everything went back to normal. Bill went back to work on other cases; Jim Scudamore went on to investigate other felons; Arnie went out with Katherine; Andreotti went berserk, and Diane started an affair with Andrew Ryan.

The other development – and one that Bill had to concede, to his disgust, was also perfectly normal – was George Webster's hiring of one of the best QCs in the land to handle his case. HM Customs and Excise, due to budgetary constraints, had to make do with someone far less expensive and with considerably less experience. He did, however, do an admirable job for the prosecution; one that resulted in five years' imprisonment for Thomas Maddern and seven for Conrad Devooght.

George Webster, on his barrister's advice, offered a plea bargain. He disclosed to customs officials all details of the illegal weapons depot in Latvia and of Mikolas. As Mikolas was a major supplier of illegal arms and chemical weapons throughout the world, Webster's move carried a lot of weight, and he was sentenced to only three years' imprisonment. Then, because of the evidence he gave for the prosecution, even that sentence was suspended.

The day after the announcement of the suspension, George Webster flew back to Portugal. He flew first class and drank champagne all the way. And he vowed to himself that, from now on, all his business interests would be strictly legal. Unless, of course, something came along that was just too tempting to resist . . .

Also available from Mandarin Paperbacks

Tom McGregor

THE KNOCK
(Series One)

One of law-enforcement's best kept secrets – a crack team of young investigators out to catch the customs and excise fraudsters. Working from top-security headquarters, often undercover, their knock is enough to strike fear into the heart of the most hardened criminal.

Bill Adams is the paternal boss who rules his teams with a rod of iron. From tough South Londoner Gerry Birch, driven to desperation by financial problems, to Diane Ralston, hard-headed senior officer at the airport, all the team members rely on the camaraderie they share to get them through the tense, exhilarating, life-threatening situations they face.

But when the teams are undermined, by illness and by personal pressures, rifts start to develop which threaten to betray the whole operation.

A Selected List of Crime Titles Available from Mandarin

While every effort is made to keep prices low, it is sometimes necessary to increase prices at short notice. Mandarin Paperbacks reserves the right to show new retail prices on covers which may differ from those previously advertised in the text or elsewhere.

The prices shown below were correct at the time of going to press.

☐	7493 19143	**Political Death**	Antonia Fraser	£4.99
☐	7493 03247	**The Cavalier Case**	Antonia Fraser	£4.99
☐	7493 08532	**Cool Repentance**	Antonia Fraser	£4.99
☐	7493 08516	**Oxford Blood**	Antonia Fraser	£4.99
☐	7493 08559	**Quiet as a Nun**	Antonia Fraser	£4.99
☐	7493 08915	**Deep Sleep**	Frances Fyfield	£4.99
☐	7493 10200	**A Question of Guilt**	Frances Fyfield	£5.99
☐	7493 10219	**Shadows on the Mirror**	Frances Fyfield	£5.99
☐	7493 0376 X	**Trial by Fire**	Frances Fyfield	£4.99
☐	7493 18422	**Wasted Years**	John Harvey	£4.99
☐	7493 1818 X	**Cold Light**	John Harvey	£4.99
☐	7493 16691	**Red for Rachel**	Frank Lean	£4.99
☐	7493 16799	**Nine Lives**	Frank Lean	£4.99
☐	7493 18201	**The Bath Detective**	Christopher Lee	£4.99
☐	7493 16608	**Home Before Dark**	Michael Molloy	£5.99
☐	7493 14532	**Cat's Paw**	Michael Molloy	£4.99
☐	7493 1883 X	**The Apothecary Rose**	Candace Robb	£4.99
☐	7493 18848	**The Lady Chapel**	Candace Robb	£4.99
☐	7493 19828	**The Nun's Tale**	Candace Robb	£4.99

All these books are available at your bookshop or newsagent, or can be ordered direct from the address below. Just tick the titles you want and fill in the form below.

Cash Sales Department, PO Box 5, Rushden, Northants NN10 6YX.
Fax: 01933 414047 : Phone: 01933 414000.

Please send cheque, payable to 'Reed Book Services Ltd.', or postal order for purchase price quoted and allow the following for postage and packing:

£1.00 for the first book, 50p for the second; **FREE POSTAGE AND PACKING FOR THREE BOOKS OR MORE PER ORDER.**

NAME (Block letters) ....

ADDRESS ....

....

☐ I enclose my remittance for ....

☐ I wish to pay by Access/Visa Card Number

Expiry Date

Signature ....

Please quote our reference: MAND